TAMING THE HIGHLANDER

May McGoldrick

SMP Swerve

AN IMPRINT OF ST. MARTIN'S PRESS

ALSO BY MAY MCGOLDRICK

Much Ado About Highlanders

TAMING THE HIGHLANDER. Copyright © 2016 by Nikoo K. and James A. McGoldrick. All rights reserved. For information, address St. Martin's Press, 175 Fifth Avenue, New York, NY 10010.

www.stmartins.com

Cover art © Shutterstock

Cover design by Ambar Ben

ISBN 978-1-250-10657-5 (e-book)
ISBN 978-1-250-15482-8 (trade paperback)

First E-book Edition: September 2016

To Jill Marsal with abiding gratitude for believing in us.

Prologue

Death one step in front of her. Death behind.

Innes Munro stood at the edge of the world, and a cold, watery grave lay ready to take her.

The gray fog swirled up the jagged cliffs. She'd run as far as she could, but another step meant certain death. Her lungs burned, and Innes stared down through moving breaks in the mist at the waves crashing against the rocks far below.

Trapped.

The brambles clinging to the edge of the precipice caught at her skirts as she turned to face her pursuers.

A dozen men, their mail shirts gleaming dully beneath filthy, dark-stained tunics, spread out like hunters at the end of the chase. They'd run their prey into the ever-tightening enclosure on the cliffs. All that remained was the kill.

They eyed her and awaited their master's signal.

The commander sat astride his black steed behind the line of men. A leather cloak, tied at the neck, was thrown back over one shoulder, revealing a heavily marked chest plate, a long sword, a pair of daggers. His eyes never left her.

Trapped.

Innes knew what they wanted. Too late she'd learned that this band of Lowlanders and English soldiers had been roaming free in the hills, looking for a certain woman from Clan Munro. Fact and rumor had been woven together into a thick noose: the Munro woman was a witch. She possessed a mysterious relic given by Satan himself. She could turn a person into stone if he looked into her eyes. Most important, gold would be paid to any man, woman, or child who pointed them in her direction.

Someone had talked. Her secret had been exposed. She'd feared this moment for so long. For years.

For Innes, the past held no mystery. She knew so well the power of the stone that passed on to her from her mother. Only one piece of the whole tablet. Three other fragments. Each carried across Scotland fifty years ago by men who'd survived a shipwreck not far from this northern shore. Innes knew the powers that the other stones held. And she knew the disaster that would rain down on their heads if the wrong person brought all the pieces together.

The commander spoke to her. "Give it to me."

Innes said nothing. His eyes were fixed on the pouch she wore at her waist.

She cursed inwardly. She should have never left the safety of the castle.

The sea breeze whipped her tangle of midnight black hair with its blaze of white. Behind her, seabirds floated on the wind, their cries breaking the silence.

"Give me the stone and I'll not harm you or anyone around here."

He was lying. He was an Englishman, risking his life here in the Highlands. He had to know. For all its ancient power, the stone was a useless bauble to anyone until the moment that its bearer died. But perhaps he didn't know. She had to touch his skin to see into his past, to learn whatever he knew, to find out which of the stones he already possessed. But she wouldn't go near him to find out. What if her fragment was the last that he needed?

"Go and take it from her."

The men advanced a step, and Innes backed to the very edge.

"Stop right there or I'll jump into the sea . . . and then you'll never have it."

The men hesitated.

Innes had been a child of seven when she sat at her mother's sickbed and learned the secret of the stone. The history, the power of sight that was soon to be hers, the knowledge that no one she touched could hide anything from her. At that moment, none of it made any sense. She'd only wanted her mother to stop talking, save her strength, and get better.

Later, standing at the funeral, she'd learned exactly what it all meant. Holding her father's hand, Innes felt his past flow like a gushing stream into her brain. Hector Munro had been so keenly disappointed with her mother, the woman who gave him two daughters and no sons, that he'd already chosen his next wife and negotiated for her hand. All of this came to Innes without speaking a word. It was at that moment, as the hot pain that came with *knowing* cut through her, that she realized what she'd been left was no gift, but a curse. The next morning, she awakened to see the white blaze in her long black hair.

"She won't jump. Get her."

Innes turned toward the cliffs.

She welcomed death. It would put an end to all of it. She was ready to part with the heavy weight she'd been forced to carry for much of her life. But she paused at the brink, thinking of him. The man she loved.

Innes winced as someone grabbed her hair, yanking her back from the ledge. She twisted and fought the men who latched on to her arms. She'd been too slow.

One of them cut the string of the pouch and ran with it to his commander.

Held captive, she watched their leader take the stone out of the pouch and hold it up. Inside her, hope fought a losing battle. Perhaps he knew nothing of the power of the relic he held. Maybe they had come because of the rumors, and he now realized that the quest had been for nothing.

Those desperate hopes sank when she saw him produce two other pieces of the tablet and fit them together. He knew what he had.

The Englishman's gaze shifted to her. He'd done this before. He knew how to take from her the power of the stone.

Innes saw a movement at the top of the rise behind the raiders. A great gray wolf appeared.

The Englishman nodded to his men.

"Kill her."

Chapter 1

CASTLE GIRNIGOE
THREE MONTHS BEFORE

Half a year, Conall thought, staring out at the folk milling about in the darkness of the courtyard. Half a year since he'd returned, and for what?

To watch his people suffer, knowing he was the reason for it.

It could have been different. If only he had died a warrior's death at the Battle of Solway Moss. So many of his kinsmen had perished there. Or if only the English had not discovered his ransom value after capturing him. After all, he had managed to hide his true identity for a year, and he would have happily continued to rot in that dungeon. If only his brother had not emptied the Sinclair clan vaults to free him. If only.

And now, six months after returning home, he had to watch Bryce make yet another sacrifice for the good of their people. His brother was about to wed again, and to a new wife chosen because of the size of her dowry.

"You won't consider me much of a martyr once you meet her," Bryce said from his chair. He put down his cup of wine. "Ailein Munro is quite beautiful. And pleasant. She also appears to be fairly capable. In fact, I'm certain she'll be able to handle the responsibilities that go with running Castle Girnigoe."

Conall shrugged but didn't look at his brother. Outside, someone was rolling a cask of ale into the courtyard. The Sinclairs and the Munros were in high glee on the eve of the laird's wedding.

"You should have been at dinner tonight," said Bryce. "My in-laws are eager to meet you."

"To see for themselves if I match up to my vile reputation? To stare at my stump of a hand? To see what a wreck of a man looks like?"

"Probably." Bryce smiled when Conall turned to scowl at him. "Of course not! They want to meet my older brother, the famous warrior, the earl of Caithness. It's only right that they would want to meet you out of respect."

"Well, they'll have to wait. You took on the torch of sociability the day you sat in that laird's chair," Conall replied, starting for the door. "The Munro woman is marrying you, not me. Her family has had all the introductions they're going to get."

"Wait. You *will* stand by me on the church steps tomorrow?"

He paused by the door. "Is that a request or an order?"

"A request."

"Good, because I won't be there. I have no time for it."

"Then it's an order."

Conall pulled the door open. "Even better, because you know that Hell will freeze over before I start taking orders from a wet-nosed stripling like you."

"But it's my wedding, Conall. It's important that you be there."

"At first light, I'm leaving for the lodge at Dalnawillan."

"Hunting? You're going hunting rather than stand by me at my wedding?"

"Leave me be, Bryce." He glared at his brother. "You're starting a new life. And you, better than anyone, know that three is a crowd."

For Innes Munro, nothing compared with the protective arms of night. She loved the dusk, the dawn, and every dark hour in between.

Night suited her. Only then could she really escape the pressures that daytime held. When darkness fell and others slept, no one demanded conversation of her. No one pressed her with unwanted attention or expectation. At night, she could follow her own solitary ways. She could come and go as she pleased. She could live safely within the walls she'd erected around herself.

That was when she was home. For another day or two, she was a guest here at Girnigoe. On some level, Innes couldn't wait to go home to Folais Castle. Before she left, however, there was something that she wanted to see.

Just after supper, by accident, she'd happened to peek into a large hall that she realized was a gallery. Now she was determined to get a better look.

As an artist, she knew how rare such things were in the Highlands. Works of art were not always highly valued, and with good reason. Life here was hard and a clan's prized possessions, other than gold, were limited to weaponry, household goods, and livestock. But this wasn't just any clan. This was Clan Sinclair.

In a land of fearsome warriors, the Sinclairs held a place of distinction. Kings of their own domains during the Crusades, they'd returned home to fight alongside Robert the Bruce. And when the great king died, no one but a Sinclair was trusted to carry his heart to the Holy Land. For centuries, a Sinclair had served as the strong right hand of every king of Scotland.

And these warriors apparently had another side to them. They had artwork that, in Innes's view, was priceless.

She stayed to the shadows, skirting the revelers who

were singing and carousing in the castle's Outer Ward, and hurried to the new North Tower. The gallery was located close to the laird's reception room and the Great Hall, where a handful of servants still worked after dinner. No one paid any attention to her when she slipped in, lit a taper, and went out.

As she entered the gallery, the mere sight of this treasure trove made her sigh with pleasure.

Along with a number of smaller works, four great tapestries covered the walls. Each of them ran from floor to timbered ceiling, and they were exquisite.

Italian, she decided, for the figures were incredibly lifelike. Each of them depicted religious events. One showed Christ with his disciples in two boats. The nets of Peter and the other fishermen bulged with their catch. In the flickering light of her taper, she could even make out the delicate golden halos surrounding the men's heads. The Galilean sea was so real looking she thought she could wash her hands in the water.

Innes pulled off one of her gloves and held the light high as she moved from one piece to the next.

She had saved the best of the treasures for last. Two paintings hung above the stone mantel of a great fireplace at one end of the gallery. She gazed at the work, awestruck.

Portraits. Two solemn boys stood together, an arched

window behind them with Castle Girnigoe and the sea in the distance. There was no question in her mind that the boys were Conall and Bryce Sinclair.

In helping to negotiate Ailein's marriage, she'd learned a great deal about this family. Only two years separated the brothers. Conall was the earl of Caithness and had served as laird until the Battle of Solway Moss. Overmatched by English cannon, many Scots had died there. Conall's people thought he was killed, and Bryce became laird. And when Conall returned, he refused to take the position back from his brother.

A rumor circulated that the earl had gone mad in the English dungeons. Innes didn't believe it. Rumors were nothing more than blunted swords of simple minds and wagging tongues.

Innes turned her gaze to the second painting. Conall Sinclair alone, decked out in court regalia. She'd seen Bryce often enough and, looking at this depiction, she saw similarities in Conall's features. But there were differences, too. Conall was darker and more handsome. The shape of the jaw, the intensity in the eyes, the broad powerful shoulders, the muscled legs. She wondered for a moment if the artist had been tasked with portraying the earl of Caithness as larger than life, or if indeed the flesh-and-blood man had the same ability to make a woman's heart flutter, even in the breast of a twenty-seven-year-old spinster.

———

Innes Munro. The bride's older sister. Dutiful daughter and trusted advisor to Hector, Baron Folais.

As he was leaving Bryce's receiving room, Conall saw the woman glide silently into the gallery. As much as he wanted to go, to get away from this place, curiosity won out. He had to see what interested her.

He entered the gallery through a door hidden in the carved wood panels behind one of the smaller tapestries. Protected now in the shadows of the cloth, Conall watched her move toward him, stopping in front of the great fireplace.

The family portraits.

She stood not a dozen paces from him. Conall studied the woman.

Smart, observant, shrewd in negotiations, albeit somewhat abrupt. This was how his brother had spoken of her. To win Ailein's hand in marriage, Bryce had needed to get by the older sister first. It wasn't easy, by all reports.

From his apartments in the West Tower, Conall had watched the Munros arrive that morning. Oddly, it was Innes, and not his future sister-in-law, who captured his attention. The woman stood apart from the rest. Calm.

Quiet. A detached bystander.

Her appearance surprised him. He had given no thought to what she would look like, but realized he had expected some shrewish old crone.

Conall's gaze moved over her now. She was hardly a crone. A modest black dress covered her diminutive frame, but there was no ignoring the soft curves of her breasts or the flare of her hips. And she was anything but old. He stared at the flawless skin of her face, the high cheekbones, the full lips. Her dark silky hair, braided into a thick rope, fell to her waist. But his eyes were drawn to the curious shock of white hair framing one side of her face.

The young woman's demeanor softened into a smile as she continued to study the paintings. This close, she was striking. Not a classic beauty, but beautiful, nonetheless. It was her mouth. Something stirred deep in his belly. Conall knew lust, but he hadn't felt it for a long time. He didn't need to be thinking such thoughts now, either.

His gaze turned to the object of her attention.

The portrait of him had been done not long before he went south to fight the king's war. Before Solway Moss. He was whole then, a man with his entire life ahead of him. Intact in body and mind, before he became what he was now. A mere shell of a man. A relic of lost dreams.

He backed away.

She was looking at a dead man.

———————

Innes started at the muffled sound of a door closing.

She glanced around, holding her taper high. She was alone. There was no one else in the gallery.

She heard footsteps approaching from the Great Hall, and the steward, Lachlan, limped in.

"I thought I saw a light here. Can I help you with anything, mistress?"

She pulled on her glove. "Nay, thank you. I'm fine. I couldn't sleep, so I went for a walk."

The man waited politely.

"The tapestries and paintings are very beautiful," said Innes.

Lachlan looked up at the walls, nodding. "I suppose they are. Some are quite old, I believe. A wee bit of trouble, too, they are," he grumbled. "Put them up for the wedding, and now I'll be taking them down and putting them back in storage. And who saw them? You, mistress, are all."

"Well, I'm grateful to you." She gestured to the painting of Conall Sinclair. "The earl of Caithness. Is he in storage, too?"

"Eh?"

"His lordship. I didn't see him at dinner tonight. Is he here at Castle Girnigoe?"

"Well, he is and he isn't."

Innes cocked an eyebrow at the man. "And will he be here tomorrow, for his brother's wedding?"

"Difficult to say, mistress. If he is, he'll be standing beside the laird on the chapel steps. If he isn't, he won't be."

Chapter 2

Castle Girnigoe sat on a narrow peninsula atop slabs of rock that rose high above the sparkling blue-green sea. Innes couldn't help but be impressed by the three towers looming over the sea and the rolling moors.

Standing amid the throng of Sinclairs and Munros waiting for the bride to appear, she looked past the happy but boisterous crowd at her sister's new home.

For the wedding celebration, the servants had decorated the courtyard with bright banners and flags. Spring flowers of yellow, pink, violet, and blue were woven into garlands and hung everywhere, adding even more color to the festivities.

The chapel stood in the original section of castle the Sinclairs now called the Inner Ward. Over the past two decades, the clan had added two more sections to the clan seat. The Outer Ward, with its North Tower, held the new Great Hall, laird's quarters, gallery, and kitchens. Beyond it, a bridge led to a walled stable and a West Tower.

Innes was satisfied. She couldn't have found a more secure home for her sister. With its impenetrable gray walls, high towers, and the surrounding sea, Castle Girni-goe was beyond impressive.

She was happy for Ailein. This was a perfect place to live, to start a new life. Her gaze was drawn to Bryce, standing alone on the steps of the chapel. She wondered if the earl of Caithness would make his appearance.

"Couldn't you change into something more appropriate, at least for today?" her stepmother urged, interrupting her thoughts. "There's still time, and this is a celebration. You shouldn't be wearing black."

"I'll wear what I please," Innes said curtly.

"And you're fine with this, Hector? Your daughter, wearing black at her own sister's wedding?"

"What business is it of mine what she wears?" the Munro clan chief replied. "She's a grown woman. Leave her be. She knows what she's about."

Her stepmother was not ready to give up. "But *why*, Innes? Today of all days should be an exception. Ailein is the only one that you care a fish egg about anyway."

"How many times does she have to tell you?" Hector intervened. "She wears black because she is in mourning."

"Mourning?"

"Aye, for the death of innocence in the world."

"By the Virgin, man, and you encourage her by repeating that nonsense?"

Innes stopped listening, looking past her stepmother

and her father. She focused on the windows halfway up the East Tower.

What could be keeping Ailein? The last time she'd checked, the women of the household were bustling about the bride with the efficiency of a small army, and Jinny was ordering them about like a warrior chief. Come hell or high water, her sister would be suitably dressed, adorned, and standing at noon at the chapel doors.

A movement drew Innes's gaze upward. A dark shape moved in a window above her sister's chambers. Another outsider, she thought, watching the events of life without taking part. She understood that all too keenly.

A young woman's anxious voice broke in. "I am so relieved to find you, mistress."

Innes glanced at her and then looked up again. The shadow in the window was still there.

"Lady Ailein is in a state," continued the serving woman. "She sent us all away, and Jinny said to search you out and bring you back as soon as I found you."

Innes allowed the young servant to lead the way. "Tell me. Who is staying in the upper chambers above my sister?"

The woman glanced back, her eyes wide. "No one, mistress. The upper chambers are shut and locked."

"Locked, you say?" Innes asked, looking up. The shadowy figure was gone.

"Aye, mistress. It's been that way for months now."

———————

Distant, quiet, observing rather than participating, Conall thought.

Innes Munro was the only interesting fish in that sea of guests. Eying the black dress, he shook his head. That's not quite right, he mused. She was more like a raven in a flower garden. A rebel. A presence.

Innes looked up and he thought she might have seen him. He backed away from the window and turned around, his eyes surveying Shona's room.

Bryce had been at Conall's door at dawn, again insisting that he at least show up for the marriage ceremony. To get rid of him, he promised to think about it.

He had thought about it. He still wasn't going. But he wasn't leaving Castle Girnigoe until he found what he came up here for.

Conall glanced for a moment at the large window from which Shona fell to her death on the cliffs this past winter. He frowned and walked to the dresser, searching for the brooch. It had belonged to his mother. He had given it to Shona before he left, thinking she would become his wife when he returned.

But his life had gone down a different path.

———

They reached the East Tower and the woman stepped aside to let her pass.

Innes moved from the bright spring sunlight of the courtyard into the damp darkness of the tower house stairwell. She started up the stone steps.

Her sister should be on her way to the chapel now, Innes thought. It did not bode well that she was sending out the very women tasked with preparing her for the ceremony. She frowned.

"Nay, Ailein," she murmured. "I know what you want, and I'm not doing it. Not this time."

Reaching the landing, Innes pushed open the door without bothering to knock.

Jinny threw her hands up and sighed with relief. "Praise be. You've come."

Innes had known Jinny since the woman came to look after her and Ailein when their mother died. Seeing now the frustration in the lined face, she shook her head. After all the years of service to their family, Jinny knew the two sisters well enough not to be bullied by a mere outburst of temper.

Ailein lay on the bed sobbing, her head buried in a pillow. She raised a tearstained face at the sound of Innes's entrance.

"I'm *not* marrying him. I've changed my mind."

"I see." Innes peeled off her gloves and stuffed them into the sash at her waist. She motioned toward the small adjoining room. "Can you give us a few moments alone, Jinny?"

"Aye, with pleasure," the older woman barked. "But she's supposed to be down at the chapel shortly. And with all this thrashing about on the bed, you can see her hair is a mess and the dress is now wrinkled and I don't know how I can possibly get her ready in time. She'll be shaming us all. Aye, lassie, I'm talking about you."

Glaring fiercely at her charge, Jinny stalked toward the other room.

"You'll do magic. I'm certain of it," Innes said quietly, closing the heavy wood door and leaning her back against it. She looked at her sister, who'd again buried her head in the pillow.

At the age of twenty-one, Ailein was like the heather in early autumn, ready to burst into flower. No Highland clan could boast a woman of greater beauty. With her deep red hair cascading to her waist and the slant of her large gray eyes and the upturned nose dusted with pale freckles, she could turn a man's head at the far end of any great hall. She was the pride of the Munros. And on top of it all, she came with a sizable dowry. As a result, for several years Ailein had attracted a line of suitors that stretched from Folais Castle to Edinburgh itself.

Innes had been at her sister's side for every first meeting. It was a mistake. Naturally, Innes read their lives like an open book. Like looking at the pebbles at the bottom of a clear mountain stream, she saw every flaw and mistake that colored their past. Men lied. Men cheated. No surprise. When a man wanted something badly enough, what he said and what he thought were often as different as night and day. Innes told her sister the truth about each man's past. That was all it took. Ailein made sure that they never came back.

Then, some three years later, Innes realized that she was robbing Ailein of any chance of married life. She'd made her own choice when it came to turning down the handful of suitors who'd come for her hand years earlier, but Ailein needed to take a chance.

Enough was enough. Her sister's weak-kneed reaction to Bryce Sinclair, the strapping young laird of Castle Girnigoe, was all the encouragement she needed. Innes decided to let them be.

Silence hung in the air. A head of tousled, red hair lifted from the pillow, and the young woman's tearful gaze turned to her.

"Please, Innes. Please do it for me. Take hold of his hand. Tell me what it is I'm getting myself into."

"I am no fortune teller." Innes approached the bed. "Get up. Right now. This moment."

Ailein rolled out of her reach to the other side. "How do I know if he's the right man for me? I have no idea how he feels. What he thinks. What if he's marrying me only for the dowry? What if he's still in love with his first wife?"

Innes lifted the mattress and her sister rolled off, landing with a thud on the floor. Her flushed face reappeared above the bedclothes.

"Ouch. That hurt, you know. What did you do that for? Sometimes you can be so cruel."

"Aye, cruel as the winter wind. Remember that. You *don't* want to spend the rest of your life with me."

"I never said I wanted to." Ailein stood up, her hands on her hips. "I'm not asking you for any more than what you've always done."

"Nay, you're asking for *much* more. This is no first meeting. This is your wedding day. This is Girnigoe, their clan seat. The Sinclairs, the Munros, and a hundred guests are waiting for you and Bryce to exchange your vows. Our father is already at the chapel steps, waiting to give you away."

"I'm not married yet. It's *not* too late."

Innes fought the inclination to raise her voice and order her sister about. She knew where that would end. As sweet as Ailein appeared to others, they had the same iron will.

Innes took a deep breath and started again. "Think this through. You love Bryce. You told me that a hundred times."

"I think I love him. I might be wrong."

"Every time you've seen him, he's been courteous, charming, attentive."

Ailein shrugged. "To me and you and the other Munros who kept a close eye on us."

"Well, that's a good start in any marriage. You already have a foundation."

"How do you know what's a good foundation?" she snapped. "You've never been married."

"Nay. I've never been married, as you well know. I've never been wooed before, either. And I've never been kissed. I've never been asked for my hand in marriage. And I will never share a man's bed or have children of my own. And no one will ever love me. And when the winter of life sets in, I'll have no memories of my own to think back on and keep me company. If I live so long." She looked into her sister's eyes. "And is this what you want for your life?"

Ailein stared at her for a moment and then batted away fresh tears. She shook her head and rushed across the chamber to hug Innes.

Cradling her sister's face, Innes looked into her soul at the fears and the insecurity Ailein was feeling about marrying this man. Bryce Sinclair was a man with much more experience. He was a widower who had lost his wife tragically. But Innes also saw the hope and love that her sister felt right up to this moment.

"I do love you, Innes," said Ailein. "I always will. And you can come and stay here with me any time you want. We'll force Father to let you come, if that's what it takes."

Her sister's surging emotions silenced Innes. Ailein had said what was in her heart. The truth.

It was a sad fact that no one could see into Innes's heart. The words she'd said—about herself, about her life, about her future—bled her inside.

"Very well, then," she said. "Sit in that chair. I'll get Jinny."

The extra hands were all assembled in the adjoining room A few minutes later, excitement again filled the chamber. Ailein sat, and stood, and stepped into layers of dress and had her hair pulled, piled, and pinned. She smiled through it all.

Innes was happy for her sister, but at the same time, she ached at the loss of her. All of their routines and arguments and companionship were ending today. Tomorrow she'd return with her father and his wife and their children to Folais Castle.

Ailein now had her own life. Her husband. Her new clan. They would always be sisters but this marriage divided them, sending them down separate paths.

As emotions threatened to overwhelm her, Innes quietly slipped out of the room onto the dark landing.

Taking a few deep breaths, she forced herself to bury those raw feelings, donning once again the hard, impenetrable cloak she wore in public. This was the way her sister's new family would see her today—brusque, confident, in charge. And in the main, she was happy with the life she had. No regrets.

She pulled the gloves from her sash and started down the stairs.

Halfway down, her foot slipped on the edge of a step, and she pitched forward. She dropped her gloves, her hands flailing for anything to grab. Her foot barely touched the next stair as she hurtled forward into the darkness. She braced herself, knowing her head and face were about to strike stone.

Suddenly, she was plucked from the air. One moment she was falling uncontrollably, and the next she was righted and placed on her own two feet. Her knees buckled.

He pushed her against the wall and, in the dim light, she saw the man who had caught her was missing his right hand. He was broad across the chest and very tall.

Her gaze moved from the black shirt he wore beneath his tartan to his face. Wild black hair hung to his shoulders, a full beard framed a swarthy face, and his eyes were dark as a loch at night.

Truth rooted and blossomed. Her heartbeat increased its rhythm. She knew who he was.

"You," she gasped. She'd been hoping to see him, to meet the great Sinclair warrior. But not this way. "You're the earl of Caithness."

"Can you stand?" His voice was deep and harsh. He sounded annoyed with her for inconveniencing him—or maybe for recognizing him. His good hand was on her shoulder, still holding her up.

"I'm fine. Thank you for catching me."

She pushed his hand away, and as she did, her mind melded with his. In a flash of an instant, she was back in the gallery off the Great Hall. It wasn't the paintings that she saw, but rather Innes herself, through his eyes. He'd been there, watching her.

Her face grew warm as she looked up into his face. But then the image changed. Her senses filled with the sight and sounds of a battlefield. A gasp escaped her as bloody corpses and the smell of blood and sweat filled her senses. Those still living cried out, filling the air with the pleading voices of the dying... and those who wished they were dead. She stared at a severed hand at her feet and a man's anguished roar blotted out every other sound.

Innes's head cleared. She blinked. She was alone.

The man was gone. The only sound was her heartbeat drumming in her ears, and a piper tuning up in the distance.

With only a brush of her hand over his wrist, his mind had swept her in. Unprepared, she hadn't seen, but felt the pain. She'd been there on that battlefield with him.

And she'd felt his shame.

She brushed away the beads of sweat on her brow and looked around. No one. No footsteps. Nothing.

A door opened and closed below.

She needed light. Air. She had to shake herself free of the horror she'd seen.

Her gloves lay on the steps. She picked them up and hurried down. Sunlight poured in through the doorway.

There was no sign of the earl. In the deep shadows at the bottom of the stairs, she noticed another door she hadn't seen before. It was heavy, with steel bands and studded nails reinforcing the thick wood. A stout timber stood against the wall to secure it on this side.

She strode to the door and took hold of the handle. As she did, she heard a latch slide into place on the other side.

———

She was as light as the wind, as soft as the finest silk. He'd inhaled the fresh scent of sea and salt on her skin. His arm had wrapped around her narrow waist and, for a fleeting moment, his hand had brushed her breast.

Conall didn't want to notice Innes Munro. He didn't want to admit that, up close, she was even more alluring than he'd imagined. He didn't want any of that, especially after she'd fallen ill at the sight of his missing hand.

He stared at the latch on the door. He wasn't attracted to her. He wouldn't allow it.

No, his problem was that it had been too long since he'd been with a woman.

Chapter 3

They had no need for words. Holding onto Ailein, Innes saw her sister's struggle to imagine what her life would be like after she left tomorrow.

No running to her for advice, Ailein was thinking. No stories to share. No outbursts or arguments. No wandering together along the beaches and through the glens as Innes collected pieces of bird eggs and feathers to add to her collection. No searching on market days through bolts of black fabric to make a new dress.

"You're making this harder for both of us." Ailein tucked the white hair behind Innes's ear, and drew back.

This was her sister's wedding night, thought Innes. She should be happy, excited. Not sad.

Innes moved around the chamber, her fingers touching the bright decorative ribbons. She fought back her own raw emotions. She wouldn't cry. She couldn't fall apart and make it worse for her sister. She stopped to breathe in the aromatic bouquets of dried rosemary, sage, lavender, and thyme. She inspected the clothes and the gifts scattered around the room, finally stopping by the open window overlooking the bluffs. The moon was rising and the sea glistened brightly. The soft breeze drifted in with the sounds of the sea, caressing her face.

Ailein was only an infant when their mother died. Six years older, Innes immediately shouldered the responsibility of both mother and sister. Their father had married twice since then, but she never relinquished her position.

She stole a glance over her shoulder at Ailein, who was pinning an ornate, jeweled brooch to the tartan arranged around her shoulders.

They were sisters, yet looked nothing alike. Ailein inherited her height and red hair and complexion from their father. Innes was their mother, dark haired, small, and reclusive. But they each had the heart of a lion, especially when it came to protecting those they loved.

Tears rushed into Innes's eyes as she realized there would never be moments like this. Not after tomorrow. She looked onto the sea and took a deep breath.

"This new North Tower. How do you like it?" Ailein asked.

"It is lovely."

"Bryce has been living here, so I chose it over the East Tower."

Bryce's first wife had stayed in those rooms, in the older section of Girnigoe. Innes was happy that her sister didn't have to battle memories of an old marriage in her new chambers. She leaned out the open window, looking down at the roaring sea.

"Not so far, if you please. That height worries me."

"Aye, good reason to be worried," Innes replied. "Perhaps there should be a bar across these windows."

"They say it was an accident."

"So I understand."

"I asked his aunt about it. I had to know how his first wife died, and Wynda told me what happened."

"I heard the tale. It was a stormy day this past winter, just after Samhain. They say she somehow slipped at the window and fell from the top floor of the East Tower. They found her body at the base of the cliffs. Her chambers were just above where you dressed for the ceremony." Innes paused. "And Bryce was away from Girnigoe when it happened."

Ailein stared at her. "So you touched his hand. That's how you know."

"Nay. I didn't. I told you before that I wouldn't. I asked questions, like you. That's the proper way one gets answers."

She moved to another window, one overlooking the courtyard. Over the years, Innes had witnessed the damage she'd done to Ailein by making all the decisions, giving her all the answers.

Ailein's life resembled that of a bairn practicing the steps but never actually walking on her own two feet. Always protected. She had no bumps or bruises, no heartbreak she ever had to deal with. Twenty-one years of age and she'd never done anything but rely on Innes to tell her what to do, whom to trust, where to go. This neverending cycle undermined the younger woman's confidence in herself, in her judgment. Innes knew. She'd played the same game with her own life when she was younger. That was why she was alone.

Bryce Sinclair was a good match. The two had to make their marriage work without any ethereal interference.

"You would not leave in the morning without seeing me?" asked Ailein.

"Are you forgetting the wedding night traditions?" Innes was sorry she mentioned it as her sister's face turned a deep shade of red.

"How can I forget? The Sinclairs will be wanting evidence that I'm the maiden our father promised them. You and the Munros won't be leaving until Bryce and his clan are satisfied."

It was barbaric, but tradition was tradition. Innes was relieved that Jinny was the one who had to do all the explaining to her sister.

Ailein hugged her middle and glanced warily at the large bed. "What happens if I don't bleed?"

"I wouldn't worry. I'm sure Bryce will know how to handle everything."

"He should. He married his first wife Shona little more than a year ago."

Innes recognized her sister's sharp tone. Ailein was rummaging around for a fight. She got this way when she was nervous or things weren't going the way she wished them. Innes hoped some solitary time would calm her.

"It's time for me to leave you." She pulled on her gloves.

Ailein looked up in panic. "Do you have to? Can't you wait with me until he comes?"

"Absolutely not." Innes backed toward the door. "He should be here very soon. You're his wife, but you're also a Munro, the daughter of a baron. In the eyes of the world, you are his equal. Remember that."

"Oh, Innes!"

"You'll do well here among the Sinclairs. They are good people. He appears to be a good man." Her voice turned husky with emotion. "You no longer need me."

The tears had a mind of their own, but she left the room before her sister could see them.

———

Moonlight flooded the rolling moors, and the starry sky

was cloudless. A perfect night to travel.

Waiting for Duff to bring out his horse, Conall glanced around for his companion, Thunder. No sign of him, but Conall wasn't worried. Thunder always turned up.

"You were here all day, and still you couldn't stand up with your brother."

Conall turned to see his aunt emerge from the shadows.

"I've decided to make a habit of missing Bryce's weddings," he said.

Their father's sister Wynda had moved back to Girnigoe when Conall's mother died. Wynda raised them and was as much a mother to them as their own had been. He studied the older woman. Even by moonlight, he could see the lines in her face that grew deeper with each passing season. Conall knew much of the preparation of this week's festivities had fallen on Wynda's shoulders.

"You look exhausted, Aunt. Why aren't you in bed?"

"I had to come and see you before you went off."

A brisk breeze blew in off the sea. He reached over and adjusted the shawl she wore over her dark dress.

"This one was much better, Conall," she continued. "Your brother has done well for himself. Ailein is nothing like the last wife."

"There could only be one Shona."

Wynda studied him in silence for a moment. "I wish

you had come, if only just to meet the sister."

"Innes?"

"You know her?" she replied, surprised.

Know was too strong a word, he thought. He recalled the woman he'd watched in the gallery. The one he'd held briefly on the staircase. He didn't *know* her, but she definitely had his attention, and those brief moments continued to linger in his mind.

Good enough reason for leaving.

He caught his aunt staring at him. "All right. Out with it. Why would you want me to meet the sister?"

"No reason." A rare smile broke on Wynda's lips. "Innes is different. Odd in some ways. Intelligent and unafraid to voice her opinion. I believe she enjoys her reputation of being difficult."

"Difficult? And why would you wish such a thing on me?"

"Birds of the feather."

Duff led Conall's horse out the stable door, saving him from continuing this conversation.

"Well, no chance of that happening," Conall said. "I understand the Munros are leaving tomorrow. And I plan to be away for quite a while."

France, perhaps. Innes heard that the mountains in the west of France had birds that were never seen in Scotland. That might be just the place for her. The time had come for change, she thought, looking out at the moon now high above the castle ramparts.

For a few years now, Innes had imagined that when her sister finally married, she'd be able to establish her own daily regimen, or lack of it. Of course, as long as she was at home, her stepmother would be an obstacle. Margaret, only a few years older than Innes, was a creature of habit, schedules, and decorum. And everything about Innes was disruptive.

No, it was now time to pursue a different path. Her father had Margaret, his sons, the affairs of the clan to see to. She would travel. It was 1544. The Spanish had discovered a new world. The Portuguese were sailing around Africa to trade with the East. The world was opening up.

She'd already told her father that she wanted to go. She wanted to see something of that world and then, possibly, settle down in some convent in a quiet part of Scotland. So far, Hector Munro wouldn't discuss it, but at least he'd given up on the idea of marrying her off. Perhaps once they returned home, she could raise the topic with him again.

Innes drifted back to the table where she'd been working on a charcoal drawing of Folais Castle. A parting gift for her sister. It should have been finished long ago. But it wasn't.

These drawings were her greatest pleasure. When she was young, she drew only on slate or pieces of wood, but German merchant ships now carried crates of paper from their mills. She treasured her store of it and used it sparingly.

She pulled out the other sketch, the one she'd drawn quickly tonight, trying to clear her mind of the disturbing image branded in her brain. She shivered as she gazed at the picture, recalling those bodies left to rot on the battlefield. Dark strokes were a pale imitation of the pools of blood. The men's faces were a gray blur, but their cries still rang in her ear.

Conall Sinclair. She doubted anyone ever had a clearer look into the earl's soul than she had today. No wonder that he had become a recluse. At the church and in the Great Hall afterwards, she'd scanned the gathered throng, hoping that he'd be there. But he hadn't shown up.

Wars and warriors. She never fathomed the brutality that humans exposed their own kind to. To pay the price for power by killing.

In the courtyard below her window, two drunken revelers from the wedding celebration wandered by, bellowing passages from *The Wallace* at the top of their voices. Innes listened as they passed by, each one embellishing on the poem in an effort to outdo the other. And the glory of wars lived on for future generations.

Innes stared at her drawing, at the severed hand lying in the grass. She'd stood in his memory. That anguished roar, as they dragged him from the battlefield, wasn't for the loss of a limb. That cry was for the loss of freedom.

She closed her eyes. She tried to think of something else—a better memory to take away from Girnigoe. Conall Sinclair had been in the gallery last night. He'd watched her. He knew she existed.

A soft tap on the door put a quick end to her folly. Innes pushed the drawing under the others and looked over. There was a second knock.

It was very late. Except for the two drunken revelers, the wedding celebration—with its shouts and pipers and singing—had died down some time ago. She wondered if perhaps one of her young brothers next door had awakened.

"Who is it?" she called.

"Open the door."

At the sound of Ailein's voice, Innes's heart dropped in her chest. She unlatched the door, and her sister, wrapped in a dark cloak, slipped inside.

"What are you doing here?" Innes looked out before

closing and latching the door.

Ailein moved to the window and peered for a moment into the darkness. "I didn't want to be seen. Not that I care. But for the sake of propriety, I suppose it's better if the Sinclairs don't know I'm spending my wedding night in my sister's bedchamber."

Even in the dim light, Innes saw Ailein had been crying.

"What happened? What did he do to you?" she asked, suddenly furious that the Sinclair might have hurt her sister. And on their wedding night! It was her fault, she thought. She should have protected her sister.

"He did nothing," Ailein responded quickly, putting up a hand to stop Innes from coming to her. "Nothing happened. He became angry because of a gift someone left for me. It was ridiculous. So, I threw him out. I told him he would not be sleeping with me until his manners improved."

Innes stared at her sister for a heartbeat, then decided this couldn't be all of it. She started toward her.

"Don't. I'm telling you the truth. He didn't touch me." Ailein dropped the cloak on a chair and pushed up the sleeves of a robe she wore over her nightgown. "When he got angry, he stopped talking. Everything just became . . . business. So I got upset. I was angry. I wanted him to explain. But he wouldn't."

Ailein had wanted a fight, or at least a good argument. Innes had seen signs of it before she left. This was what her sister was accustomed to. Looking at her storming about the room now, Innes decided Bryce had done nothing to damage her sister's fiery spirit.

"What was this gift he was so upset about?"

"The brooch I had on."

"I saw it. It was lovely. It looked like a family heirloom."

"Perhaps it was." Ailein waved a hand in the air and started pacing the room. "But I'm not a simpleton. The brooch must have belonged to his first wife. And I have no idea who put it there for me."

"It sounds as if this is easily resolved. If it wasn't Bryce, then it had to be Wynda or—"

"It doesn't matter. What upsets me most is that he went from ordering me to take it off to lecturing me about my duty and his duty. It was upsetting. And he says he's keeping separate chambers! Our time together will be for one purpose only. And I should expect nothing more. It's all just a sham. My marriage is a fraud!" Ailein stopped and faced her. "That was all I could take. I told him he had to leave."

"And he left?" Innes needed to make sure.

"Oh, he tried to look threatening, but I wasn't having any of that. So in the end he just yanked the sheet from the bed and stomped out."

"The sheet," Innes repeated. She was relieved that Bryce Sinclair was not some brute who would force his wife against her wishes. There were more than a few of those around.

"Aye. I found it spotted with blood outside of my bedroom door. There it lay, for anyone to see it," she said angrily. "My maidenhead, my lost virtue, on display."

"But your virtue wasn't lost. Was it his own blood on it?"

"I suppose so, but for all I care he might have cut his own throat. And you wouldn't believe how much blood! Like I was a stuck pig. It was right out there in the open. His manly badge of *honor*." She moved off to the window, muttering words of violence under her breath.

"Ailein, listen to me now. You need to understand this. He did you a favor."

"He did no such thing."

"Think it through. Where would we be if everyone knew that you refused your husband on your wedding night?"

"Everyone can go pound sand!"

"Nay. I don't mean to sound callous, but this is clan business."

"You sound like him."

"Of course it's not *just* business, but there were agreements made."

Ailein glared at her.

"Bryce covered your tracks for you," Innes continued. "Protected you. So now—as far as everyone is concerned—you're his wife. Whatever argument you have with him, it's only between you two to sort out. The clans will have no part in it."

Hands clenched at her sides, Ailein stamped her foot. She stared at the door, trying to restrain her temper. "I told him I'd stay. But I think I gave in too much. I want to go home."

"Ailein," Innes remonstrated. "You are showing less sense than a child."

Ailein sent her a hurt look. "I know I'm already married. And I really *don't* want to go. I just want him to go back to being the man who courted me. I would have been fine if he'd just been civil. Just talked to me."

Innes sank down on the edge of the bed. This was the newlyweds' first argument. And knowing Ailein, it wouldn't be the last, by any stretch of the imagination. She actually felt a twinge of sympathy for Bryce. She was certain the Sinclair had no idea of the strength of his wife's temperament until tonight.

"He probably had too much ale or wine. I can't tell you how many times they toasted his health and yours. He'll be back to himself tomorrow."

"What if he isn't? As you say, everyone thinks we've

consummated this marriage. You'll all be gone, and I'll be left here with no one."

"You're married. You want this to work. So tomorrow night, you pick up where you left off today. You work through your trouble. This is your new home, my love."

Ailein shook her head doubtfully, then sat next to Innes on the bed. "I'll stay if you stay."

"That's impossible." Innes shook her head. "I'm going back to Folais Castle."

"It's not impossible. Stay for just a short time. For a month. That's all I'm asking."

"This is your life now, Ailein. There is nothing I can do to help you or improve your relationship with your husband."

"A fortnight, then. That's all. Please, Innes." Ailein threw her arms around her. "With you here, it will all work out. I'm certain of it."

An unexpected image took shape in her mind. Conall Sinclair. Innes pushed it away.

"This is a mistake. I'm telling you. With me here, you'll have someone to run to every time you have a disagreement with him."

"I won't come running. I promise. I want you here because I love you. You're my sister. A fortnight. Please, Innes. Do this for me."

Chapter 4

"Here begins a short treatise on the history of the Wheel of Lugh, writ down for the edification of ignorant and sinful wretches, wherein they may learn of our sovereign Savior Christ Jhesu, who sheds His Light and His Goodness and His Power on us in ways his people can little understand. This narrative being the truly spoken words of Ian Wallace, as told to Gilchrist Scribe, in this year anno Domini 1494.

"This is my true understanding of the Wheel of Lugh, of where it came from, and how it came to be broken into four, and where the fragments of the Wheel have gone, and of a terrible power that can belong only to a true High King, Lord save us all.

"I undertake to have all this chronicle writ down now to preserve what I know. Plague rides on the wind across my beloved land, and folk are dying all about me. I fear that I too shall be struck down and rendered unable to keep my vow. I shall be unable to pass on the history of the Wheel and my fragment which, through the grace of the Lord and Lugh his warrior king, gives me a knowledge of the past that no other man possesses.

"And so this history begins . . ."

From the *Chronicle of Lugh*

"So, what are you trying to do?" Innes muttered to herself as she walked. "Stay here forever? Grow old here? Die and be buried here?"

The fortnight she promised Ailein had passed, but the newlyweds seemed no closer to resolving their problems. So, she allowed herself to be persuaded to extend her stay for another sennight. The two behaved perfectly well whenever they were in public, but Innes knew that Bryce continued to avoid his wife's bed.

He's a laird, Innes thought. And he's a man. All that's needed, in all likelihood, is an apology. When she suggested that to her sister, Ailein countered that she'd do a penance of a thousand Ave Marias before admitting she did anything wrong.

Two pigheaded people, locked in a standoff.

Pushing her cloak over one shoulder as she walked the hard ground, Innes admitted that the living arrangements here were better than she had at home. After the wedding guests left, she moved to the second floor chamber in the East Tower—the same rooms where her sister had dressed for the ceremony. Here in the Inner Ward she was a bit removed from the bustle of daily activity in the castle's newer Outer Ward. And as the sole occupant in that building, she was free to come and go, and to keep her own schedule as she pleased.

Though she didn't want to admit it, even to herself, her only disappointment was that she hadn't seen Conall Sinclair even once since her tumble into his arms on the staircase. She couldn't ask about him directly, but Jinny told her that the word among the servants was that the earl often went off to the Sinclair hunting lodge unannounced, and for weeks at a time. Some thought he'd gone there the day of the wedding.

It was for the best, Innes told herself. Her fascination with the man was futile. It would be better for all parties if she scratched out those brief moments from her memory.

And she enjoyed her routines. Most days, she wrote and sketched. She listened to and argued with Ailein whenever her sister tired of her daily tasks as the laird's wife. Only on occasion did Innes join the others in the Great Hall for meals, and no one complained when she visited the kitchens for a tray of food.

And she explored. Innes loved this shoreline. The wildness of the sea and the variety of birds thrilled her, giving her ample material for her sketching and her collecting. And the long stretches of stony beach provided solitude that she cherished. Once she traveled beyond the gardens protected from the wind by stone walls and the fields filled with flocks of sheep, she could walk for hours without seeing or talking to a living soul. Away from Girnigoe, she would occasionally come upon deer that immediately bounded off, and red shaggy cattle that regarded her with mild interest for only a moment before lowering their great heads again to graze.

Every morning at dawn, regardless of the weather, she made her way down to the rocky strand. As she walked, she was often joined by the seals who would follow her just offshore, their sleek heads and brown eyes appearing, focused on her, and then disappearing. In the evening, she stayed on the path along the bluffs where she could look down on the roaring sea and the occasional stone huts of the families that fished the waters, or sit in a protected spot and watch the golden sun descend slowly in the western sky.

Tonight, she had no setting sun or rising moon to enjoy. No sky above her, no sea stretching into the distance. A chill gray fog obscured everything, limiting her vision to a few yards around her. She was glad she'd left her leather case of charcoal and paper in her chambers when, a mile or so from the castle, the rain began to fall.

Innes pushed back the hood of the cloak and raised her face to the sky, welcoming the touch of rain on her skin, in her hair. Closing her eyes, she listened as the sounds of nature came to her like a melody. Waves crashed over the rocks beyond the cliffs. Sea birds cried out as they hovered above her in the breeze, warning of the impending storm. The wind whirred and rustled as it caressed the hills.

A growl, deep and menacing, raised hackles of fear in her scalp.

Innes's eyes opened and her head jerked toward the sound. The animal was huge, larger than any dog she'd ever seen. He stood only a dozen paces from her, at the crest of a low rise. When he took a step toward her, her heart pounded in her chest. In an instant she took it all in: the shape of the head and the ears, the lips pulled back, the show of teeth that could tear out her throat, the piercing glare of eyes almost orange.

This was no dog. It was a wolf.

Cold sweat broke out on her face. She couldn't breathe. She hadn't heard him approach.

"Hello," she said, finding her voice. She once heard her father's lead huntsman say that wolves were more afraid of people than people were of them. She hoped that was true. But this one did not look frightened.

"Where did you come from?" Her voice quavered.

She realized she was hugging the basket tight against her chest, as if that could possibly offer some protection.

"I didn't know any of you were left in these parts, and

yet here you are. I think someone might have warned me, don't you?"

The wolf cocked his head, looking at her as if she were an idiot, thinking he would talk back.

"As handsome as you are, why don't you just go your own way?" She was surprised at how calm she sounded, in spite of the terror clutching her insides. "Really. You go your way and I go mine."

The dogs and cats that roamed free in Folais Castle and in the farmland surrounding it generally kept their distance from her. She always thought it was because they sensed her power. But to a wolf, especially one the size of this one, she was the next meal.

"I promise not to tell anyone I saw you."

She took a step backward. The wolf moved with her, lowering his head. Cold sweat spread to the rest of her body. She couldn't outrun him. She had a small knife at her belt, good for little more than cutting her food.

"You seem well fed," she said, taking another step back. "As you can see, I have little meat on my bones."

She didn't want to do anything to appear hostile. In all the pasts of the men and women whose lives she had peered into, not once had there been a wolf attack. Not that any of that mattered at this moment.

The wolf moved in closer, his eyes never leaving her face. Suddenly, the beast bounded toward her.

Innes froze, unable to move, unable to think, unable to even cry out.

The animal circled, sniffing her as he went.

The wolf was even larger up close, and he exuded power. Raw power that showed itself in his smooth, fluid movements.

She was dead; she had no doubt now.

Even as she thought with cold dread of her imminent demise in those jaws, Innes recognized the sheer beauty in this animal. His thick coat wasn't just gray, but banded with black, white, gold, and brown. His eyes, so clear and alert, had thin bursts of green amid the orange.

He nosed her elbow, her hip. She stood still, not breathing, every muscle in her body tense. Her hands were shaking. She'd heard that people often fainted in situations such as this, but she decided she must be too frightened to pass out.

"You see, beast? I'm no threat. Go on your way. Find a fat rabbit for your supper."

He sniffed at the empty basket and then raised a paw and batted at it. It fell from her hands, but she didn't dare reach down for it. He cautiously put his nose in it, all the time keeping an eye on her. Evidently satisfied that there was nothing in it to eat, the wolf turned his full attention back to Innes.

"This is it. I'm going to die," she murmured. "Blessed

Virgin, intercede for me at this moment of my—"

She got no further. Raising himself up onto his hind legs, the wolf put both front paws on her shoulders. She gasped and staggered back a couple of steps under his weight, but the animal moved with her.

Somehow, Innes managed to keep her balance.

And then, with a mix of horror and astonishment, she stood still as the beast licked her entire face—her nose, her cheeks, even her eyes. He nibbled at her jaw and chin, but never scratched her skin.

Affection! The realization struck her suddenly, and her fear dissolved like a morning mist in summer. She heard herself laugh, which only seemed to encourage him.

She tried to back away, push him down, but she couldn't do it. "Do we know each other?"

The absurdity of the situation and the way he paused at her question made her laugh again. She reached up and touched the thick fur at his shoulders. Her fingers sank into softness.

Suddenly, his weight was too much and she went sprawling onto her back.

The wolf danced in a circle around her, nipping her hair, kissing her ear, tugging at her clothes and shoes. Clearly, a game had begun.

"Hey, what do you think you're doing?" She pushed him away, only to have him jump back at her.

Innes put her arms over her face to protect herself. She was no longer frightened, but overwhelmed by the speed and enthusiasm of the animal. The wolf's heavy paws landed on her chest, and he put his full weight on her. His teeth wrapped around her elbow, mouthing her arm but clearly with no intention of hurting her. She peered into the animal's eyes, and a thought crossed her mind.

She'd never done anything like this before, but curiosity compelled her now.

Her free hand reached up and she touched the soft fur by his ears. He paused, watching her warily. She caressed the ears and nose. And as she did, an image rushed into her mind's eye. A man was lifting the pup into his arms.

She knew the man's face. Conall Sinclair.

"Thunder!" The shout rang out and the voice was as familiar to her as the face in her vision. An unexpected thrill raced through her.

The ground shook as a horse approached, and the wolf released her elbow and looked back at the rider.

"Get away from her, you beast."

The wolf gave her face a final tongue lashing before following his master's orders.

Boots hit the ground. Innes tried to wipe her face and eyes clean with her sleeve. She was covered with the wolf's kisses. The earl's dark figure appeared over her.

"Are you hurt?"

The gray mist made his bearded face even darker. He knelt down beside her, and she stared into blue eyes so dark that they seemed almost black. They were the color of a clear sky an hour before dawn. She was speechless, seeing him this close. The long hair was now tied back, revealing his face. Since the time of the portrait, his nose showed signs of being broken. A scar ran across his cheek. One might consider this a fearsome face, but his eyes showed nothing but concern.

The wolf's face now appeared next to his master's, showing no concern at all. The animal was ready to play again.

"Did he hurt you?"

Innes stared from one beast's face to the next and couldn't stop a smile from forming on her lips. "My dignity is a wee bit bruised. But nay, he didn't hurt me."

She tried to sit up. He stood and stretched out his hand. She didn't know where her gloves had gone. Bracing herself for what she knew would come next, she took his hand.

Her mind joined his, and this time she was in the dark stairwell, caught in the protective embrace of his arms. He was staring at her lips with desire.

The image disappeared, replaced by a darker moment. The place was dank, foul smelling. A dungeon. She felt the weight of the shackles on his arms and legs. The air stank of human waste and death. She could taste blood in her mouth. She grunted in pain as a heavy lash cracked across her back.

A voice came from a great distance. "You're not well."

She clutched desperately at his shirt, feeling faint from the agony of the whip.

And then she resurfaced from his past. His arms were wrapped around her, holding her upright. The scent of man and horse and fresh sea air flooded her senses. Her face was pressed against his heart, and she felt the solid, steady beat against her cheek. The painting, their brief encounters, her mind conjuring him while he was gone—they all combined to make this moment seem more like a dream than reality. The closeness and the sense of protection were unlike anything she'd ever experienced. And, for a few brief minutes, she welcomed it.

Sanity and propriety returned. She pushed herself out of his arms and took a step back. The light rain had eased to a fine mist.

"I'm fine," she said. "Just a moment of light-headedness."

He stood looking at her. She tried to straighten her clothes. Her hair was loose. One shoe lay in the wet grass a few feet away. The basket lay farther off. The wolf sat beside it, alert and poised, with what looked like a smile on his face.

The earl towered over her, watching her every move. She was flustered by his nearness. Here in the open, he was taller than Bryce, wider across the chest, more impressive than she remembered from the East Tower stairwell. Like the last time, he wore black beneath his tartan. She noticed the way the shirt hugged his powerful arms.

"I believe you're not well."

She shook her head. "I'm fine. Truly. I can manage."

He fetched her shoe and gloves and handed them to her.

Innes was still ruffled by all that just happened, and the shoe slipped through her fingers. He bent down and offered it to her again. This time, he put an arm around Innes's shoulders to steady her.

She pulled on the gloves and slipped on the shoe before going to pick up her basket. The wolf simply watched her. The few early bluebells she'd cut were scattered on the ground.

She could breathe again, now that he wasn't looming over her. It was easier now to break free of the spell of attraction. She glanced over at the chestnut steed he rode. The animal pawed the ground.

"I don't believe we've ever been formally introduced. I am Innes Munro, sister to your brother's wife."

"And what are you doing out here in this weather?"

She was surprised by the reprimand. "Perhaps I could

ask you the same question."

"Aren't you aware of the dangers?"

"I'm taking my evening walk." She motioned in the direction she'd come. "I'm not so far from Girnigoe."

"Clearly, you're not familiar with these lands. Dangers abound here. You should not leave the castle unescorted."

"I don't see what business it is of yours." The roughness of his tone irked her. "But as it happens, I've done the same thing every morning and night of my stay while you were gone. I've seen no sign of any danger."

"Fortune has been kind to you so far, despite your disregard. Don't tempt her."

She liked him better when he was worried.

The memory of him holding the pup came to her mind. The wolf now watched the two of them with great interest.

"I survived a vicious wolf attack today," she said. "I believe I can face whatever dangers these hills hold."

"What would happen if this were a real wolf attack?"

She looked at Thunder. "He looks real enough to me."

"Bandits? Outlaws? Any traveling renegades who found you alone on these moors?" he snapped, not amused by her answer. "Don't you see the danger you'd be in?"

"I carry nothing of value. People like that would hardly

bother with someone like me."

"Foolish woman," he muttered under his breath. Striding to his horse, he swung up into the saddle.

"Oh . . . thank you," Innes called out. "And I really enjoyed the pleasant introduction."

The great horse tossed his head and stamped his hoof, as restless and agitated as his owner.

"Return to Girnigoe before you trouble someone else."

She had no chance to reply. He tugged at the reins, and his steed wheeled and galloped away. The wolf bounded off after him.

Innes watched the three disappear into the fog.

If the man were this gruff because he saw her as a difficult guest, she could only imagine how upset he'd be if he realized she was privy to his past without his knowledge or permission.

She'd make sure he never knew.

The rain began to fall in earnest during her trek back, and she was soaking wet by the time she crossed the drawbridge.

The stable yard and Outer Ward, quiet when she left, now bustled with activity. It was as if the castle had awakened. She attributed it to a key presence that was missing and had now returned.

An upper chamber in the West Tower drew Innes's

gaze. A dark shadow watched her, waiting for her safe return.

In spite of their brief skirmish on the moor, Innes was glad that the earl had come back to Girnigoe.

Chapter 5

Conall stood with his back to the fireplace, warming himself.

What a luxury, he thought, having a fire and clean, dry clothes. After a year in the English dungeons, he'd never again take these things for granted.

Two candles flickered on a table by the window. Two more burned on either side of a chessboard that he'd laid out on a low table.

Conall knew word would reach his brother the moment he was back.

The West Tower had been built to provide one large room on the top floor that Conall used as his bedchamber, and this floor directly above the stables where he could work. Duff, his servant, occupied a small alcove sectioned off from the rest. It continued to be a bone of contention with Bryce that, in a castle as large as Girnigoe, Conall chose to live here.

But Conall was adamant. He needed to be able to come and go freely. A year ago, he'd been in chains. He had no future. He wanted none, not at his clan's expense.

And where would he be a year from now? He had no idea. For the present, he would stay at Girnigoe to help Bryce and try to repay a small portion of what he owed his people.

He glanced over at Thunder. The beast had shared Conall's supper and now lay contentedly in his corner.

It had been an uneventful ride from the lodge, until the end. He frowned. When he rode over that hill and saw Thunder standing over Innes Munro, the rush of mixed feelings nearly overwhelmed him. Fear for her, anger that she was out alone, concern that she might have been hurt. What other feelings? He didn't want to admit them, never mind feel them.

Damn the woman!

Conall only returned to the castle when he thought she'd be gone. Why didn't she leave after the wedding?

This complicated everything.

The problem was—and it *was* a problem—he loved holding her in his arms. Twice now, he'd done it. Knowing she was safe in his embrace warmed him, satisfied him. It was so strange, especially for him, since he barely knew her. There was something primal and right about being close to her, touching her, and for those brief moments his inner demons weren't so close to the surface.

He realized now that he'd thought of little else but Innes while he was away. And something had swelled inside of him when he saw her laughing while Thunder licked her face.

"Damn it," he swore aloud.

The wolf raised his head, looked at his master, and laid it back down.

Before any knock came, Thunder was on his feet. The animal flew at Bryce as he came in, but he was ready. Grabbing the wolf by the scruff of the neck, Bryce held him a safe distance away from his face as the excited animal tried to nip and play.

"Easy, monster. I'm happy to see you, too."

The wolf circled, jumped, and pulled at Bryce's boots, doing everything possible to knock the laird down.

"Control this wild animal."

"Thunder," said Conall. The oversized pup immediately retreated to his place beside Conall's chair "You'd think he'd be tired after running behind me all day."

Conall studied his brother for a long moment. He didn't like what he saw. Bryce looked weary, wounded. He didn't seem like a bridegroom floating in the euphoria of wedded bliss.

"How was Dalnawillan?" Bryce wandered over to the fire and pushed at a log with his boot. The lodge on the windswept moor by Loch Dubh had always been a favorite place for the two of them when they were growing up.

"Quiet. Just the way I like it."

"Did you hunt?"

Conall shook his head and set down the pitcher of wine and another cup next to the chess set. "Not in the mood."

"Did you make your rounds of the tenants? Like I asked?"

"That's your job. You're laird." He sat down and gestured at the board. Something was bothering his brother, but he would wait for him to bring it up. "You have the first move."

"I asked you to do it."

"Good for you." Conall filled the two cups.

"You're as ornery as an old bull."

"I knew you'd finally catch on."

Bryce sat down and eyed the board. "The day of my wedding. You were still here. Why didn't you come?"

Conall cocked an eyebrow. His brother should have let that go by now. No, it was something else. "You need to move one of those pieces to begin the game."

"You don't stand beside me, but you leave my wife a gift." Bryce moved a pawn. "You gave her Shona's brooch."

Conall frowned. This couldn't be the reason he looked like someone just took his last mutton chop.

"The brooch was our mother's," he said. "It should be

worn by the laird's wife."

"Aye, in good time."

"I waited until your wedding day to fetch it from Shona's room. You didn't do it. So I did it for you."

"That brooch was given to *you* by our mother. You were the one who gave it to Shona. And now to Ailein."

Conall picked up his cup of wine and sat back. "And you've been stewing about this for the past fortnight?"

"Nay, but it was our *mother's* brooch, and maybe you were a little premature in giving it to my bride."

"You have nothing better to do with your time but worry over a wee bit of metal and stone?"

"Your move."

Two years ago, when he was still whole, Conall would have taken the younger man to the training yard and let him vent his frustration. But that was their old life. This was their new.

And Conall knew Bryce better than he knew himself. This was not what was sticking in his craw. There was still something else.

"Listen to me," said Bryce. "I want you to meet my wife. It's time."

"And how is married life?" Conall moved a piece.

"Why will you never answer a question or carry a coherent conversation?" Bryce slid the next piece into place. "I'd have a more intelligent chat with Thunder."

"That you would. I've heard you both howl at the moon." Conall captured a pawn. "Are you two off to a good start with this marriage business?"

"Of course. Why wouldn't we be?" Bryce leaned forward and took a black pawn with a flourish.

"I don't know. The sister is still here."

"How do you know that?"

Conall placed his knight next to his brother's king. "Because I've spoken to her."

"You've spoken to Innes?" Bryce took the knight with his king, his expression brightening.

There weren't many occasions when Conall allowed the other man an upper hand in this game. But every now and then, he had to let it happen or he feared Bryce would quit playing.

Conall sat back, drinking his wine. "What's the woman doing, traipsing about in the hills with no escort so late in the evening?"

"How do I know? She is a grown woman."

"And do you allow your wife to wander off in the dark with no one accompanying her?"

"Of course not," Bryce told him. "Wynda and Lachlan keep her busy. She's too tired by the end of the day."

"Innes is a Munro. She's your responsibility while she's a guest here."

"You don't know her. No one tells her where to go and

what to do." Bryce groaned as Conall's queen took his knight, putting the king in check.

"Then ask your wife to do it."

Bryce moved his king out of check and stared at the board. "I'm telling you. Innes is bloody independent. She minds no one. She follows no direction but her own."

Conall took his time before taking the next piece.

"What else do you know about her?" he asked vaguely, trying to sound conversational, indifferent.

"I know the Munro relies more on that daughter than is customary. They say Innes is his most trusted adviser." Bryce shuffled his piece. "I already told you she was there at his side during the negotiations regarding Ailein's dowry."

"Why does she wear black?"

"I never asked."

"Was she married?"

"Not that I know of."

"Why didn't she marry? Her dowry should have drawn suitors by the boatload."

"True, if wealth were all that they were after," Bryce said, studying the board. "But as I said, the woman is independent, abrupt, intimidating. Maintains her distance. She's always studying those around her. And as you say, she wears black at all times. And that peculiar shock of white in her hair."

"It's quite soft."

"What's soft?" Bryce's gaze snapped up to Conall's face.

"Her hair."

"How the devil would you know that?"

Conall caught himself. He was talking too much, asking too many questions, sounding too interested. Even so, he wanted to know more about her. Much as he hated to admit it, he wanted to know *everything* about Innes Munro. He moved his queen.

"Checkmate."

Bryce stared in disbelief at the board. Conall had cornered his king with the queen and bishop.

"Bloody hell. You distracted me. I was certain I had you."

"The only one around here you might beat at chess is Thunder. And that's only if he's having a bad day."

———

"Seriously, Ailein. I'm tired and wet and hungry. Where are you taking me?"

The rain-drenched courtyard of the Inner Ward was deserted, and Innes was beginning to be somewhat annoyed at being dragged along by her sister without an explanation.

"I told you," said Ailein. "You'll see in a moment."

Ailein had been waiting for Innes in the stairwell of the East Tower and pounced on her as soon as she returned from her walk. Whatever it was Ailein wanted to show her, Innes clearly had to see it right now.

"Shouldn't you be in the Great Hall, dining with your husband?"

"One of the servants came in, whispered in Bryce's ear, and then he left without a word of explanation. Just got up and went. But everyone else is still there, so this is the perfect time."

"The perfect time for what?"

The rain began to come down again in earnest, and sharp gusts of wind whipped their cloaks around them.

"Soon," said Ailein.

They reached the chapel. Ailein passed through the arched entryway into the small kirkyard.

"Why are you bringing me here? And why now?" Innes complained. "If we're planning to rob a grave, we need shovels. Wait. We're going to bury your husband. That's it, isn't it?"

As Ailein pulled her against the protective shelter of the chapel wall, the wind coming off the sea fought them with every step.

Innes stole a glance at graves topped by slabs of stone. The rain was beating down and small wisps of mist, like souls released, curled around the larger rock markers.

They stopped at a doorway in the shadows.

"A back way in," Ailein whispered, looking past her toward the courtyard. There was not a living soul except for them.

"It's probably locked."

With a knowing look back at her, Ailein pushed open the thick oak door.

Innes waited just inside the door as her sister crossed the chapel to a small red globe glowing in the sacristy. The odor of old dampness mingled with the sharp smell of ritual incense. A moment later, the flame of a taper brightened the space between them. She hadn't been inside here since Ailein's wedding a fortnight ago. The flowers and greenery that festooned the walls were gone now, and the chapel looked as simple as any other.

"Will you explain to me now what this is all about?" Innes asked.

"The crypt. I want to take you down there."

"I'm not going. Not unless you explain yourself."

"I asked for your help, but you wouldn't give it to me. So I had to find the answers in my own way."

"So why the crypt?"

"I'll show you."

Innes watched her sister start down a half dozen steps, and there was nothing she could do but follow. As they descended, the air became mustier. Innes held onto the wall as she went down into a low, square chamber. Stone tombs lined the walls. Some were adorned with the effigies of knights, their carved stone swords held in their hands. Others had chiseled silhouettes of faces.

"Very well. We're here. It's time you told me what this is about."

"I need you to confirm that what I've found here is real and not my imagination."

"Stop being mysterious," Innes ordered. "Just tell me."

"I've been following Wynda and Lachlan around every day, doing whatever they ask of me. I've been so agreeable that you wouldn't even have recognized me." Ailein put the candle in a sconce on the wall. "In return, I've been asking questions. Quietly and discreetly."

"About Shona."

Ailein nodded sadly. "I'm not an idiot. The more time passes since my wedding, the more I realize how much Bryce loved her. He lost his temper that night because I wore a reminder of someone he'd lost."

Innes considered lecturing her sister about the futility of trying to change the past, but there was no purpose to that. Ailein had to follow her heart and her instincts until she somehow came to terms with her husband's history. This was her nature. There could be no other way.

"What have you found?" asked Innes.

"Those two never say a word about her. Whatever I ask, they ignore. They won't so much as mention her name. You'd think she never existed. So, I followed a different track. I've spent the past couple of days coming here and visiting with Fingal."

"That strange little priest?"

Ailein nodded. "He's opened the church ledgers and allowed me to ask questions. He thinks I'm trying to learn more of the history of the Sinclairs."

"Which is true in a way, isn't it?"

Her sister shrugged and turned to one of the walls, touching some inscriptions etched in the stone.

"I've looked at the record of every birth, baptism, marriage, and death that has happened here in the past hundred years," said Ailein.

"The chapel at home has a similar book. You've seen it."

"This crypt is where they bury only the immediate family." Ailein pointed to the inscriptions. "And the names are here."

Innes's gaze moved from her sister's troubled face to columns of names on the wall. "What have you discovered?"

"When she died, Shona was carrying a child."

During her sister's marriage negotiations, Innes recalled learning that Bryce had been married to his first wife for eight months. The Munros had asked about heirs. They were told Bryce had no children—no heirs.

"In the book that Fingal keeps, her name is listed with the day she died, along with a notation, 'with child.'"

Innes rubbed her arms. The chill seemed to have seeped into her bones. She imagined what such a loss would have meant to Bryce. His wife and his bairn.

"Perhaps knowing this will help you understand your husband better. He needs you."

"But that's not the worst of it," Ailein replied, her distress evident in her voice.

Innes looked up into Ailein's gray eyes, shining with unshed tears. "What else?"

"I can't confirm that she was buried here."

"Perhaps her body was sent to her own people."

"If I die, where will I be buried?" she asked.

"You're a Sinclair now," Innes said in a hushed tone. "You'll be buried here."

"I think Shona might be buried outside somewhere, not on consecrated ground."

"What are you saying? That she took her own life? While she was pregnant?"

A tear rolled down Ailein's cheek. "I don't know. I was hoping you'd help me find out."

Even now, as I look down at the bluffs where she fell, where her body struck and broke, where her unborn child died in her womb, my guilt is not strong enough to make me confess. And if she lies buried in an unholy field or in a consecrated crypt, what difference? It is all the same. Ashes to ashes; dust to dust.

Whatever pain and sorrow I feel, nothing can make me cry out, "It was I! I did it!" Nay, that will not undo what has been done. The lass is dead, and she cannot come back to life.

But, to speak truly, I would not want her back.

Still, they cannot know. I shudder at what would happen if they found out the truth. I would be ruined. Destroyed.

The devil take me before I let them find out. And if he does take me, so be it.

Chapter 6

Innes couldn't sleep.

Standing in her window, looking down at the bluffs, she imagined Shona jumping to her death from the floor above. What would drive a woman to do that?

They'd known she was with child. So how far along had she been? The Munros were led to believe that the first wife's death was an accident. But the church clearly held a different view. Why else wasn't she buried in the crypt with the family?

Before they went their separate ways, Innes convinced her sister that her discovery might be nothing. There could be a rational explanation for all of it. Somehow, Ailein needed to put the questions delicately to her husband and trust his answer.

Ailein went off to her chambers glummer than Innes had ever seen her. This was marriage. Real life. Innes had seen enough of people's pasts to know happiness was a momentary illusion. Everyone had pain. No one was spared hardship and toil in this life. The difference between people was simply that some were better at masking it than others.

She moved across the room and gazed out at the lit windows in the upper floors of the West Tower. Conall Sinclair. Another restless soul.

It would soon be dawn. The rain had stopped. The smell of bread baking in the kitchens mingled with the sea air. She donned her cloak, pulled on her gloves, and grabbed her basket and leather case before heading out.

During the first days of their stay, Bryce's aunt Wynda had shown her the way to leave the castle on the sea side. A small door in the fortress wall, just above the high-water line, led down stone steps to a *goe*, one of two rocky inlets thirty to forty yards wide that created the high peninsula on which the castle stood.

Innes went past the kitchens toward the stairwell down to the door. Most days, the kitchens were just stirring as she passed. This morning, the place hummed with activity. Beneath rafters hung with a multitude of meats and great bunches of herbs, workers bustled about their tasks, and fragrant steam from a score of cauldrons and pots rose like a cloud to the vaulted stone ceiling.

"Ah, Innes. Come here, mistress, if you please."

She stopped at Wynda's command. Bryce's gray-haired aunt stood straight as an oak, and her pleasant demeanor did not fool Innes. The woman ran Girnigoe with strict authority and ruthless efficiency. Innes thought her sister could have no better teacher for her role as mistress of a castle.

Approaching the ovens where Wynda was supervising the baking, Innes was once again surprised by the snow-white muslin apron the aunt wore as she performed her duties. The apron was never soiled nor spotted. Never. Considering how busy Wynda was at all times, Innes decided the woman had to change a dozen times a day.

Wynda was speaking to the cook. "The mistress here went without her supper last night. She didn't even ask for a tray to be sent up."

"I'm fine, Wynda. I wasn't hungry."

"Aye. I'm sure that's so, lass." The aunt turned back to the cook. "Put something together for her, before she disappears. We'll not have it said that the Sinclairs allowed her to waste away here during her stay with us."

The cook, a stout red-faced woman of indeterminate age, nodded sternly at the older woman and, with a covert wink at Innes, began to assemble some food for her.

"The kitchen workers are at it early this morning," Innes commented. "Are you expecting guests?"

"No guests here these days. Just us." Wynda took the cloth packet of food from the cook and handed it to her. "Be mindful of the tides now."

"And watch out for the seabirds," Cook added. "Larger

lassies than you have been carried off, you know."

Innes nodded her gratitude, placed the food in her basket, and walked out.

No guests. The earl's return must be the reason for the excitement.

She descended the dark, narrow stairs and unbarred the stout door. A few moments later, she stood on the stony strand and looked back up at the formidable combination of nature and man's work. Above the sheer cliffs, Castle Girnigoe loomed. The peninsula, projecting out on an angle from the shore into the German Sea, provided a site for what was said to be the most impregnable fortress in Scotland. Innes believed it. Only at the lowest tides could one even manage to circle the base of the castle. Beyond the farthest point of land, high stacks of rock rose above the waves, some reaching fifty or sixty feet into the air.

Dawn fire was streaking through the sky as Innes climbed and settled down on a flat rock, facing the sea. Just offshore, the heads of a dozen seals popped up, watching her before slipping beneath the surface again.

The storm from the night before had washed many sea creatures ashore. The gulls were in a frenzy, flying high with clams and oysters and other shellfish and dropping them on the rocks before diving on them. Innes drew paper and charcoal from her leather case and started to sketch. Her thoughts returned to the crypt and to Ailein.

Her sister needed causes to champion. She needed purpose in her life to avoid wasting her time on the trivial. This mystery of Shona's death, serious as it was, remained for the younger sister to unravel.

Perhaps such a search would result in healing the rift between Bryce and her sister. Perhaps this was a good way for Ailein to develop more empathy for her husband.

It was time for Innes to leave Girnigoe. She only complicated her sister's life by staying. She was a confidante to Ailein when none was needed.

Another thought hovering on the edge of her mind was that she'd stayed long enough for the earl to come back. But last night he'd treated her as if she'd overstayed her welcome.

From the corner of her eye, she saw the wolf racing toward her.

"Thunder! Come back here." At the sound of Conall's voice, something stirred deep within her. This pointless attraction wasn't going away. More reason for her to return to Folais Castle.

Innes quickly slid her drawings into the leather case and clutched it to her chest. She drew in her legs as the excited animal jumped over her, pulling at her cloak and licking her face before bouncing down the rocks toward his master.

Innes smiled. The unsolicited affection tickled her and she loved the wolf for it. She wiped the wetness off her face and watched the Highlander throw a stick into the sea. Thunder jumped into the water after it.

Conall's long black mane was loose this morning. With the wind in his face, he resembled a lion. Her gaze traveled the lines of his powerful body. The span of leg from kilt to boot top was muscled. The shirt was open at the neck and her gaze caressed every inch of the exposed skin. She bit her bottom lip, feeling a gentle tug low in her belly.

He looked up, catching her perusal, and she glanced away, embarrassed.

He tossed another stick of driftwood for the wolf and started toward her.

"You're an early riser," he said. The earl of Caithness didn't believe in formal greetings and small talk.

"I keep my own schedule," said Innes.

"Nocturnal, eh?"

"As much as I'm allowed."

"Allowed?" He raised a brow and climbed the rock to where she sat. "I hear there is no man nor woman alive that you mind or take orders from."

She looked up at his face framed by the early morning sky. "I had no idea that I've already established such a reputation at Girnigoe."

"It's not bad. They could say worse."

"Worse than being called a shrew?"

"I've heard no one call you a shrew." He sat down on the rock beside her. His shoulder bumped hers, and he seemed to make no effort to move away. "But they call me the 'mad' brother. I'd say that's worse."

Innes slid over to make room. "I see no evidence of madness." She nodded at Thunder scattering seabirds by the water. "Unless you suppose keeping such a wild creature as that one enhances your reputation. Then I'd say you're indeed mad."

"Did you just insult me *and* my wolf?" His bearded face was fierce, but his eyes showed amusement.

"Did I?"

"You implied that he's not a wild creature and I'm mad to think so."

"Look at him. I'm just saying he's far too sweet to be wild, and that must come from you."

"So now you insult my manhood."

Her gaze flew to his, and heat rose into her face. "I did no such thing."

"You said his sweetness comes from me."

"I meant your training and treatment of—"

"That animal is a killer. A dangerous beast. Ask anyone at Castle Girnigoe. I need to keep him on a chain or he'll rip apart the throat of any man that comes within his reach. In fact, not a month ago, a woman about your size made the mistake of—"

Thunder bounced up onto the rocks and shook himself directly in front of them. Innes shrieked and Conall cursed, sending the animal scampering off the rock and down to the water again.

She laughed. "That one is a terror."

Innes dried her leather case on her skirts and placed it on the rock. He picked it up.

"That's mine," she said. She held on to one end, he the other. Innes didn't share her sketches and paintings with strangers. Her work wasn't for display. She sought no audience. Their gazes locked in a challenge of wills. She was agitated and excited at the same time. This close, she saw her own reflection in his blue eyes.

"May I?" he asked.

Her defenses crumbled. She hesitated for a moment longer and then shrugged, glad she'd left the sketch of his battlefield memory back in her room. Conall pulled out her sketches. Innes ceased to breathe as he spread them on his lap.

"This is German paper," he said, looking up with surprise.

"It's the only luxury I allow myself."

"An artist."

"Hardly."

He studied them, taking his time with each drawing. "You have an interest in birds."

"All animals interest me, but birds especially, I suppose."

"Why?"

"Because they're free." The words sounded hollow to her ears. She recalled the months that he'd spent in captivity and felt obligated to explain. "Because I imagine that they've traveled so far, to places I'll never see." She stared up at the seagulls floating in the wind. "When I draw, I share in their stories of far-off lands. They whisper to me tales of adventure."

"Do they also whisper of sorrow and loss and grief?"

Innes looked into his eyes. He was serious now, all joking forgotten. If he only knew that she had already seen into his soul. Felt his anguish and pain.

"Aye. They do. Too often." She tore her gaze away and reached for her basket. Her gloves lay at the bottom of it. He sat too close. She needed to put them on.

"I see you came prepared." He took the basket off her lap and lifted out the cloth filled with food. "I smelled Cook's bread from a hundred paces off."

She snatched the basket back and took out her gloves. Realizing she was being watched, she tucked them in her belt.

"Wynda told me she'd have Cook prepare a feast for

today." He tore a small loaf of bread in half and offered her a piece. He had no difficulty manipulating things with his one hand.

She accepted the piece, making sure her fingers didn't brush against his.

"I'm surprised you didn't see them when you passed by the kitchens," she said. "The two were in there quite early, leading their troops."

"I came out a different way."

"Oh?" A sea breeze lifted his kilt, exposing more of his muscular thigh. She forced her attention onto the bread in her hand.

"I don't move around the castle as others do."

"I see. A secret passageway. The door at the bottom of the East Tower. You disappeared through that door the first day you caught me falling down the steps." She took a bite out of the warm bread and licked her lips. A glaze of butter and sage coated the crust. "I keep testing it every time I go by, but it's always latched."

He was watching her mouth. She lowered the bread to her lap, suddenly self-conscious. Her cheeks burned. She wasn't used to having a man sit this close and watch her.

"And what will you do if one day that door is un-locked?" he asked.

Her heart beat so loud that he had to hear it. Was he making a proposition?

"Perhaps I'll open it and see what lies beyond," she said.

"There are tunnels."

She glanced over her shoulder at the towers of Girnigoe looming over them. "I wouldn't wish to get lost. I won't take them."

"What if someone left you directions? Signs to show you which passage to take?"

"I might follow the signs, but only if the paths led me to the hills. You know how fond I am of my solitary walks."

"I thought we were done with that foolhardiness."

She intended to be amusing, but the gruff tone made her bristle. "And I thought we made it clear last night that I won't be dictated to about where I go and what I do."

"Nay, you can do what you like when you're at Folais Castle, in the bosom of your family."

"I am free to conduct myself as I wish wherever I am."

His distaste for her answer showed plainly in his expression. "From now on, you will take an escort with you when you go for your walks."

"And if I choose not to?" she challenged.

"You know my duty as host is to keep you safe," he said curtly. "You will abide by the rules of the Sinclairs while you're staying at Girnigoe."

"When you were away, no one appeared to mind my

harmless jaunts. So are these rules of the laird of the castle or the earl?"

The sharp look made her cringe inwardly. She stopped herself from inching away. He threw a piece of crust to a waiting gull.

He ignored her question. "We shall provide our hospitality and protection. In return you will behave like a gracious guest and abide by our instructions."

"You mean your *orders*."

"Call it what you want," he snapped, pushing to his feet. "You'll do as I say."

Innes couldn't let it go. It wasn't in her nature to let someone else have the last sharp word. "So now that the occasionally present earl has returned, and hospitality has been restored, are you planning to introduce yourself to my sister?"

He shot an accusatory glare at her. "Since you bring it up, we need to talk about your sister and my brother."

"What about them?"

"Only a fortnight into this marriage and they're having a row."

"And why should you care? You didn't even show up at church. You could not be bothered to be introduced to my father while he was at Girnigoe."

He climbed down from the rock, but he was obviously not done with the argument.

"There are three people who have a right to be possibly offended by my actions. Bryce, Ailein, and your father. You are not one of them."

Hot anger rose into her face. She was not about to let him dismiss her. Innes threw her things into the basket and yanked on her gloves. "Then when it comes to Ailein and your brother, I have nothing to say to you."

"I—"

Innes cut him off. "And I've clearly worn your 'hospitality' thin. But I've agreed to stay six more days. Then I return home."

"A bit hot-tempered, I see," he said. "Poor Bryce, if your sister is anything like you."

"Poor Bryce?" She shook her head and came to her feet. "Don't you dare judge my sister before even meeting her."

He walked away while she was still talking. It was impossible to miss the storm brewing in him the way he tossed the next stick for Thunder.

Innes climbed down and eyed the door back into the castle. She took a couple of steps toward it, then changed direction and headed right at the scowling giant. "And another thing. My temper is justified."

His dark gaze fixed on her face, and she decided to let him know exactly what was on her mind.

"You provoked me," she continued. "I am not leaving

while you speak ill of my sister."

"The fact remains that they are having matrimonial issues."

"They'll solve it. I'm not getting involved, and I'd advise you to do the same. Stay out of it."

"I happen to care about my brother," he growled into her face.

"Do you think I don't care about my sister?" she retorted.

"It's only because of my brother that I am alive," he snapped, towering over her. "He's the only reason why I continue to carry on with this muddle of a life. He is the strength that keeps the Sinclairs together. I care deeply for him. And if you had a fraction of that feeling for your sister, you'd do whatever needs to be done to help them."

Innes rose on her toes and poked him hard in the chest. She might as well have poked a rock.

"Do not presume to think you understand how I feel . . . or why I do or don't do anything. Do not assume that you know me. And don't you *ever* question my loyalty to my sister. You know *nothing* about me!"

Without waiting for a response, she turned and marched off.

Chapter 7

" . . . And the stories came down from the distant past
how Lugh used his many skills to make better the lives
of men and eventually became High King. When the
Spirits of Hell rose up and threatened the people, Lugh
defeated them. Knowing their magical powers, he
forced them to take the sling-stone that he used to kill
Balor the Poison Eye and harness four of his many skills
within it. Each spoke of the Wheel held great power:
the first being the ability to heal grievous wounds and
sickness; the second, to speak to the dead; the third,
to read a man's past; and the fourth, to read a man's
future . . ."

From the *Chronicle of Lugh*

Innes was numb and isolated. Walking back to her chambers, she tried to comprehend what had happened. One
moment, Conall's attention delighted her. The next they
were arguing.

He was authoritative and she'd lost her temper. Innes
scorned petty rules. For too many years she'd been al-

lowed to go about her life as she pleased. But she was a *guest* at Girnigoe. An unwelcome one at that. And there was no reason for her to lash out at him for failing to meet with her father when she knew the inner wounds that continued to fester and cut him off from society.

Was she just looking for opportunities to push him away?

Innes's mind turned to what he had asked about the newlyweds and her refusal to get involved.

She was defensive of her own actions. Having composed Ailein's life for too many years, Innes knew it was wrong to meddle in their marriage. What could she say to them? They went about their business day to day. They appeared to behave with civility toward each other. They never raised their voices. They never made derogatory comments about the other in public. What advice did she have to offer? What did she know about marriage? About men? In all certainty, she was the least qualified person on earth to help someone with matrimonial issues.

Two weeks was a long time to be at odds, but Innes believed Ailein and Bryce's quarrel wasn't serious. He'd protected her reputation on their wedding night. She'd decided to stay at Castle Girnigoe. Perhaps they needed this time to get accustomed to marriage.

Innes hoped she was right.

Back in her room, the lack of sleep from the night before caught up to her. She stripped off her dress and fell asleep, only to have Shona haunt her dreams.

The young woman stood before her in the window of the top floor of East Tower, dark eyes pleading, hands cradling her swollen belly. Innes reached out, but Shona slipped from her grasp and disappeared out the window.

The sound of the woman's screams as she fell awakened Innes.

There was persistent knocking on her door. Innes was upset about the nightmare, but she still needed to sleep.

Whoever was at the door, they were not giving up.

She groaned and peeked out from beneath the quilted counterpane. A brilliant sun blazed outside her window.

"Innes, you open the door this very moment or by the saints, I'll fetch a couple of men to come and knock it down for me."

"Blast you, Ailein," she called out. "Go away."

The knocking only got louder.

"Now, Innes. This is your last chance."

Innes kicked aside the covers and marched toward the door. "Sister, you'd better be in pain. There'd better be blood or protruding bones. Because otherwise, I'm going to kill you for disturbing my sleep."

The moment she unlatched the door, Ailein pushed it open and marched into the room. Behind her, Jinny and a line of servants followed, carrying a tub and buckets of steaming water.

"What do you think you're doing?" Innes asked.

"You're putting on your best dress and accompanying me to the Great Hall tonight for dinner."

"I'll do no such a thing."

Ailein motioned to the others. One by one, the women poured water into the tub and laid out the towels and pitchers of oils so fragrant Innes could smell them across the room. Then, like a well-trained army, they filed out in the same order they entered. Jinny closed the door on the last one and turned to Innes.

"This is lovely, Jinny, but I have no intention of going to the Great Hall."

"Come, mistress. This petulant creature of a sister has grand plans for you. Don't you look at me like that, Ailein. You know it's the truth. Come now, Innes. Let me wash your hair and dress you."

"Very well, Jinny. But you know I can do it myself."

"She can't," Ailein warned, standing like a sentinel by the bed. "She won't. She'll crawl back into that bed the moment we leave the room,"

Innes turned on her sister. "I am this close to taking a stick to your backside, brat. And don't you have some-place you need to be?"

"This is where I need to be." Ailein's tone became

pleading. "And I need you at dinner tonight . . . desperately. So you need to prepare yourself and accompany me. Please, Innes."

"We had an agreement. You promised to leave me be while I stayed. No ceremonial functions. No clan dinners. No interrupting my sleep."

"I've done as I promised. And I will continue to. But not now." Ailein turned her doe eyes on her. "Please, Innes. Do this for me."

"You know how I feel about public displays. Why must you parade me in front of your new clan?"

"It's not that." She crossed to Innes. "I'm to meet Bryce's brother tonight. I need you to stand by me."

For an instant Innes lost track of their conversation. Her mind slipped back to her meeting with the earl, to the sharp words they'd exchanged.

Ailein was still talking. "I'm not surprised that you look dazed. Aye, the earl of Caithness. I'm to be presented to him." She started pacing the room. "The mad brother. But I understand there's some question about whether he's entirely out of his head. Except that he keeps a wolf with him. And the beast somehow got loose in the kitchens today. Who keeps a wolf as a pet?"

The wolf must have gotten into the kitchens after Innes left. "The wolf's name is Thunder. He's completely tame."

Ailein paused. "You've seen him?"

"Aye. Strangely, Thunder has taken a fancy to me." Innes realized that Jinny was already undressing her and pushing her toward the tub.

"And the earl?" her sister asked. "Have you met him, too?"

Jinny was listening to every word. Innes didn't think this was the time to go into detail about any of this.

"I have. Briefly."

"Is he as mad as they say?"

"I don't know how such rumors begin. The man seems to be completely sane. Intelligent. Well-spoken. A wee bit arrogant, but that's to be expected, I suppose."

And he is terribly protective of his brother, she thought, *so you and Bryce better mend your differences or his wrath will be upon you.*

"They say he was a fierce warrior and that the Regent trusted him like a brother," said Ailein.

"I remember hearing that."

"One of the serving women told me he's scarred horribly from battle."

Innes lowered herself into the tub. The water was warm on her skin. *Scarred* and *horrible* did not belong together in any sentence describing Conall Sinclair. He was a bit unkempt and wild looking, but that only added to his appeal.

"He bears a few scars, but they hardly disfigure him," she said. "He's lost one hand."

Ailein considered that. "Not a good thing for a warrior."

"I shouldn't think so."

"Is he short?" the younger sister pressed.

"Tall. Taller than Bryce."

Jinny motioned to a washcloth and Ailein held one out. Innes took it, her hand brushing against her sister's.

A kiss. Her gaze snapped up to Ailein. The younger woman moved to the bed, arranging the dress she wanted Innes to wear tonight. A kiss. In the brief brush of their hands, Innes saw her sister being kissed—and kissed passionately—by Bryce.

"And his build?" Ailein asked.

That kiss must have happened today or Innes would have seen it before. How funny, she thought. The newlyweds had apparently mended their differences while she and Conall bickered about them.

"Is he as muscular as Bryce?" Ailein repeated.

"From my perspective, the man is a giant."

"And, uh . . . is he as handsome as his brother?"

Innes paid closer attention to her sister. She didn't need to use her gift to see the truth. Ailein's face was flushed. She was lively, talkative.

"Well, is he?" the younger woman asked again.

Innes waited until Jinny had emptied a pitcher of water over her head. She was delighted for her sister. At the same time, she could play this game, too. If Ailein was choosing to hold back the news that she and Bryce had made up, then Innes could keep her own counsel, as well.

"It's difficult to tell. His hair is long and he has a thick beard."

"Is there *anything* pleasing about his looks? His person? The way he conducts himself?" Ailein asked. "Are there any positive qualities that I can comment on when I meet him?"

He saved Innes on the stairs. He came to her rescue again when his wolf decided to use her as a playmate. She was on his mind and he'd watched her in the gallery. This morning, he'd complimented her on her sketches and stared at her lips. *Her lips.* When had she ever been so near a man and experienced such internal tumult? *Never.*

"None. I can't think of any."

"Devil take me if I spend another moment with the woman."

Bryce stared at him. Conall knew this was quite different from the way he'd spoken about Innes the night before. But their time together this morning had taught him a lesson. Innes was unbending and blunt and stubborn. She could go off like a cannon blast when provoked. But she was also striking and enchanting and he could easily get lost in those gray eyes. More than once he'd wondered about the taste of her lips.

He couldn't be near her and remain detached.

"Innes is a guest at Girnigoe. She's accompanying Ailein to the Great Hall for dinner tonight," Bryce repeated. "It doesn't matter if she's there or not. It's time for you to meet my wife."

"The same wife who keeps you locked out of her bedroom?"

"Don't listen to rumors. There's no truth in them."

"Then tell me, what is this quarrel between you?"

"It's nothing," Bryce said. "You know I can be somewhat commanding, and Ailein is a proud woman. We're steadily and quietly finding our way."

Conall sat back from the chessboard and studied Bryce in silence. He seemed much more at ease now than he'd looked last night. Still, he decided to speak his mind. "In a clan such as ours, there is no such thing as *quietly*. This morning, the second sentence out of every Sinclair's mouth pertains to some worry about you and your bride."

Bryce sat back and smiled. "I'm relieved that you're finally seeing the truth in what I've been telling you for the past six months. Everyone talks to you."

Conall knew where his brother was going with this. It was the same argument Bryce used to keep him at Girnigoe. He was connected to their people. He might no longer be laird, but the clan still reached out to him, spoke to him, respected him, and sought his advice.

"You are talking nonsense," he said.

"Conall, you're their warrior lord. I'm at peace with that. Our people come to you when they are troubled."

"Keep pushing me and I'll ride out again today."

"I won't push." Bryce put both hands up in resignation. "But just remember, for the thousandth time, I need you at my side to protect and rebuild the clan."

He would stay, Conall thought, for the time being. He turned his attention back to the chessboard.

"We still need to talk about your marriage."

"Very well." Bryce shook his head. "What is your advice in dealing with Ailein?"

"You're asking me? Blast me if I know."

"You wouldn't bring it up unless you've thought about it."

Conall moved a chess piece and looked up. "Blowing on a fire only fans the flames. But a great gust of wind can blow out the fire completely."

"Oh my Lord." Bryce laughed. "That's your advice? Did you go to the hunting lodge or to that drunken old gypsy fortune teller down the coast?"

"It's good advice," Conall growled.

Bryce took his brother's knight and became serious. "Are you saying I should be that great gust to her fire?"

"Something like that."

"Very well. Then help me."

"How can I help? This is your fire."

"I'll tell you how you can help. Ailein is fond of her sister. More than just fond. Her mood seems to depend on how the sister is feeling. I told you that when I was courting her, if I wanted to win Ailein's hand, I needed to gain Innes's approval."

Conall stared at the board. He'd have Bryce in checkmate in six to eight moves. "So you're married now. Send the bloody sister back home, and your problems go with her."

"Ailein won't allow her to go until we're settled into our marriage."

"Seems to me you have three ropes tied together in a knot. And that's one too many."

"This is where you can be a great help to me."

"I don't like where this is going." Conall moved the bishop across the board.

"Until we work through our difficulties, be nice to Innes. At least, be civil."

He'd like to be much more than civil, Conall thought.

"You ask far more than you know. The sister is small, but she's a force. She's short-tempered. Rude. I believe the woman could be a real terror if she set her mind to it."

"Then can I offer *you* some advice?"

Conall started a path of bloody destruction to his brother's king. "Advice?"

"Take a different approach with her."

"And what does that mean?"

"You spoke of fanning flames before. There's also a saying that when two raging fires meet, they often consume the thing that kindled them."

"At least my advice wasn't a riddle."

"Don't be the raging fire," Bryce said. "If she rants, tell her that she sings as sweetly as a nightingale. If she flushes with anger, say her complexion looks like roses newly washed with morning dew. If she's silent, praise her piercing eloquence. If she orders you to leave her—"

"I'll strap her to the back of a mule and point the beast toward Folais Castle." Conall slapped his piece on the board, putting Bryce's king in checkmate. "Bloody hell. All right. I'll give it a go."

"Just be nice to her."

He'd be nice, all right. He'd be civil *and* nice, blast him. Just to help his brother. "Very well, by the devil. I know what I have to do."

Chapter 8

"After a long reign of peace and prosperity, the High King Lugh died and was laid to rest. He left his powerful Wheel to the priests to safeguard for generations of future High Kings. But when the new religion of Christ Jhesu came to those shores, great battles raged across the land for the souls of the people, and the Wheel fell into the hands of a missionary. Knowing its power, he smashed it and hid the four pieces away from the eyes of men . . ."

From the *Chronicle of Lugh*

Sinclairs crowded the Great Hall, and Innes knew the reason. Conall.

Whatever the expectation of the clan, however, the earl of Caithness stood handsome and aloof in a corner, deep in conversation with a swarthy, battered warrior, paying no attention at all to the hopeful glances of others who sought his company.

In the role of laird, his brother Bryce played his part well. After opening the gathering from his great chair and receiving the greetings of his people, he moved from table to table, addressing people by name, asking questions and listening to the answers, laughing at jokes, drinking to their toasts. He was the perfect host.

But Innes's gaze never strayed too far away from the earl. His reaction to this event matched what she expected of him. He was injured—not just in body, but in soul.

"You'll notice that they've moved our table from the dais," Ailein said. "We'll be eating there."

She pointed to a table to the side beneath a tapestry. Innes didn't have to ask why. That was certainly the work of the earl. He stood near it, close to the door through which he could escape to his lair at any time.

As she was looking at him, he glanced over and, embarrassed to have been caught, she looked up at the tapestry. It was a highly imaginative and colorful work, depicting two monstrous, bearded, club-wielding creatures holding between them a shield with the Sinclair coat of arms. This was a much newer piece than the ones she'd seen in the gallery. Displays of gleaming weaponry flanked the tapestry.

Bryce crossed the Great Hall and joined his brother and the warrior. The two men exchanged a few words, and Conall's gaze swept across the packed hall. He shook his head.

"You were correct. He's taller than Bryce," Ailein whispered in her ear. "And broader in the shoulders."

Innes felt the small nudge, pushing her toward the men. Before coming down, she'd warned Ailein that her stay at the dinner would be brief. Now she wished she hadn't come at all. A skittish feeling deep in her stomach unsettled her. She was nervous, excited, out of her element. Would he remember every word they'd said to each other on the strand or would he only recall her sharpness? She dug in her heels, refusing to be moved toward them.

"He has beautiful eyes," Ailein whispered. "Very intense."

Innes wholeheartedly agreed, but she wasn't going to admit it. "And how would you know? You haven't even been introduced to him."

"Look at the women standing by those tables near them. Look at the way they try to get his attention."

Innes didn't care for the unexpected stab of jealousy that went through her like a hot blade. She glanced at the nearest door but before she could move in that direction, her sister grabbed the back of her dress, steering her toward the three men.

"I think I like his beard and that wild mane of hair," Ailein added. He hadn't tied it back for the occasion. "It definitely gives him an air of danger and mystery."

Innes looked from Bryce's clean-shaven face to Conall's. Beauty and the Beast. Still, she agreed with her sister. And, though she'd never let on to Ailein, she preferred the Beast.

Bryce said something, and a rare smile appeared on the older brother's face. He had perfect, straight teeth. But as quickly as the smile surfaced, it disappeared.

They were near enough now that Innes had an uninterrupted view of the men.

Ailein took hold of her arm, stopping her. "Let's wait here for a moment, shall we?"

Innes nodded, turning to her sister and trying to look at anything but Conall.

Wynda, the matriarch of the clan, was circulating in the hall as Bryce had been doing. The steward Lachlan limped about on the periphery, ordering the servants. The only other Munro in the hall was Jinny, who appeared to be happily settled at Girnigoe. Innes watched her laughing with a group of women at something one of them was saying. The priest Fingal sat nearby, drinking steadily as he lectured men sitting at the far end of the table. None of them appeared to be paying the least attention to him.

Innes's gaze uncontrollably returned to Conall. Tonight he wore a white shirt under his tartan. She admired the fit of it on his chest. Her gaze moved downward. He had one foot up on a stool, exposing a knee and the muscles of a powerful calf. She stared at his leg, unable to understand her fascination with this man's body. Twenty-seven years of age. She thought she was immune to such a reaction to a man. Why now? Why him?

"He's staring at you."

Innes glanced up into his face, realizing she'd been caught again. She turned to her sister. "Can I go now?"

"You are *not* going." Ailein grabbed her by the elbow. "You're here for me, remember?"

The third man walked away, and Bryce and Conall approached them. Introductions and formalities were exchanged between Ailein and the earl. Innes thought about their conversation this morning. She stayed behind her sister and listened.

"I want to apologize, m'lady, that this is our first meeting and for missing the opportunity of meeting your father at the wedding."

Though his face was stern, neither his words nor his tone revealed any hint of accusation. She relaxed slightly.

Her sister was at her gracious best. "We're brother and sister now, so please, no more formalities. I am just Ailein. And I'm certain you and our father will have many other occasions to meet."

"I hope so," Conall said with a slight bow.

At that moment, their aunt Wynda called to Bryce. He

excused himself before crossing the room to her.

Ailein moved to Conall's side and gestured toward Innes. "I understand that you've already met my sister."

His gaze traveled from the hair that Jinny had insisted on braiding, down the length of her black dress to the tips of her shoes, and then back up. When he reached Innes's face, he lingered over every flaw.

"Indeed. I've had the pleasure."

Innes let out a breath that she didn't know she was holding.

"Very good. Then I can leave her in your hands. Watch her. You'll find she's a slippery sort, and I know she'll try to escape the hall before dinner is served."

Innes sent her sister a baleful glare, but she had no chance to respond before Ailein ran off to join Bryce and Wynda. Conall stepped over beside her.

"She's not what I expected," he said in a low voice. "She's quite pleasant."

Innes had a hundred and one complaints about her sister right now, but she held her tongue. This was Ailein's new home. She needed to be accepted, and the Sinclairs only needed to see her virtues.

"Aye, she is pleasant," she agreed. "And Bryce is clearly a patient man. That will be a blessing for both of them."

"She's also beautiful. They're well suited."

"The two of them make a striking pair."

"And they need to settle whatever this quarrel is between them."

Her resolve this morning that she didn't want to get involved evaporated, considering what she knew. "I believe their relationship is already mending."

"How do you know?"

For a lengthy moment, Innes struggled trying to come up with a logical answer.

"Did your sister say something?" he pressed.

Innes shook her head. "I can tell from the way she talks about Bryce. She is definitely smitten."

"Good. Because I believe he is, too."

Their gazes were drawn to Bryce escorting his wife to their table. The newlyweds smiled and talked to a group as they passed, but there wasn't a word spoken between them. There were no smiles. No touches. No displays of affection.

"They still need more fixing," he said close to her ear. "Are they always this formal?"

"I believe so," she admitted, her skin tingling from the brush of his breath. "Although I am rarely here to witness it."

"But you made an exception tonight." He looked at her.

Innes was running the risk of drowning in those eyes. "I was forced to attend."

"So was I."

"I can't imagine anyone forcing you to do anything against your will."

"Very well. I felt obligated."

"You mean Bryce asked, and you came."

"The same with you?"

"Hardly. I screamed and fought, but Ailein wouldn't hear it. She brought in a small army of servants, who bound and gagged me and dragged me down here. I only slipped my ropes at the door of the Great Hall, but by then it was too late."

There was a brief flash of white teeth again, and her heart beat faster in her chest.

"Bound, you say." He leaned closer and whispered. "I had no idea of how interesting your sister's approach could be."

There was a delicious twist low in her belly. "I don't recommend that you use her methods," she told him, feeling bolder. "I have claws."

"I'd be willing to feel your claws, under the right circumstances."

Her cheeks caught fire, but she couldn't tear her gaze away from his. "Beware, Conall Sinclair. You'll find my teeth are sharper than your wolf's."

"I taught Thunder to kiss, rather than bite."

"He's still barely more than a pup. I, on the other hand,

am well past the age of instruction. You know what they say about teaching old dogs."

"Old? You? If you're old, then Hell's lake has iced over. And I could fly this castle to Jerusalem. You, old?" He snorted. "Hardly."

"Is this your idea of sweet talk?" She smiled. "I may swoon at any moment."

Bryce and Ailein were already seated at the table. Conall extended his arm for her to take. "So another challenge. I'll show you sweet talk and look forward to seeing how strongly you resist my charm."

"Did you say 'charm'?" She put a gloved hand on his arm. He looked down at it. "You underestimate my defenses."

"I find it interesting that you wear gloves at all times. Much like dressing in black. No doubt, they form a part of your armament."

Innes said nothing. He had no idea how close he was to the truth.

As they neared the table, the exchange between Bryce and Ailein reached them.

"Bueford is a fine name," Ailein said.

"For a horse, maybe," Bryce retorted with a huff. "Nay, I wouldn't even use it for a horse."

"Osnot?"

"Osnot? By all that's holy, what are you thinking?

Would you condemn the lad to a life of mockery?"

"You're never satisfied with anything I say." Ailein spread her hands in frustration. "Very well. What about Frang? You surely can't object to Frang."

"Are we deciding on a name for our child or a gargoyle?"

Innes and Conall exchanged a look as they arrived at the table.

"I have the perfect name." Ailein smiled. "Nevaeh."

"What does that mean?"

"Heaven, said backwards."

"Heav . . . ?" Bryce slapped the table in obvious exasperation. "Woman, why don't you just call him Hell, or Lucifer, or Thunder's Arse?"

"Are they really arguing over a name for their bairn?" Conall whispered in Innes's ear as she sat.

Innes knew her sister well enough to recognize that Ailein was attempting to act. But for what purpose? "I believe they are."

"Well, Thunder's Arse won't do," he murmured. "I won't have them naming their child after my wolf. It would be too confusing."

She bit her lip to keep from laughing.

He sat himself next to her, continuing to speak in a low voice to her alone. "I could be mistaken, but I always thought the birth of a child required a certain physical activity for the joyous event to take place."

"I believe you're correct in that."

"Well, listening to them now, I'm not holding out much hope."

"But I am," Innes replied, and turned to Wynda on her other side so she wouldn't have to explain further.

The feast is long over, the castle slumbers, and the morning breaks. I watch the bloodred dawn and remember.

This is the day—so many years ago—that my love was taken from me. Aye, they took him from me. My own blood kin tracked us down, seized him in his own great hall, tore him from my arms, dragged him into the courtyard, and killed him.

He was dead. Never to return to me. I was already carrying his bairn, but he was a good man and we would have married. I cried out, "Our love is true!" But the laird would hear none of that. He looked at me with blind rage. I thought he would kill me then, as well. How often have I wished he'd done it! How will I ever blot out the memory of those screams, of his life's blood running down between the stones?

I see him still. His beautiful face, now battered; his eyes that once looked at me with nothing but love, now lifeless and blank. Aye, all that was left of him, lying there in my lap, staining my apron and my hands and my cheek with his thickening blood.

They looked on me with disgust, as if it was I who'd gone mad. I, who simply wanted to be with the man I loved. And later, when darkness fell and they stood around me—a circle of torchbearers afraid to come closer—I realized that the cries echoing in the Highland hills were my own.

Chapter 9

The path followed a meandering brook through green meadows dotted with sheep and red, shaggy cattle. Patches of forest broke up the regularity of the rocky moorland, and a warm sun shone down on gray stone farm cottages snuggled into low hillsides. Cresting a hill, the two women descended into a broad, flat area where in the distance Innes saw a dozen men cutting peat from a bog. The distinctive old-egg smell reached her long before they drew close. Children stacking the peat blocks to dry waved to them as they passed.

Innes was glad she'd accepted Wynda's invitation. Once a sennight the aunt delivered baskets of food to the sick and needy. The older woman was not a talker, but the occasional conversation between them came with a natural ease that Innes found as pleasurable as it was surprising.

Each of them carried a large basket, and the first three cottages where they stopped received the supplies of bannock bread, meats, and dried fish with expressions of sincere gratitude.

Wynda gestured to a large oak grove some distance ahead. "Our last delivery is there, just beyond the edge of the wood. My basket is empty. Do you want me to carry some of what's left?"

"I'm fine."

"I'm glad you came. It's very pleasant to have the company," she said. "I brought Ailein along the last time. But today she seemed anxious for the return of her husband. Better that she does her pacing at Girnigoe than fret her day away wishing she were there."

Innes hadn't seen Conall since the night of the dinner. The following morning he and Bryce rode out unexpectedly with a few men. She learned from her sister that a messenger had arrived, bringing them a summons to meet with other Highland leaders.

"Do you expect your nephews back soon?" Innes asked Wynda.

"No way of telling. I suppose it depends on the reason for the meeting. They didn't tell me."

Innes was sorry she hadn't gotten a chance to see Conall again. Something had happened to her during that dinner, and since then she barely slept at all, thinking of every word they exchanged. Lying there in the dark, night after night, she tried to attach meaning to every brush of his clothes and every glance or smile.

In two more days, she'd be leaving Girnigoe. A feeling

somewhat akin to sadness overtook her. But perhaps this was the break that she needed.

She'd gone over the events of the dinner again and again. In the course of the evening, no one spoke of the wars or his past. No one asked any question that might evoke the memories of what he went through. No one wanted to risk upsetting him.

Having the stretch of days and nights to think, Innes came to realize how foolish it was for her to entertain any dreams of a future that might include him. Conall was a wounded man, inside and out. Two times she touched him, and in each instance she wasn't prepared for what she saw. He was a man who wanted to keep his past buried inside of him. Why would he want a woman who could see right into his soul?

"I believe we will continue to see a lot more of that now that he has returned to us," said Wynda. Innes looked at the older woman. "Conall being called away."

"Why?" Worry clutched at Innes's heart. "Surely, they won't expect him to fight again. He's sacrificed so much already."

"Not called to fight, but to serve as an advisor. To offer guidance and direction."

Innes was relieved. She remembered that Conall had been a close confidant to the late king.

"And it's a blessing that he's no longer laird of Girnigoe," Wynda continued. "He'll have no time for that."

Her interest was piqued. "No time for what?"

"He is still tending to his wounds, but I am sure it's only matter of time before he's summoned to court to serve as a member of the Regency Council," Wynda said confidently. "He's the earl of Caithness, the strongest peer in the north. As you say, he served the crown in war. Conall is greatly respected for his bravery and sound judgment. He's never been one to seek power or profit for himself. Who is more qualified to serve Scotland?"

It pleased Innes to think that a rewarding future awaited the earl if he chose to consider it.

The smell of smoke from a small fire drew both women's attention. She and Wynda passed an outcropping of rocks, and a camp on the bank of the shallow stream came into view. Two young men were up to their knees in the water, a net spread between them to catch fish. A third lad tended the fire and watched the others.

"These are not local boys, I'm sure," Wynda whispered to Innes. "I don't recognize them."

The one by the fire jumped to his feet and called to his fellows in the stream. The two dropped their net and waded out of water.

"Good day to you lads," Wynda called, pulling Innes along.

"Oi, old woman, wait up there. Just a word, if you don't mind."

Striding up the hill, he stepped in their path. The other two followed him.

"We've got a sick family to see to," Wynda told him. "You'll need to step aside. Get back to your fishing."

The young man pulled his cap off and scratched his head. "Aye, that's the problem, you see. My friends and me have been trying to coax a fish or two out of that stream, and have naught to show for our trouble."

Innes glanced behind him at the other two. They were young, she realized. But they definitely looked hungry, and she knew that hungry men of any age could be dangerous. She recalled Conall's warning on the strand.

Innes handed the basket to Wynda. She peeled off her gloves, tucking them into the sash at her belt.

"If you're tired of fishing, not far along this path you'll find men cutting peat," Wynda said. "Go and tell them you'll work the rest of the day for a meal and a roof over your head for the night."

"And why would they do that for three strangers, I'd like to know?" asked the lad.

"Tell them the laird of Castle Girnigoe said so."

"And you speak for the laird, I suppose?"

"As a matter of fact, I do," Wynda said sternly. "So you'll do well to let us pass."

"As a matter of fact, m'lady," the young man said, sarcasm evident in every word, "we'd never forgive ourselves if we let you carry that heavy basket on your own. Would we, lads?"

"This food is for a family with sick children," Wynda said angrily. "It's not for three able-bodied young men who can be earning their own bread."

"So it's bread, is it?" The ruffian's tone grew sharper as he motioned to one of the others. "Help the lady with that basket."

"Don't you dare," Wynda snapped.

Innes took the basket back and put it at her feet, pushing the aunt behind. She faced the three of them.

"The old crone has a protector," he said mockingly. His gaze fell on the pouch at Innes's waist. "I'm thinking there might be a coin or two in this one's purse. Get that too."

"I have no coins to give you."

Innes watched the burliest of the young men as he approached. As he bent to retrieve the basket, Innes seized his wrist and he looked up in surprise. They were nearly eye to eye.

"What would your family think of this? You stealing a sick child's bread?"

He hesitated, and that was enough for her.

"Jock, you don't want to do this," she said quietly. "I know you. You and your brother and this other one live to the south, in the village by the falls. Your sister Makyn, she tends the sheep for the blind cotter. I know it's been hard for you since your father went off to fight in the king's war and never came back. But your mother is doing her best."

The lad tried to pull his hand free, but Innes held on.

"Do you think it's right that you and your brother left them to fend for themselves? And what happens when word gets back to your village that you harmed two women trying to steal bread? You don't want to be shaming your own mother. You and your brother Finn are better lads than that, I know."

The surprise turned to wide-eyed panic. The burly young man wrenched his hand away as if she'd burned him. He staggered backward and spun to face the other men who stared, openmouthed.

The leader was the first to bolt down the hill. The other two soon followed on his heels.

Innes waited until the three of them were over a low hill before she let out a nervous sigh.

"Did you know him?" asked Wynda.

Innes broke into a cold sweat, realizing what she'd done. What choice did she have? She'd acted without thinking. She had no way of protecting them. Innes pulled on her gloves before turning. Wynda was waiting for an answer.

She couldn't lie. "I didn't know him."

Wynda stared at Innes's gloved fingers.

"I have a gift. One that my mother had before me." The words spilled out. "I can touch a person's hand and read their mind, see their past. This is the reason for wearing the gloves."

Wynda's face paled. Innes reached out to steady her for fear of the older woman falling. "It's not witchcraft," she quickly explained. "There is a relic. One that has been in our family for many years. It's completely innocent. Harmless. You saw the extent of its power."

"Does Ailein have this 'gift' as well?"

Innes shook her head. "She doesn't have it. Only I do."

Wynda clutched at her arm, wanting the support. Innes understood how difficult it must be to accept what she just witnessed. The two stood in silence for some time.

"No one knows of my gift except Ailein and my father," said Innes. "I wear the gloves because I have no wish to intrude on people's lives or their past. Many could judge such an intrusion harshly, and I—"

"You don't need to explain more." The older woman nodded and caressed Innes's arm gently before pulling away. "Your secret is safe with me. We'll tell no one what happened here today."

Wynda drew the shawl around her and bent to pick up the basket. Innes lifted it first, relieved.

"Thank you," she said. "I can't tell you how much—"

The sound of hoofbeats drew their attention. Four riders appeared on a far hill. Even at a distance, Innes recognized Conall's black mane flying in the breeze.

Her heart leaped in her chest and a jumbled rush of emotions nearly brought tears to her eyes. The upset of what they'd just gone through with those young men, the revelation of her gift, and the longing that she was feeling now churned her insides.

Thunder provided the distraction she needed. His nose lifted and the wolf came racing across the moor toward Innes and Wynda. The riders immediately changed direction and approached, but Thunder was happily jumping at Innes long before the men reached them.

"Good day to you, too," she said, petting him. "Aye, pup. I'm glad to see you, too."

Conall rode past the fire, glancing at it before dismounting. Bryce's boots hit the ground a moment later.

"Cooking dinner, Aunt?" the younger man asked, smiling.

Conall looked at Innes and she had eyes only for him. Her gaze took in the boots and the kilt, the wide chest and the face that she already found extremely handsome, regardless of the scars and the beard.

"I didn't expect to find you out here," the earl commented.

"Innes has been helping me deliver the baskets," Wynda answered. "We've one more family to visit."

Conall glanced at the forest. "The woodcutter's child. Still sick, is he?"

"Mending, I believe," the aunt replied. "Well, was the meeting as urgent as they said?"

"It was good that we went," Bryce said.

"Why?" Wynda asked. "What's happened?"

"The English attacked. They sailed up the coast, landed at Leith, and went on a rampage."

Innes turned to Conall. His face was grave. Would there never be an end to this, she thought? Must people continue to suffer because of these incessant wars?

Conall spoke up. "Our defenses at Leith were smashed and the raiders swept into Edinburgh town. The castle held. The gunners fired straight down the Royal Mile, but that was the best we could do, they tell us. The English took what they wanted and destroyed the rest."

Leaving more lives shattered, she thought.

"The English burned the town and the palace and abbey at Holyroodhouse," Conall continued. "And dozens of villages, churches and all. When they left, they even took two of the crown's ships. Just loaded them with looted goods and sailed south."

"And it isn't over," Bryce added. "They have a new butcher tearing up the south. A devil named Evers has come up from the Borders. They say some renegade Scots have joined his army."

"I know this man," Conall told them. "Sir Ralph Evers. He calls himself the Scourge of the Borders and revels in the title. He's the English commander in the north and holds other positions courtesy of his king. He sees all Scots as vermin and believes it is his duty to flush us out and kill us wherever he can."

Innes's heart was heavy as a millstone, hurting for those innocents who fell into the clutches of such men as Evers.

"This was the reason for the meeting," Bryce said. "The Highlands are no longer safe as they once were. We need to organize. We must stop this madman and his bloody marauders."

Conall looked about him and at the unattended fire. "We need to get back to Girnigoe. But I don't like the two of you doing this alone."

"Why don't you leave your two men to escort us?" Wynda suggested. "If we get started, we can be back at the castle long before dinner."

Conall considered this for a moment, his eyes never leaving Innes. His reluctance was evident in his face, but finally he nodded and directed his warriors.

He cast one more look at Innes as he mounted his horse, then called to Thunder and rode off with his brother.

Chapter 10

"For centuries, the Wheel of Lugh was lost. The religion of our Savior ruled supreme, but the old religion did not die. And then, when the four of us were still young men, the pieces of the Wheel surfaced. The priests of the oak gave one to each of us and commanded that we travel over the sea to our homeland. We were to protect each tablet until summoned to the Crypt of Lugh, where a high priest, a giant, and a great bird would take them and protect them for all time . . ."

From the *Chronicle of Lugh*

After a walk along the bluffs, Innes returned to the East Tower to find her sister pacing in the Inner Ward, waiting for her.

"Nothing you say will convince me to change my plans again. I'm leaving tomorrow," Innes warned.

What had happened with Wynda on their outing continued to prey on her mind. She didn't say a word of the incident to her sister. She hoped the old aunt would remain true to her word and stay silent about it. Ailein didn't need the worry.

The morning sun was just clearing the castle walls, and the courtyard lay half in shadow.

Ailein frowned, glaring at Innes with that stubborn look she used when she wanted something that she'd have to fight for. "Come and walk with me, at least."

"Nay. Come inside." Innes headed for the door.

"This is your last day. Am I less deserving of your company than your precious birds?" Ailein turned and stalked off toward the bridge leading to the Outer Ward.

Innes sighed. She didn't want this. She didn't want to leave Castle Girnigoe feeling that her sister harbored ill will. She hurried to catch her.

"What's this all about?" she asked. "Say it."

Ailein barely slowed down. "You didn't show up to dinner last night. You avoided him."

Innes knew perfectly well who her sister was talking about, but for the sake of pretense she had to say it. "I wasn't trying to avoid your husband. But Wynda and I walked for miles. I was tired."

She was also troubled that her secret had been exposed. Those young men had to know. She shivered, thinking what the consequences of rumors could be.

A cart carrying sacks of milled grain passed in front of them, heading for the kitchens. The drover lifted his cap and smiled toothlessly. Innes looked around the courtyard at the faces that had become familiar to her over the three weeks of stay. She knew some by name.

Ailein took her arm and spoke quietly. "I'm talking about the earl. Conall Sinclair."

"I wasn't avoiding him. I saw him yesterday with Wynda."

"In passing," she said. "What do you have against him?"

"Nothing." Innes had nothing against the earl. In fact, her problem was that she liked him too much. "Last night, I got to bed early. I need to readjust myself to the schedule I'll have when I return home."

"You mean Margaret's schedule. You can't be looking forward to her constant harping."

"Not the harping, to be sure. But I do miss Father and the boys and our own folk."

"They'll be there waiting for you whenever you get back," Ailein said. "Father will be anxious to have you sit in on clan meetings."

"Aye, but he'll have Robert for that after this year."

Robert, their brother from Hector Munro's second marriage, would be returning from university in Paris. They both knew he was to be the next laird and Baron Folais.

"Which means Father is certain to bow to Margaret's pressure and marry you off before he steps down."

"They could try. They've tried before. It will not happen." There was only one man she'd ever been tempted to dream about. Conall Sinclair. But she would learn to forget him. She had no other choice. "Did you ask me to walk with you so you could remind me of the difficulties that await me at home?"

"Aye." Ailein smiled. "Stay another fortnight."

Innes was relieved that her sister didn't try to lie about troubles with her husband as a reason to stay. They were together now, although for some insane reason they still tried to keep a pretense of disagreement in public.

"Please?"

Innes shook her head. "You're incorrigible. This is your home. These are your people now. You don't need me."

Growing serious again, Ailein stopped and looked about her. "I've discovered something. Actually, Jinny found out. It's about Shona."

Innes frowned at her. "Let the woman rest."

She shook her head. "There's an elderly woman who lives in a village a half day's ride from here. Her name is Teva. She was Shona's nursemaid, and later her maidservant. She only left the castle after Shona's death." Ailein started walking again. "I want you to come with me in a few days when I ride over to see her."

"I won't be here in a few days . . . or in a fortnight, either," Innes reminded her. "But even if you speak with her, what makes you think she'll say any more about the past than you've been able to gather already?"

"Jinny says the word among the household is that Teva talked too much. *That* was why Wynda sent her away."

"Wynda sent her away?"

"She did."

They turned around and started back toward the East Tower. Innes liked the aunt a great deal. She could believe that Wynda might find the serving woman's gossiping unsuitable. On the other hand, what if she sent her away for openly saying things that were true?

"You can get an escort of Sinclair warriors and ride over there yourself."

Ailein sent her an exasperated look. "Don't you think Bryce would find out? And what excuse could I use? It's one thing if I say I went riding with my sister and we ended up in that village. It's quite another if I—"

"Your husband has been gone for most of the week. Why couldn't you tell me this two days ago? A day ago? We could have gone today," Innes said shortly. "I swear, I believe you're plotting this whole thing."

"Ask Jinny yourself. She only told me this morning."

Innes was tempted to use the gift of the relic to get the answers Ailein wanted. The challenge was that a person's past didn't come to her in one sweep. Like yesterday, the past came to her in bits and pieces. Often they were images or thoughts that were on a person's mind at the time. Recent nightmares. Secrets they didn't want revealed, but that were always weighing on their minds. Often, she saw recent events that had strong emotional connections—both good and bad. The key was to ask a question that triggered the memory of that specific moment or event. She could read the truth then, even if the person refused to answer or lied to hide it.

She pushed the temptation away. She wouldn't do this to her sister, not when she planned to go away. Besides, Innes had a nagging feeling that this would only open Pandora's box. The past was never as neat and tidy as Ailein naively believed.

"I promise this will be the last time I ask. Only a fortnight," said Ailein.

Innes shook her head and started toward the door.

"Please, Innes."

"Let me think about it," she said over her shoulder. "But I doubt I'll stay."

Stepping into the East Tower, she welcomed the cool darkness of the stairwell. As always, her gaze drifted to the latched door. Could she stay at Girnigoe and not encounter Conall? And if she did, could she keep herself safe from him? And what about those young men from yesterday? Would they talk? Would her mere presence here complicate her sister's life?

Innes climbed the stairs, knowing that she needed to go home.

As far as Teva, there was no urgency in the information that Ailein sought. Shona was dead. Why she took her own life—and the mystery of where she was buried—mattered less with each day that Ailein spent at Castle Girnigoe. Ailein needed to look to the future and give up her obsession with the past.

Innes spotted something enfolded in silk cloth at her door. Picking it up, she went into her room and unwrapped the object. It was a book.

She gasped in delight when she opened it and saw the contents. An emblem book of birds. She'd seen only one before. Her fingers touched the delicate illustrations and moved under lines of French poetry.

She pressed the precious gift to her chest and saw the letter left in the silk wrappings. She broke the Sinclair seal and stared at four words scribbled in a rough handwriting.

The door is unlocked.

She wasn't coming.

Conall turned his back on the window and peered

over at the table where Duff had laid the new sword.

Bryce had sent it up to him. He was being a pain in the arse, plain and simple. He wouldn't give up until Conall joined the men in the courtyard and began training again.

"The laird says the armorer worked on it all night to finish it this morning." Duff tooled a harness as he spoke. "It's a bloody fine sword. The blade edge looks sharp and true as anything Toledo-made. You can see I wrapped the grip the way you like. O' course, if you want to use one of your old swords, they're ready in the back room."

"Did I tell you how pleasant it was at the hunting lodge without you yammering in my ear all the time?"

"Nay, m'lord. I know that's hardly the truth. Why, Thunder was just telling me you both missed me." The wolf raised his head at the mention of his name.

Bloody hell. Even Duff had been instructed to harass him. And there was no need, especially after everything they'd heard these past few days. They were far to the north, but he'd fought against bloodthirsty English raiders before. This commander, Sir Ralph Evers, sounded like the worst of the worst.

Conall agreed that it was time to work on strengthening his left arm. He could swing a sword with skill using either hand, but it had been a long time since he'd tried.

He picked up the weapon. It was lighter than he'd been

accustomed to when he still had his other hand. The grip was perfect. He swung it in the air a few times, pivoting and lunging.

Thunder jumped up from his bedding and rushed out the door and down the steps.

Duff grinned. "You scared the beast, m'lord."

"Is the door into the stables closed?"

"Aye, I closed it tight. Won't be making that mistake again." Duff tugged on his ear. "But if he goes out that bloody window and tears up the scullery . . ."

Duff caught hell from Wynda *and* Cook the day Thunder got into the kitchens. Conall feared that the stable workers would be even less forgiving if the wolf got in with the horses.

He'd trained Thunder since finding him as a newborn pup. But with the exception of his own steed, the horses in the stable became downright panicky whenever the wolf was around.

"This will do." He laid the sword back on the table. "Give my regards to the armorer. Looks to be a fine weapon. On second thought, I'll tell him myself."

When he looked up, Duff had snatched the hat off his head and was bowing politely. Conall turned around and saw Innes standing in the doorway with Thunder beside her. The heat rose in his face and he smiled despite himself.

"I'm sorry to interrupt," she said.

"Not at all. We're done here."

Duff bowed at least three times more as he moved hurriedly toward the door. She stepped aside, letting him pass.

Conall had hoped to see her before she left. Yesterday, with the audience of Wynda and Bryce, their meeting had been restrained, impersonal. He wanted so much to sweep her onto his horse and take her away someplace where the two of them could be alone. Lately, those were the times when he felt the most alive. He behaved, however, forfeiting that moment with the hope of this one.

Conall let his gaze take in all of her. She wore another of her black dresses, and with her matching gloves every inch of her from the neck down was covered. But her face, as always, fascinated him. Her wide mouth with those full, pink lips. The straight nose and high cheekbones. The gray eyes, large and beautiful. The pale, flawless skin. His eyes were drawn to the patch of the white hair, some of which had escaped the braid and hung down the side of her face.

"So you were able to read my terrible handwriting."

"Of course." Her gaze darted to his right hand before returning to his face.

"And you found your way with no trouble."

"I followed the trail of broken bread crusts and found myself at the bottom of these steps. That's where Thunder greeted me."

"I couldn't risk having you get lost in the tunnels and caves that honeycomb the shore."

"It was a good idea leaving the bread." A smile tugged at the corner of her lip. "But the first ones tasted a wee bit stale, so I left the rest."

"Thunder will like you all the more for it. He's not quite so fussy." He motioned to her to come in.

She stayed near the door, looking as skittish as a colt. "I only came to thank you for loaning me the book. I'll leave it with Ailein to return to you."

"It was not a loan. It's a gift."

"I cannot accept it. That is far too precious a volume."

"Nay. It's yours now," he said firmly. He leaned against the table and motioned to the shelves along one wall. "That book is better off with someone who has an interest in the topic than collecting dust here."

Her gaze moved over the shelves and the weaponry in the room to the chess set. Her frown told him she was still bothered by the value of what he'd given her.

"If you want to thank me for the gift, then come in. We can sit and chat for a few minutes."

"About what?"

"About my brother and your sister. I have no one else

to talk to about them once you return home tomorrow." Thunder nudged her hip.

"You see?" laughed Conall. "Even *that* beast agrees with me."

He tried to hide his pleasure when she moved away from the door.

"These are the only comfortable chairs I own." He gestured to the seats on either side of the chess set.

She didn't sit but moved around the room, looking out each of the windows, crossing to the shelves, running a gloved finger lightly across the volumes. Conall tried to imagine what she was thinking. The Munros were a wealthy clan, and the baron was especially generous with his daughters. Bryce's complaints nudged into his thoughts. An earl shouldn't be spending his time in two rooms above the stables like some pauper. Still, Conall had no regrets about living here, especially at this moment.

"Wine?" he asked.

She shook her head. "Are you a reader?"

"I wasn't always. As a peer, I needed to learn, of course, but I always preferred hunting and riding and fighting as a young man. These days, I have much more time on my hand, so I've begun to read more."

"And you play chess."

"I enjoy it, but it's difficult to find a worthy opponent at Girnigoe. Thunder prefers to eat the pieces rather than play the game. Bryce doesn't do much better." He motioned to the board. "Do you play?"

"I have an elementary knowledge of it."

"Excellent. Then we shall play."

He moved to her chair, holding it for her to sit. She bit her bottom lip, taking hesitant steps.

"I doubt that you'll find me a worthy opponent," she said.

"I promise to be gentle with you."

She smelled of fresh sea air. He recalled the day in the hills when she held on to him as he helped her stand after Thunder knocked her down. He'd wanted then to continue holding her, protecting her. It wasn't until he rode off that the desire crystalized in his brain. That was the second time that they met, but the incident was different. For those few moments she was in his arms, Conall felt a bond forming between them. He couldn't explain it, didn't understand it, but he'd never felt such a connection with any woman before. He still felt it.

Today, knowing she was going away, he'd set his mind on seeing her, alone. Conall was glad that she came and he didn't have to go to the East Tower in search of her.

He pushed in the chair and she sat down. Thunder forsook his bed to curl up at her feet.

"Thank you for being gentle with me," she said, smiling sweetly.

For a few seconds he found himself only staring at her lips. He guessed she would object if he leaned down and tasted them.

She pointed to the board. "This is the queen and this the bishop, if I recall."

He carried the pitcher of wine and the cups to the table, and took the seat across from her. As he poured the wine, he explained names of each piece and how they moved and captured the opponent's pieces on the board. "Am I being too elementary?"

"Nay. I'm grateful."

Her eyelashes were long and dark and they fanned the translucent skin of her cheekbones as she watched the board. He explained just enough not to bore her. "The best way to learn is to play. But have no fear. As I said, I'll go easy on you the first time."

"First time? Don't forget, I'm leaving tomorrow."

"How can I forget?" He motioned to her to make the first move. "You're going to abandon me here with a pair of feuding newlyweds."

She moved a pawn forward two spaces. "I'm certain of it now. They're no longer fighting."

Conall pushed one of his pawns forward. "I heard them arguing last night at dinner, even though they've been apart for most of the week."

"They're making a good show of it, but that's all." Innes

took her turn. "They're only doing that for your sake and mine. It's a ruse."

Some loose strands of hair brushed her lips. He struggled not to reach over and tuck them behind her ear. "And their bedroom difficulties?"

"It's difficult to say for sure. I believe they've mended their differences, but they've decided to continue to play their game."

He stared at the column of her neck and the small buttons stretching down to her waistline. What would it be like to open them one by one?

"How do you know this?"

"I know my sister too well." She shrugged, moving her bishop back to remove the danger from his pawn. "I let her think what she wants. She believes their plot is working."

He leaned on an elbow, hiding the growing evidence of her temptation beneath the folds of his kilt. "What is their plot?"

"To keep me at Girnigoe a while longer."

"I'd like to help them with their plot."

She bit her lip and took his pawn with a bishop.

He studied the board, then looked up at her lips. She had the power to drive him crazy. He held out his hand to take the piece, and her gloved fingers placed it gently in his palm.

"Why do you always wear the gloves? Is it habit? Fashion?"

A soft blush immediately crept into her cheeks. He watched her face. Her enticing lips. Her gaze refused to lift from the board.

"Habit more than fashion, but that's not entirely accurate," she said. "It's just my way."

"Like wearing black."

"Like never trimming your beard or cutting your hair."

He smiled, looking down at the board and the moves she'd been making. "Like being an expert in this game and lying about your skills."

"I didn't lie." She smiled.

"'I have an elementary knowledge of the game.'" Conall tried to do an imitation of her tone. He put her king in check with his queen.

"You're mocking me," she said, sounding insulted. Her knight blocked the check.

"This will not be the only game we play."

She sent him a challenging look. "Are you forfeiting already?"

Her bishop put his king in check. He moved his king and glared across the board. She glared back, but Conall saw the trace of a smile on her lips.

Her second bishop put him in check.

"You are a bloodthirsty wasp," he said, moving the king.

"Then beware of my sting."

In the next few moves, her queen began carving a bloody path while his king went on the run.

He couldn't believe it. He'd been distracted by her looks, by the allure of her lips, by his body's response to her. He hadn't seen it coming. The last time he had lost a game had to be when he was a student at the university.

"Checkmate."

"Bloody hell." He sat back in the chair. "How many moves was that?"

"What makes you think I was counting moves?"

He shook a threatening finger in her direction. "I know you were."

She laughed and her face transformed before his eyes. Whatever he'd thought of her beauty before, it was nothing compared to how he saw her now. When she laughed, her somberness disappeared, age melted away, her wariness evaporated. Suddenly, she was young and carefree and happy, and her smile shone with a brilliance that knocked the breath from his chest.

"Twenty-two," she finally admitted.

Setting up the board again, he scowled at her. "We are having a rematch right now. And this time, m'lady, be prepared to learn how this game is played."

———

Innes lost the next game, and she rose to her feet. Thunder stood and stretched beside her.

Conall motioned to the seat. "Sit. We play again."

She watched him set up the board. "Can't we leave it at a draw? We each won a game."

"We can if you agree to postpone your journey to Folais Castle."

A delicious knot formed again in her belly. Years ago, one of her tutors had taught her the game. From the very beginning, she found she was excellent at it. Now she only played occasionally, when a guest arrived at Folais who was fond of the game. To her, chess was just a diversion, something with which to pass the time. She never saw it as a battle of wits. She never imagined the joy that would fill her heart when she watched him as he studied the board and made a move.

His gaze met hers. She thought she might melt from the intensity of it.

"Nay, I'm leaving tomorrow." She sat down and stared at the board. "But we can play one more game, and that is the end of it. The winner is the champion. You go first."

He started to play and then sat back, watching her.

A charged silence hung in the air for a few moments. Thunder sat on his haunches, looking from one human to the other and then at the board.

"Let's make a wager," said Conall.

Innes was forced to look up at him. "What should we play for? Coins? A book? A tutor to teach you to play chess properly?"

"We play for you."

Her face went warm. Her heart began beating so hard that she feared it might burst from her chest.

"If you win, you leave tomorrow. If I win, you extend your stay here by a month."

She shook her head. "I'm not going to stay longer because of a silly game."

"Then do it for your sister."

Innes thought about Ailein's request. Staying here would make her sister happy. And the men they ran into yesterday? There were rumors everywhere. She could deny them. But what about the complication sitting across the table? After today, she would lose whatever shield she had to resist her deepening attraction to him.

"I can't. Ailein doesn't really need me."

"I say she does. And I know what it's like to be alone."

Innes looked down at her hands folded in her lap. Why did he have to pull at her heartstrings like this? She knew what he'd gone through. But she also knew what it was like to be alone. That was her life. Her future.

"Your sister still needs you," he said softly.

He was tempting her. Manipulating her. He was playing her heart like an instrument. She was torn by which road to take. Reason or . . . was it passion?

And why did he press her? What did he want?

"What do you say, Innes?" he prodded. "Why not let our talent in this game decide?"

She took a deep breath. "Very well." She focused her attention on the board. "And so a month of my life is about to be decided by a foolish game."

"I don't believe this game we're playing is foolish, at all," he said quietly, picking up his knight.

Chapter 11

Thunder leaped out of the water and raced across the strand before the door began to creak open.

As the gate swung wide, the wolf went in and Innes stepped out. Thunder immediately reappeared, bouncing happily in circles around her.

Conall climbed the rocky beach toward her. Thunder was hopelessly in love—jumping up, licking her face, kissing her lips. She petted him and tried to push the animal away.

Conall never thought there would come a day when he'd be jealous of a wolf, but that day had arrived.

"Get down, you beast," he commanded.

The excited animal ran from Innes to him, and then back. This time he knocked her down.

"Thunder!"

At Conall's harsh tone, the wolf crouched down at Innes's side, kissing her face as she lay flat on her back laughing.

Conall went to her and leaned down, his hand on his knee, looking down at her smiling face and sparkling eyes.

He thought of her looking up at him in his bed, naked, her limbs tangled with his. His gaze drifted to her lips.

"Did he hurt you?"

She pushed up onto her elbows. "I believe my backside is severely bruised." She reached under herself and produced a large shell. "You're not to blame after all, Thunder. It's what I landed on."

The wolf's tail wagged.

"You stayed," Conall said. "I'm glad."

"I lost," she said. "I always make good on my wagers."

He wanted to be able to take the same liberties with her the wolf did. He imagined having the freedom of sweeping her into his arms and kissing those lips.

How long had it been since he'd felt this way? He'd dreamt of her last night. She came to him in his bedroom. Naked, her skin glowing, reflecting a full moon. She pushed him back on the bedding and climbed on top of him. He looked into her eyes, the blanket of her silky hair caressing his chest, his arms. And then Innes lowered herself, inch by inch, until he was fully embedded in her tight sheath. He'd awakened fully aroused, wanting her.

He offered her his hand, and her gloved fingers grasped it. He pulled her up and inhaled her scent; his hand lingered on the small of her back before letting go.

"I hope you realize that just because I stayed, that

doesn't mean we'll be playing chess three or four times a day," she said.

"Once a day will be fine." He picked up the drawing supplies that Thunder had knocked down and walked beside her as she headed toward the rock slabs near the water's edge. "But I'll need to think of other things to keep you occupied for the rest of the day."

"You don't need to entertain me. My understanding was that I was staying to be a help to my sister."

He waved a hand dismissively in the direction of the castle, looming high behind them. "You were right. I paid closer attention last night at dinner. The attraction between them is obvious and mutual, and they're doing a poor job of hiding it."

She sent him a knowing look. He liked this feeling of being a coconspirator with her.

The sea had grown rougher since he'd come out at dawn. He and Thunder had come down early, not wanting to miss her. Now, as they drew close to her favorite spot, a wave crashed on the rocks, spraying them with mist. As always, the blaze of white hair danced free in the wind, and it blew across her eyes.

He acted without thinking. He touched the hair, felt its texture, and curled it around a finger before pushing it back behind her ear.

Her lips parted and her eyes grew wide. A blush covered her cheeks, and he wasn't able to stop himself. He leaned down and brushed his lips against hers. It was a chaste kiss. A peck of the lips that gave him a sampling of her. Her lips were so soft.

It was a good thing that she turned and quickly climbed the rocks, or he would have done it again, this time taking it further.

"I doubt you'll find a dry place to sketch this morning. Not this close to the surf."

She kept her face away from him and continued to climb. Thunder followed her, making it known to his master that his allegiance at the moment was with her.

"It's no use," Conall continued. "The sea has a mind of its own when a storm is brewing."

"So we're in for a storm, you think?" she asked as she reached the top.

"All the signs point to it." Conall looked up at her standing on the rocks and lost track of whatever else he was going to say. Her face lifted to the sky, and she squinted into the wind. The wind whipped her dress, molding it against her breasts and hips and legs. Her braided hair was coming loose and long locks flared out behind her.

He wanted her.

She drew in her cape around her.

"Do you ride?" he asked.

"Of course," she responded, looking down at him. "But most animals—my four-legged friend here being an exception—are not comfortable around me. I ride when I need to, but I prefer to walk."

"Where I'm taking you is too far to walk."

"This doesn't sound enticing."

"Do you know that we have some of the rarest birds of the Highlands near us here?"

Her gaze fixed on him and she smiled. "How would you know that?"

"I'm very knowledgeable about subjects of importance." The truth was that his late uncle used to drag him and Bryce all around Caithness showing them the nesting places of birds that had been far more abundant in his own youth.

"Name some of these *rare* birds."

"Are you doubting me?"

"To be sure, we have birds one rarely sees," she said. "But I am doubting your ability to name them."

"How could I have fallen so low in your estimation in so short a time?" he said as pitifully as he could muster.

With a frown at the ominous skies, she began to climb down.

He slipped an arm around her waist and lowered her next to him—allowing his fingers to linger on her waist. He eyed her lips again, wanting another taste, but sensed her hesitation.

"Very well," he continued. "Have you ever seen a purple heron?"

"I . . . well, I haven't."

"Or a red-throated diver?"

He affected her when he came close. He saw the difference in her every time. Her breathing changed, and she would not let herself look directly into his eyes. She moved away from him now.

"I know *of* those birds. But I've never seen them."

"Then this week you will," he told her. "I've told Bryce I'd train with him and the men some of the mornings. But I'll be free any day you're available. What do you say to that? Give me a day."

"I don't know. I have to check with Ailein. She might need me with her every day." She started back toward the castle.

He fell in beside her. "By going with me, you might actually be helping her."

"What do you mean?"

"I'll tell Bryce that you and I won't be around for a day. Imagine what those two will be able to do with the hours that we're gone."

The blush colored her cheek again. She sent him a quick glance. "There are certain things I'd prefer *not* to imagine."

Conall chided himself inwardly. The words came out coarser than he intended. He had little practice in the art of wooing. He'd never needed to learn.

"I promise you we don't even have to think about them when it's just the two of us."

"I'll have to consider that excursion. It might not be . . . well, it might not be the best thing to go out on our own for any distance from Girnigoe."

"You are concerned because of propriety."

"I care nothing about propriety. I care nothing about what people think. My reputation is my own to keep."

"Then what is it?"

They reached the door into the castle. She pulled it open. His attraction to her grew every time they met. Suddenly, he had to know. He took her elbow, stopping her from going in.

"Is there someone else? Another man?"

Innes's face lifted. Her gray eyes looked directly into his. There was no fear in them, no shyness, no reserve. "There is no one else. And there has never been."

He was relieved. "Then why do you wear black?"

She paused for the length of a breath and looked away before speaking. "Why I wear black . . . who I am . . . cannot be explained in a few casual words between friends."

"Then we *are* friends."

She hesitated and then nodded.

He took her chin and lifted her face until she was again looking into his eyes. "Friends trust each other, don't they?"

"Aye," she whispered. "I am sorry. Perhaps someday I'll tell you the real story of Innes Munro."

Conall watched her disappear through the door.

———

From the window of Ailein's bedchamber, Innes watched the men training in the courtyard of the Outer Ward. Her attention was focused on only one of them.

Sweat glistened on Conall's bare chest as he hammered the straw-covered post with the sword in his left hand. Spinning and slashing, backing and charging, parrying and thrusting, he pushed his body through the fierce training.

"Even with one hand, he's still a fearsome opponent."

Innes jumped. She hadn't realized her sister had left Jinny and the seamstress at the far end of the room.

"Your husband is a great fighter, too," Innes said.

She hoped Ailein wouldn't press her for details, for her gaze barely strayed for a moment from Conall's muscular frame. Even from this distance, Innes could clearly see the marks on his back. She hugged her middle, recalling the day that she felt his pain, felt the lashes cutting open his skin. She blinked to stop the tears suddenly burning her eyes.

"Why do you continue to avoid Conall?" Ailein asked.

"I don't know what you mean." Innes fixed her gaze on the yard again. The training regimen he followed was brutal. Ten had started with him. As she watched, two more put up their swords and left the area. Now only Conall and Bryce remained.

"You've been avoiding him this week. He asked me at supper last night if I could ease the chores I assign to you so he could take you on a day of riding."

Innes bit her lip. She'd repeatedly used her sister as an excuse to delay their excursion. She was afraid, afraid of what could develop between them if they were left alone. She remembered what it was like when his fingers brushed the hair behind her ear. And then the kiss. However chaste, she remembered the pressure of his lips, the excitement rushing through her. And before she left the strand, she couldn't forget the intensity of his eyes when he asked if they were friends. She thought of him night and day.

She had no armor left to keep Conall at bay. Spending more time with him simply meant that she would have to lie. About her gift. And she couldn't do it. She couldn't lie to him, and that meant she had to reveal the power of the stone. Would he understand and accept a woman who saw and felt the pain of his past? Innes was confused, plagued by her own wants, her own fears.

"Chores?" Ailein repeated incredulously. "Shall I tell him that your *only* chore has been coming here and watching him train down there every day?"

Innes turned away from the window. "That is utter foolishness. I come here to see you."

"Foolishness? Really? Well, he knows that you spend your mornings here with me watching, and he's been pushing himself harder each day. He's trying to impress you."

"What makes you say that?"

"Br . . . I have my ways of finding things out."

Innes rolled her eyes and joined Jinny. The woman finished her pinning and handed the seamstress the dress.

Staying had been a terrible mistake, she thought.

Innes drifted across the chamber to the window overlooking the bluffs. She looked down at the crashing waves.

"You can't spend the rest of your life hiding from relationships," Ailein whispered in her ear.

"Please," she snapped. "Do *not* give me advice."

Ailein was not deterred. "Father's only wish in this world is for you to find a husband worthy of you. A man who can be trusted."

Innes leaned out the window. She needed more air.

The wind swept the hair back into her face.

"This man is worthy of you, and it's obvious he's taken a fancy to you."

"Oh, Ailein! Go away."

"You're in my room."

"Very well, then. I'll go away."

She left her sister's room in a huff. This was becoming their daily routine. Innes showing up so she could watch Conall from a distance, and her sister buzzing in her ear as if she were now expert in all matters of the heart. Actually, compared to Innes, Ailein *was* an expert.

As always, the men had retired from the Outer Ward by the time Innes slid into the sunshine and directed her steps toward the East Tower.

"Wait a moment."

The call came from behind her, and she knew to whom the voice belonged. Her heart pounded in her chest. She quickened her steps. Perhaps she could pretend she hadn't heard him.

"Do you wish to make a scene?" he shouted. "I will chase you, if you prefer. I'll make you listen to me."

She slowly turned around.

He was shirtless, a cloth draped over his shoulder. Her eyes were drawn to his muscular chest, his powerful arms. An ache deep in her belly moved even lower, setting her face on fire.

"Tomorrow," he said.

She looked up at him. "What?"

"Tomorrow you and I are going with Lachlan over to Wick harbor. A ship we were waiting for has arrived, and I need to help Bryce and the steward with a few things."

Innes guessed her sister was no longer a viable excuse. "Why do I need to come?"

"Because I'm asking you to."

"Why?"

"Because you reneged on our wager."

"I did no such thing. I stayed, as we agreed."

"You've reneged on the *spirit* of the wager, and you know it." He took her chin and lifted it until she was looking into his eyes. "Be ready tomorrow."

"What if I decide not to go?"

"I'll be at your room at dawn. If need be, I'll break down your door. Carry you out to your waiting horse. Tie you to the saddle. And the three of us will ride to Wick together." He whipped the cloth off his shoulder, and she looked at a chest about a mile wide. "You'll have a memorable time. You can trust me on that."

Chapter 12

" . . . but before we reached Scotland, the crew heard us foolishly whispering about our powers and went to the ship's master. When he forced the fragments from our grasp and joined the Wheel as one, the ship was torn twice asunder, and death claimed many lives. The four of us, each carrying our portion, knew what we must do. Not knowing if the sea or man would kill us, we set out to the four corners of Scotland to wait for our summons . . ."

From the *Chronicle of Lugh*

The trip to Wick was far better than Innes thought it would be. Choosing to ride in the cart with Lachlan, she could watch Conall riding ahead on his chestnut steed without feeling the pressure of being too close to him. She glanced back at the mare, tied to the back for her, in case she changed her mind.

In the stables around dawn, Conall and Innes had exchanged nothing more than casual pleasantries. The farther they got from the castle, the more at ease she became. The steward loved to talk. Each patch of land they passed seemed to have a story, and Lachlan had to tell her about it.

"Do merchant ships arrive at Wick often?" she asked.

"Nay, m'lady. The harbor takes heavy swells from the bay when the wind blows from the east. Makes coming into the port dangerous." She waited, already knowing the man would say more. "Wick has two harbors, which you'll see shortly, but they both sand up bad after the fall and winter storms."

"So this is the best time for merchant ships to come in."

"Aye, and that's when the fishing is at its best, too. Wick is a great herring port, don't you know. We at the castle get our share, of course, but the lads take enough to supply fish all the way to Edinburgh."

Innes imagined riding back with a cartload of herring. She deserved to reek of fish after refusing to ride the beautiful mare trailing behind them.

"Does the earl accompany you to Wick often?"

"Only when it's time for setting the prices."

"Setting the prices for what?"

"Sinclair wool and even cloth, of late. Also, he helps to negotiate the price of herring for the fishermen," the steward added. "What they decide on today will support many a family through the long winter months."

Innes's gaze followed Lachlan's as they both stared at the back of the man sitting so comfortably on the horse. She couldn't look at him without the twist of attraction.

"Many lairds rely solely on their tenant folk for income," she said. "The Sinclairs are doing things differently."

"That was the way with Sinclairs, too, until this one stepped in. No disrespect to their father, but Conall and Bryce have their own way. The first thing Conall did was to put a stop to our people sending the wool south and getting practically nothing for it," Lachlan explained. "He said the cottars needed to bring all of our wool in together and sell it as one. He said we buy what we need when the ships come in; it's time we sold our own goods the same way."

"And the farmers went along?"

"Oh, there were a boneheaded few. There always are. But Conall brought them in and convinced them."

"And it worked."

"Aye, mistress. It worked all right."

Innes's eyes were again drawn to the earl. In a way, she realized she'd been disappointed this morning when he didn't complain that she preferred the company of Lachlan to his own. She tore her gaze away, disgusted with herself. She was a whirlwind of contradictions, and that was not her way. He did this to her. She moved forward one step, then ran back five. She welcomed his attention, but as soon as he reached out, she scurried away and hid. She was surprised that he hadn't already tired of this game.

"The clan had a tough go of it when the earl was away," said Lachlan.

Innes studied the steward's lined face. Everyone knew the Sinclairs to be tight-lipped about their affairs, and she already sensed the old man's loyalty to Conall. For Lachlan even to utter such a thing, Innes knew that he must have accepted her on some level.

"After Solway Moss, you mean," she said gently.

"Aye. Word came back he was among the dead. We lost so many brave men there. The news arrived from Falkland Palace along with word of King Jamie's death. It wasn't until months and months later that we learned Conall was rotting in an English dungeon and there was a chance we could get him back."

And none of his people had seen what she'd seen. How he'd suffered.

"I'm not one for rumormongering, mistress, but they said he wouldn't tell them who he was. They knew he was highborn and good for ransom, but he wouldn't tell."

Innes shivered, once again remembering the pain of the lash. Her heart ached with sadness imagining what other torments he was exposed to while in captivity. She stared at the black gloves encasing her hands. Her gaze drifted to the pouch at her waist containing the relic.

Perhaps no one knowing of the scars on his soul allowed Conall to keep going. He was a proud man, and he bore his past alone. And here he was clearly pursuing her, not knowing how exposed he'd be.

"There it is, m'lady," Lachlan said as they came to the crest of a small rise. The village lay before them, and they descended into it.

Three miles south of Girnigoe, Wick was a prosperous-looking village. Spreading back from the river and the harbor, the place consisted of rows of squat stone houses topped with thatch, a church, a square tower with a bell, and a market cross at the center that teemed with merchants and buyers. Two ships lay at anchor in the harbor, and another sat tied to a good-sized dock. Men were busily moving goods off her.

Conall appeared beside the cart and helped Innes down.

"You stay with Lachlan," he told her. He nodded toward a large barnlike structure and a number of long, low stone buildings by the docks. "My business shouldn't take me past noon. I'll come and find you then."

The sun was well up in the sky, and the good weather and market day seemed to have brought the entire village out. Merchants and farmers looking to sell their goods to the castle accosted Lachlan before he was even out of the cart.

Innes tugged at his sleeve. "I'll just browse around for a while. Don't worry about me. There's nowhere I can go to get lost."

The steward sent a wary glance at the back of the earl disappearing through the crowd.

"Trust me. I'll be fine," she said, striding off before the old man had a chance to object.

Innes walked the streets, smiled at people, shook her head at the merchants eager to make a sale. She no longer did this when she was at home at Folais Castle. She no longer visited the Munro villages for she felt the disappointment of the clan elders. As the older daughter of the clan chief, she recognized that they expected her to marry. But she didn't welcome suitors. And when she sat with her father at the clan gatherings, she knew many of the men did not receive that well. So, she gradually retreated from the world. And the more she retreated, the more difficult it became to change. The more she withdrew, the more she feared . . . and the less she trusted.

Today, she didn't have to worry about any of that. No one knew her here. She was a stranger, like so many others walking the streets of the bustling village. She was free.

Innes lost track of time as she continued to explore.

For a while she sat on the bluff to the south of the harbor, watching the fishing boats. All along the stony beach below, seabirds were in a constant frenzy over the buckets of herring being brought in. She wished she had her paper and charcoal.

As the sun rose higher in the sky, she started walking again. At the bottom of a hill, she took another intersecting lane. She turned her steps toward the dock. As she reached the long, low buildings, a swarm of children surrounded her, running in every direction. A young lad barreled into her legs, and she caught him before he fell back.

Innes was still smiling when she spotted Conall in conversation with a man who must be the master of one of the trading vessels moored in the harbor.

As if he were expecting her, he turned and looked directly at her.

———————

The man continued to speak, but Conall heard nothing more. He stood gazing at Innes as time stood still. She looked so serene, so at ease in the midst of the chaos. She didn't try to hide her smile.

He'd been so relieved this morning to find her already in the stables when he came down the stairs. Perhaps she was just heeding his warning. Or perhaps she *wanted* to spend the day with him. He preferred to think it was the latter.

He finished his instructions to the ship's master and strode to her.

"How do you like the village?" he asked.

Another child ran around her, using her skirt to hide from a pursuing toddler. Innes laughed, and he had an almost overwhelming urge to pull her into his arms and kiss her.

"It's lovely," she said, looking around. "Such activity. You don't have to stop what you were doing, you know. I'm quite capable of amusing myself."

"Let *me* amuse you," he said, taking her gloved hand and tucking it into the crook of his arm. "But first I need to look in at one of the warehouses."

Leading her toward a building near the wharf, he felt such a sense of well-being, of possibilities for the future. He loved this feeling, but knew he had to rein himself in.

"Are you finished with your business dealings?"

"I am. Lachlan told you what we're doing?"

"He's quite proud of all you've accomplished. He feels that he's a part of something quite special. I think it's brilliant." She squeezed his arm. "I know my father would love to speak to you about the wool exporting."

He guessed she knew the business herself. "What do

the Munros do about it?"

"The wool agents go from village to farm, paying the least they can."

"Agents, transporters, traders, merchants, other merchants selling to still more merchants, and eventually it gets to Edinburgh," he said, shaking his head. "And the farmers haven't much to show for it, do they?"

"Just as it's always been."

"I know. We were in the same place not too long ago. Now, we're cutting out a number of those middlemen and garnering the profits ourselves." He pressed his hand on hers, relishing the warmth of it, even through the thin leather glove. "I would be happy to speak with you and your father about it. It took some planning, and there were initial costs, but it's achievable and worthwhile."

Moving past several rows of buildings, Conall led her inside one closest to the dock.

"This is no warehouse," she whispered in surprise. "You have *looms*. You're using your own wool to produce cloth."

"Aye, and fine warm stuff, too, as you can see."

They walked by rolls of woolen cloth, stacked and ready for shipment. Workers bustled back and forth, some carrying large spools of spun wool, and others carrying rolls of finished material.

"I need a few minutes' time to discuss my morning's

meeting with the master weavers."

"No hurry. I'll wait right here." She withdrew her hand from his arm and walked away.

The people that he needed to speak to gathered around him. Conall gave them the terms that had been agreed upon this morning, drawing comments of approval. Meanwhile, his gaze never strayed too far from Innes.

As she moved along, she nodded to the workers, asking questions. By one of the drawlooms, she pulled off a glove and caressed the cloth. He stared at her delicate fingers, so pale against the vibrant colors of the wool. A worker stepped up and said something. Innes smiled and responded, pulling the gloves back on.

She repeated the same thing at another loom. She tested the quality while speaking with the seated weaver and the drawboy. A few moments later, as she stepped away, Conall saw the glove being donned once again.

When his business with the weavers was finished, he followed Innes to the next building. Here, in a room beyond the dyers, the spinners plied their trade, preparing the combed wool for the looms. Gesturing to the women not to give him away, he approached her from behind. Her naked fingers sank into the puffy shreds of wool. She picked up a piece and tested the softness against her skin, held it to her nose and breathed in its smell.

Her slow, delicate movements and her smile bewitched him.

The image of her fingers on his own skin pushed into Conall's mind. He wanted her hands on his body. He imagined himself holding her, touching her. He looked at her mouth, wanting to ravish it.

Her fingers sank into the pile again, and she didn't know he was upon her until his hand dove in and joined hers. The skin was softer than silk. A surprise gasp escaped her lips as he entwined their fingers, holding her captive. She turned, her gaze flying to his face.

He wanted to kiss her and explore every sweet recess of her mouth.

She swayed and her lips parted. Her gloved hand flattened against his chest.

He wanted to undo the buttons of that dress and press his mouth to her throat, down the neckline of the dress. He wanted to taste her flesh and run his tongue against places that would make her cry out with pleasure.

The gray eyes darkened, and her gaze dropped to his lips.

He wanted to run his hand over her naked body, cupping her breast, touching the folds of her sex.

Innes gasped and leaned toward him.

She had no idea the effect she had on him. An urgent need rushed into his loins. He wanted her, and he wanted her now. She was in danger of being ravished in the middle of a room filled with women at work at their spinning wheels.

"We have to leave," he muttered. "Now."

She nodded. Her face was bright red. She pulled her hand away, and Conall saw the fingers trembling as she hurriedly pulled the glove back on.

Those few moments gave him every answer he'd been searching for. He'd seen the desire banked like hot coals in her eyes. He wouldn't let her play that hiding game again. As long as she stayed at Castle Girnigoe, he would draw her out and pursue her.

He led her out of the building. Neither said a word. He directed her up a small rise toward the place where she'd left Lachlan.

They hadn't gone ten paces when the sudden wail of a child yanked her to a stop. They both looked over at a toddler facedown in the dirt. She went over and helped him up.

"There, there. This is not so bad."

The child's cries only became shriller. A lump the size of a goose egg was quickly forming above the boy's eyebrow. His chin was scratched, as well. His nose was running, and dirt mixed with his tears.

Innes lifted the boy into her arms and rocked him as she checked his injuries.

Conall looked around for a mother or for other children. No one showed any interest in the wailing boy who now called for his mama.

"Where is she?" he asked. "Where is your mama?"

The lad buried his face in Innes's neck and only cried harder.

"Why don't we take him back inside?" Conall suggested. "One of the workers is sure to know who this urchin belongs to."

Innes was taking off her glove. Using her skirts, she wiped the boy's tears and then caressed his face. She took his hand and pressed soft kisses on his scratched forearm.

She suddenly stood and looked away down the lane. "I think I saw him this morning and he *was* with his mother." She started back toward the harbor.

Conall was surprised. It was market day, ships were being unloaded, and so many people were about in the village. Gangs of children played underfoot everywhere. And to him, one child's face looked much the same as any other. But she seemed fairly certain.

"I remember," Innes said when Conall caught up to her. "They were near the water's edge. A sandy place, it is."

"There's a wee stretch where the fishing boats are dragged ashore," he said, taking the road. "This way."

She continued to hold the boy's hand, whispering soothing words to him. The child's cry was now more of a mournful hum, with occasional calls for his mother.

"And bread," she said. "His mother sells loaves out of a basket."

The lane became a mere path that hugged a stretch of sandy beach. They passed a number of bakers—male and female—hawking their bread, but Innes ignored them.

"This way, I'm sure," she said, glancing at the lad in her arms.

She turned away from the water and unerringly weaved through a cluster of cottages at this end of the village. At the center of it, a woman with a basket over her shoulder was just drawing water from a well.

With a cry of recognition, the child dived into the young woman's arms.

The mother's surprise turned to a scowl after Conall explained where they'd found him. "Och, them brothers of his were supposed to be watching after him. Wait till I get my hands on them. I'm so sorry, m'lord. And m'lady. I cannot think what got into them lads of mine."

Innes immediately made excuses for them. "Your boys must be searching all over for Kade right now. I may have reacted too quickly. Probably worried sick, they are."

"And with good reason." The mother pushed a lock of hair back from her face. "They know I'll be worrying their backsides for them when they come home."

The toddler dived back into Innes's arm and allowed

her to give him a kiss on his muddy cheeks before wanting to go back to his mother.

Conall gave the woman a coin and dragged Innes away by the arm before she could say more.

"How did you know his name was Kade?" he asked as they walked back in the direction of Lachlan, the cart, and the horses.

"The boy?" she asked.

"I didn't hear the mother mention it, but you knew the lad's name."

She stretched the gloves over her fingers. A blush had once again crept into her cheek. "I must have overheard it. Perhaps when I saw him playing with the other children in the lane. Or perhaps it was earlier when I passed the mother selling bread."

He placed a hand in the small of her back, pulling her toward him as a cart went by. "You always find a way to impress me."

"Then you impress easily."

He shook his head. "Your talent in drawing. Your sense of direction. Your memory. Your intuition in seeing through Bryce and Ailein's pretense of marital problems."

"You forgot to mention my brilliant chess play."

"That is where I draw a line," he told her. "Happily, in that at least, you could use some instruction."

She smiled up at him. "And let me guess. *You* are the

man best suited to provide that instruction."

"You see? That intuition again. Very impressive."

When they reached their horses, a lad was waiting with them. The steward and the cart were gone.

"Where is Lachlan?" asked Innes.

"He took a few things back to the castle."

Innes eyed her mare and then frowned at Conall. "You planned this, didn't you?"

"That I did. Very clever, wouldn't you say?"

She shook her head, but it obviously amused her. "Should I assume you have another destination in mind before we return to Girnigoe?"

He nodded, leading Innes toward her horse. "I want to introduce you to a rare bird or two."

She allowed him to help her onto the mare's back. "So I finally get to meet some of my own kind."

———

There was sadness in the castle when I returned. My brother's wife was dead. Two boys need raising, they told me.

But where is my own child? Torn from my arms in that convent in France. A bastard. A devil's child. A product of my sin. Do not concern yourself with this one, they said. Concern yourself with the penance that may someday redeem your blackened soul.

So I prayed and I worked and I became useful in the eyes of God and men. I wore an apron of purest white in memory of the love that died in the courtyard of his keep. In memory of the angel they took from me.

And then my brother wanted me back. My hated father, who murdered my beloved, was dead. And now I was needed to raise my brother's sons.

He needed me. His sons needed me. His wife had been taken, like so many, when the fever struck. So I came.

I think of it now, seeing them for the first time. They stood by the doors of the Great Hall. Conall, so dark and sad and noble. Bryce, so young, focused entirely on his older brother.

And from that moment, I loved them. I love them still. More than life itself.

In loving them and raising them as my own, I found a life that I never imagined would be mine.

And I shall not lose it now.

Chapter 13

When Conall stripped out of his kilt, Innes tried to look up along the shoreline of the loch, at the sky, at the stretch of trees curving up and over the crest of the low hill on the far side of the valley. She tried to look at anything but the man striding to the edge and then diving into the crystal clear waters. She tried, at any rate.

Loch Watten was a two-hour ride from Wick. As they followed the river, the sun became warmer with each passing mile. As soon as Conall helped her down from the horse, he pulled a blanket from his steed and a satchel packed with food. Placing them on ground, he headed for the loch, saying he was going for a swim.

The invitation was implied, if not stated. The view of him shedding his clothes and moving toward the water was magnificent.

Innes spread the blanket on a grassy rise by the shore and emptied the satchel. Cook had packed a delicious assortment of food.

She hazarded a quick glance in Conall's direction. She would have gone swimming too, if not for her concerns about her slipping sense of caution. The day was the warmest so far this year, and her nervousness on the mare only added to her rising heat.

Where she set out their meal, she could see the water was shallow and stony along the shore. Pulling off her gloves and boots, she peeled off her stockings and unfastened the neckline of her arisaid. The breeze was warm but refreshing against her skin.

She walked barefoot along the shoreline until she reached a stretch of high weeds. Innes hitched up her skirts and sighed with pleasure at the cold water on her feet and her ankles. She splashed her face, scooping handfuls and wetting her neck. She untied the top of her shift and splashed her chest above her breasts. She lifted her skirts higher, tucking them more securely into her belt, and stepped in deeper until she was up to her knees.

She moved through to the edge of the high weeds. Suddenly, a flock of birds took flight from a grassy patch on the shore. She watched them climb and wheel and sail off on the wind. One of them didn't go with the others, but hung suspended in the air, watching her. An ivory gull, she thought, admiring the circles of silver this one sported.

"Do you see, away there, standing still in the shallows? A purple heron."

Startled, she looked around. Conall stood on the

beach watching her, pointing at the majestic bird.

His hair was wet. Drops of water still sparkled on his skin. He'd wrapped his kilt around his waist and belted it, but he wore nothing else. Her gaze lingered over his broad chest, marked with the scars of countless battles. She forced herself to breathe and turn her eyes toward the heron.

"They say this loch has magic, and after all these years, I finally understand what they mean," he said.

"Magic?" she asked, her eyes returning to his body.

"Aye. The folk say that fishing here requires great patience, that nothing may happen for a very long time. But then suddenly, the magic happens and the fish simply rise, ready to be caught."

"Is the magic happening now?"

"I believe it is."

He waded into the water, and Innes watched him come. When he'd taken hold of her hand in the wool bin back at Wick, she'd seen into his mind and read what he was thinking. Even as their fingers intertwined, she had known she needed no special gift to understand him. She knew how much he wanted her. She'd thought about it every moment of their ride here.

He continued to come toward her, and Innes's heart soared, knowing his desires were her dreams. His gaze caressed her skin. His eyes lingered on her throat, and she wondered if he could see the wild beat of her pulse.

As he moved still closer, his gaze focused on her mouth. When his body met hers, her lips parted involuntarily and she gasped. He looked into her eyes, and she was suddenly lost in a storm of passion.

Innes saw his eyes darken. Her breath hung suspended in her chest. She hid her hands in the folds of her skirts. She now understood what longing meant. She now knew what it was like to ache with desire. She wanted this. She wanted him. She welcomed the press of his hard, wet body against hers.

His mouth descended upon hers, and her eyes closed. His lips possessed her, and the molten heat uncoiling in her middle jolted her.

Stunned at first, she stood still, trying to understand the sensations racing through her. She loved the feel of his fingers on her skin as he held her face. She hesitantly opened the eyes that she had shut so tightly and watched him as he drew back briefly before lowering his head again to suckle her lower lip.

She couldn't move, couldn't breathe, but she thought her heart would explode in her chest at any instant. And still, the undulating mass of molten sensations threatened to set her insides on fire.

"I've been waiting for this. For you," he murmured against her lips. "Kiss me, Innes."

She had no experience in this. She didn't know how to react, how to please him. But she refused to touch his hand. She refused to use her gift to learn. Not until he knew.

His fingers dug into her hair. The braid loosened, the thick waves sliding down onto her shoulders and back. His lips again lowered to hers and heat rushed through her body.

Innes's startled hands jerked away from their hiding place, clutching at his back as the pressure of his mouth increased and his tongue started teasing the seam of her tightly closed lips.

"Kiss me, Innes."

She opened her mouth to tell him of her ignorance in such matters, but no words came out. It wouldn't have mattered. His lips descended again, and he thrust into the opening, exploring her mouth with his tongue.

Bolts of lightning shot through her. The images from his mind mingled with hers. She saw the extent of his desire. His tongue rubbed against hers, and Innes vaguely felt his hand move down her back and encircle her waist. He pulled her even tighter against his solid torso. She felt nothing but the incredible heat that possessed them both.

In that moment, a life of solitude transformed into an eternity of desire.

Innes became frantic to satisfy this sudden hunger for him. Her hands traveled down his back. She touched the powerful muscles. It was miraculous, the way her body softened and molded itself to the hard contours of his.

As if from a distance, she heard his low growl of pleasure. And as he pressed his hip against hers, she felt something else. The kilt did nothing to conceal the evidence of his arousal. And in his mind, she saw him wanting to lay her down in the shallows, lift her skirts, and bury himself deep inside of her.

Clarity returned instantly and with it, sanity.

They had to stop. But who was going to stop them if she didn't?

And what was worse, if their positions were reversed and he was the one with the ability to delve into her mind and read her past, how would she feel not knowing?

She pulled back, wedging her hands between their bodies. He grew still, and then released her, stepping back. Her face burned with embarrassment.

"I am so sorry." She brought her hands to her cheeks. They were wet with sudden tears. Her body trembled. She was still affected by what they'd done, by how she continued to feel, by what he wanted to do next.

He took another step back, taking a deep breath. "Why should you be sorry? I thought ... I felt ..." Embers of passion glowed deep in his eyes. A muscle in his jaw clenched and he looked away. A battle still raged inside.

She wanted to reach out and touch him, but she couldn't. "I . . . it's just . . . it's all moving so fast."

"I know. You have nothing to fear from me; I promise you that. But for the moment, perhaps you should go back to the horses." He paused and looked around at the lake and the sky like a man just awakening and getting his bearings. "In a wee bit, we can eat something and go back to Girnigoe."

She hesitated to move, hating herself. Hating the curse that was hers for the rest of her life.

"I won't touch you," he assured her, misunderstanding. "I won't pressure you. You can trust me, Innes."

She had read his mind. When her mouth joined with his in that kiss, her mind joined his, as well. She closed her eyes. She knew how much he wanted to make love to her. But he had stopped. In the midst of his rising passions, he'd stopped.

She did trust him.

A moment later, she reached the stony beach and hurried along the shore. Coming to the blanket, she looked back, searching for Conall. He was far out in the loch, swimming hard through the cooling waters.

Conall dove beneath the surface, trying to clear his mind. He wanted her more than he'd ever wanted a woman. His desire for her was deep and explosive. He hadn't thought himself capable of such a passion. If she hadn't stopped him, he would have taken her right there in the water, or on the beach.

But he didn't just want to make love to her.

There was so much more to Innes. He admired her intelligence, her wit, her stubbornness, her independence, even her temper. Bryce claimed that these qualities alienated men from her, and yet they were the very things that drew Conall to her.

She'd erected a façade in the way she dressed and acted. She consciously created that protective distance, and he wondered what had so wounded her that she needed it. He knew about wounds and the need for distance. She saw the stump that remained of his hand. She saw the scars on his body. But he was blessed that she would never see the blackness, the guilt, and the shame that filled his soul.

He waded out of the water and donned his kilt. His shirt and boots lay in the grass not far away.

The manner in which she first responded to him and the way she put an end to it, all pointed to her inexperience with men. He frightened her, and the last thing he wanted was for Innes to run away. He needed to go slow.

He needed to give her time to adjust to him and to the passion he knew she felt.

Give her time.

Marriage? Was he thinking about marriage? The realization was sudden and startling. He'd never thought a day would come when he'd again plan for a future. He'd buried that probability the day he was captured and dragged away from the battlefield. What could make him think, or even dare to hope, that he deserved a chance at happiness?

He found her sitting on the edge of the blanket, dressed and cool-looking in the warm sun. She had her boots and gloves back on. Her hair was still loose, cascading in silky waves around her shoulders.

He couldn't look at her and not remember the taste of her lips, the softness of her skin, and how much he still wanted her.

"We have a very nice selection of food." She avoided meeting his gaze and spread out what had been packed for them.

He sat down on the blanket, making certain to give her enough room to be comfortable.

"Wynda, Lachlan, Bryce, Cook—the whole lot of them were beside themselves when they heard I was bringing you here." He unwrapped a cloth from a piece of pastry and took a bite. "My brother went so far as to suggest that I give you a lame horse to ride so we could spend more time in each other's company. If we had a three-legged beast in the stables, you could have been riding that one."

"Matchmakers." She groaned and shook her head. "I worry about Ailein and Bryce. They continue this pretense that they're at odds with each other."

"He slips into her bedroom when they think no one notices."

She laughed. "They had a great surprise last night. I arrived unexpectedly at Ailein's door."

He stretched out on the blanket, leaning on an elbow. It gave him such pleasure to see her at ease. "What happened?"

"I believe they were busy at . . . well, they were busy when I started banging away, insisting that she let me in." A blush bloomed on her cheeks. "I heard some noises, but I wasn't certain."

"And?"

"Bryce hid under the bed and Ailein pretended that nothing was amiss."

"And?"

"And nothing. I took my riding boots and left."

"You saw more."

She shook her head. "I'm already embarrassed that I even brought this up. Please don't make me say more."

He laughed, wondering if she knew that he couldn't refuse her anything.

A breeze lifted strands of her hair and made them dance around Innes's face. Sitting there, sharing stories, she looked so young and carefree, so much at ease with herself and the world. He wanted to know more about her. About her childhood. He was curious about what, if anything, happened to make her the person she was now.

"Tell me, what you were like at, say, six or seven," he said. "Were you as prim and proper and hard on yourself then?"

"I lost my mother when I was seven," she told him. "You might say that was a year of rather large changes for me."

"Losing a mother is difficult."

"It is." She stared at the gloved hands in her lap. "I needed to grow up. I needed to take on some rather large responsibilities."

"If you mean a father, a younger sister, and a household that needed to function, that's a great deal of responsibility for any woman. But for young lass who's mourning her mother . . ." He shook his head.

"Perhaps I'm too loose with the word *responsibility*. Maybe it was knowledge. I was told some things, and there were other things I needed to learn in order to carry out a bequest my mother passed on to me."

He waited for her to say more, but she stopped. Her gaze never lifted. She tugged at the fingertips of the gloves, pulling them off very slowly, and putting them back on again. Conall sensed that she was withdrawing into her shell. He had to change the topic, distract her.

"I was a hellion at seven," he said. "I caused trouble, got in even more of it, and made life miserable for Bryce. He was forever following me around, happy to be part of whatever mischief I arranged."

She looked up from under her lashes, a smile starting at the corner of her lip.

"Only two years older but I was definitely the gang leader." He picked up another pastry and took a bite. "And I know what you're about to say—I look old enough to be his father now."

"I wasn't going to say anything of the kind. When anyone meets me and Ailein, they never even guess we're sisters." She stretched out her legs, leaning back on her hands. "I'm six years older, and I do behave more like a parent than a sister to her. I have for years."

Conall remembered the day on the rocks when she warned him never to question her loyalty to Ailein.

"I am fascinated." She smiled. "Thinking of you as a child running wild through Castle Girnigoe, with Bryce in your wake. Did you carry a sword?"

"Aye. When we were lads, they'd only trust us with

wooden swords. We were great ones for stabbing each other and anyone who wandered into our path. We were brave and bloody Sinclairs, saving king and country."

"No damsels in distress?"

"Nay! We had dragons and Tudors to kill. We had no time for damsels."

"I'm glad."

He thought back on those years and how simple their lives were. "Our mother died when we were just lads. That was when Wynda came back to Girnigoe. She was our father's sister. We raised more hell than ever, then. She looks like a stern one, but we could do no wrong in her eyes. After that, we only needed to mind our father, but he was mostly away at the wars and at court. Whenever he was home and we got into trouble, we knew to keep our distance."

"So you two ran wild for your entire youth."

"Well, not entirely," he admitted. "Everything changed, of course, when Shona arrived."

She looked up at him in surprise. "Shona came to Girnigoe as a child?"

He met her gaze. He thought she knew this. "Aye. She was a Sinclair, but from another sept. The daughter of the laird. She was about nine, I think, when she arrived at Girnigoe. She'd just lost her whole family to the sweating sickness. Her father fought in the Borders that summer and came home sick with it. So many died of that foul pestilence that year."

"I was only eleven then, but I remember hearing about the deaths," Innes said. "What happened to the rest of her people?"

"Their losses so weakened them that they made the decision that my father would combine their lands with his own. The two septs would become one through marriage, and Castle Girnigoe would be the clan seat."

"So your family arranged the marriage between Bryce and Shona when they were very young."

"Not Bryce and Shona," he told her. Conall was glad Innes was hearing this information from him. He didn't want any misunderstandings to drive her away. "Shona was to be my wife. The countess of Caithness. We never had a legal contract, her people all being dead. But it was understood. Then, after the news reached Girnigoe that I'd been killed at Solway Moss, she married Bryce."

Chapter 14

"Ian is dead, dear old fellow. I now have the stone relic that he passed on to me, along with this chronicle of the Wheel of Lugh. Even with the final pains wracking his body, he told me all he knew and told me what I must do. In truth, I did not believe him until now, but I truly have the power that he carried to his deathbed. And I know that I must prepare and one day pass this gift along to another woman, for Ian told me that a man surely would be tempted with such power. Only a woman can carry such a secret in her breast, and I must find the right one . . ."

From the *Chronicle of Lugh*

As soon as she and Conall returned to the castle, Innes went looking for her sister.

Hearing that Ailein and Wynda were in the chapel oratory, tending to an injured farmer, she hurried across the Inner Ward. At Folais Castle, they used the oratory as an infirmary as well, for anyone needing immediate doctoring. Having the priest nearby was also convenient in case

Last Rites had to be administered.

She came upon the priest Fingal sitting on a stone outside the chapel. The golden rays of the late afternoon sun slanted across the kirkyard, and the long shadows cast by the chapel nearly reached the man. The cleric, a small slightly built man with a pale complexion, sat lost in his thoughts.

Innes hadn't spoken to the priest since the formal introductions on the day of the wedding. Anytime she'd seen the man after that, she got the sense that he was watching her, studying her.

Roused from his reverie by her appearance in the kirkyard, Fingal stood quickly, half turning as he reached for the cross hanging from a chain around his waist. For a moment, she wasn't sure if he was going to run away or ward her off like some demon.

She nodded in greeting. "Good day to you, Father."

Fingal recovered himself quickly, bowing to her.

"Lady Innes," he replied in a deep, gruff voice that did not match his diminutive stature. "What a pleasant surprise."

His movements were quick. He reminded her of a ferret as his eyes darted from her face to the bodice of her black dress to her gloves. She thought that his gaze fixed for a moment longer on the pouch at her waist.

"How did you find our village of Wick?" he asked, his

gaze returning to her face.

It surprised her that he knew they'd gone. "I found it a very pleasant, busy place. If you please, I am looking for—"

"And Loch Watten?" he continued solicitously. "Did you find that pleasant, as well?"

Innes's gaze narrowed. Something in his tone put her on guard. He was being affable and chatty to her, but she sensed that more lurked behind the man's sudden sociability.

He didn't wait for her to answer. "I take the lads I teach out to the loch a few times every summer. The angling is quite good there, if one has the patience and waits for the fish to rise. A very pleasant place indeed."

"If you don't mind me asking, how did you know I went to Loch Watten?"

"Lachlan told Cook to prepare some food for the earl, telling her that Conall planned to take you out there. Cook told Wynda. Wynda told me. I confirmed the information with your sister. I made certain to say a prayer this morning for continued good weather, and here we are."

"Aye, and here we are." And she thought the Sinclairs were tight-mouthed folk.

Just then, Ailein came out of the chapel door, saving Innes from any further discussion with the priest regarding her day with Conall.

Following her gaze, the priest quickly bowed and went to Ailein, stopping her and whispering loud enough for Innes to hear every word. "Be sure to let me knew the next time those two go out. I'll pray for more than good weather."

Innes's jaw dropped in astonishment. Fingal nodded to them both and then darted toward the chapel. He stopped abruptly by the door, pretending to look at a bird's nest above the stone cornice.

"You're back," Ailein said, hugging her. "And so soon."

"What do you mean, so soon?"

She wasn't going to say anything more while Fingal lingered, listening to every word. She led her sister out of the kirkyard.

"Tell me," Innes asked as they crossed the courtyard. "Was *anyone* in this castle unaware that I went out riding with Conall today?"

"I don't think the farmer with the broken arm that I just left in the oratory knew. Wait . . . actually, I think he knew, as well."

"This behavior is ridiculous. Fingal, the steward, Cook . . . Wynda, for heaven's sake!"

"Aye, and as I'm now a Sinclair, I'm expected to join in."

"This is not funny." She frowned at her sister. "This is matchmaking, pure and simple. And these people know me, know my reputation. I'm the beautiful bride's shrewish old spinster of a sister. Who in your clan would be so foolish as to want that for their beloved earl?"

"Foolish? The Sinclairs are elated! You're the first person who's been able to draw Conall out of his lair in months, except when he disappears with his wolf for weeks at a time." She looped her arm through Innes's. "So when is the wedding?"

"Stop."

"And you'll not wear black to your wedding. I'll not allow it."

"I'm *not* getting married."

"I think you will."

"If I ever do, you're not invited."

"That will be very unlikely since the wedding will take place right here at Castle Girnigoe." She patted Innes's arm. "Father will be thrilled. And Wynda and I will take care of all the arrangements. You and Conall have to be agreeable, though, and do as you're told."

A month ago, such talk would have set her temper roaring. Now, after all she'd gone through these past weeks and after the kiss she and Conall shared at the loch, her heart ached with the mere possibility of it.

Innes whispered, "He's made no mention of marriage."

"He will." Ailein squeezed her arm. "But Bryce says he'll take his time. He doesn't want to chance a rejection.

And he's smart enough to know you might do just that."

"Just when is it that you and your husband have time to talk about us? Is it when you are in the Great Hall pretending to argue over your bairn's name or when he's hiding under your bed?"

Ailein laughed, a beautiful blush darkening her cheeks. After walking a few steps in silence, she leaned over and kissed Innes on the cheek. "We did start out with our marriage in an uproar. But we mended our fences soon enough."

"Then you decided to keep up the ruse to keep me at Girnigoe . . . and match-make."

"I had no doubt you knew the truth all along the way." Ailein smiled. "Thank you for not giving me away. I am so enjoying this. And I think he is, too."

"Your happiness is my greatest joy." This time Innes patted her sister's arm. "But I *am* worried about the way everyone here is trying to push us together. You know what stops me, what has always stopped me."

Ailein slipped her arm around Innes. "Aye. The relic."

Her sister was the only one who understood. She was the one person that Innes could confide in about her fears and about the responsibility she carried.

"From all I hear from my husband, Conall is a brave man," said Ailein. "And a proud one. Bryce says he's become extremely unpredictable since returning from the wars, but that he's not the beast he wants everyone to see. Perhaps it's time to take a chance."

"It's not about trust. I know him now. I have no doubt about his honor. And I know he wants me. And he's no beast." Innes paused as emotions welled up in her. "But what happens when he knows? He's not the only one to fear rejection."

"You care for him."

Innes nodded, fighting sudden tears that threatened to spill over. What she felt was much more than caring.

She'd loved their day at the loch, him sitting across the blanket telling her about his childhood, his life, his years of service fighting for King James. And of leading his warriors against the English at Solway Moss. There he stopped, a dark cloud closing in around him.

She wanted to take him in her arms and hold him. She wished she were brave enough to admit that she knew what blackened his spirits. She wanted to let him know that she felt his pain, all of it, and wept for his despair, for his loss. But she'd held back.

"I love you, sister." Ailein touched Innes's chin, forcing her to look up. "Tell him the truth, sooner and not later. If he is going to react unfavorably to the responsibility you bring with you, it should happen before you are in love with him."

A single tear escaped and rolled down Innes's cheek.

Her heart ached. She already loved him. And she could do nothing to shed herself of her mother's gift.

Ailein wiped the tear away. "We'll talk more of it tomorrow, when we go for a ride."

"Where are we going?" asked Innes. They started walking again.

"I've sent word to Teva, Shona's old serving woman. We're going to see her tomorrow."

Innes wiped away the rest of her tears. "That reminds me of why I came to find you. I learned something today from Conall about Shona. Shona came here as a child. She was intended to be *his* wife, not Bryce's. The clan made the arrangements when they were both children. When Conall was presumed to be dead, Bryce married her to fulfill the obligation."

Ailein took her hand, and Innes saw the glimmer of hope in her sister's mind. She also saw how much she already loved him.

"We still need to go," Ailein told her. "I want answers to all of my questions. I want to bury the past for good."

Innes wanted to go, too. She was curious to know more about the woman who for years was Conall's intended bride.

How everything had changed, she thought, since she'd arrived at Castle Girnigoe. Innes had found fault in her sister for her insecurity over a dead wife. Now Innes herself fought the same feelings.

Unwanted conjectures edged into her mind. Shona, pregnant with Bryce's child, died when the younger brother had gone to bring back Conall, the man she should have had. Was she perhaps so torn by her love for him that she would end her life?

Innes shivered. Like her sister, she needed to know the past so that she could face the future.

"How do you woo a woman like Innes?"

Conall shook his head when his brother choked on a mouthful of ale. Bryce had arrived at the West Tower as soon as he was back. Conall figured the younger man expected a hint of an announcement, not a chess game and this question.

"Woo her? You're Conall Sinclair. You're the earl of bloody Caithness. Tell her."

"Tell her? By the devil, you are useless. You couldn't play a decent game of chess if your life depended on it. And you clearly have no understanding of women . . . and Munro women, in particular."

"Wait, give me a chance." Bryce took another sip of his ale, cleared his throat, and put down his cup. "I happen to understand Munro women quite well. I am married to her sister, don't forget. I can tell you anything you want to know about Innes."

"That wasn't my question. But as to that, Thunder can tell me more about her than you."

"That wolf doesn't talk." Thunder raised his head from his master's foot and stared at Bryce. "If you say one word, I'll have you stuffed."

The wolf bared his teeth.

"Enough, the two of you," Conall snapped. "Wooing Innes. How? I need ideas."

"Are you telling me you've never tried to impress a woman?" Bryce asked.

Conall was far from celibate in his youth. But that was different. "When did I ever need to? My wife was decided for me."

Bryce was no stranger to the truth. From the time she arrived, Shona was to be mistress of Castle Girnigoe. There was no courting or wooing. He also understood that, from Shona's perspective, whoever filled the position of husband was of little consequence.

"Well, how about the suggestions I gave you before. Remember? Singing her praises regardless of what she says."

"That seems so insincere now."

"You might sneak into her room and lie in wait for her under the bed."

"I hear that's what *you* do these days."

Bryce smiled. "*We* are married. You are not. If *you* do it, her reputation will be so compromised, she'll have to marry you."

"*That* is the worst idea yet." Conall pointed to the chessboard, reminding his brother that it was his move.

"I don't know. I'm starting to think you're not cut out for courting."

"I'm shocked that you could think such a thing."

"Forget about wooing," Bryce rolled on. "Tame her like a hawk."

"Like a hawk?" Conall shook his head. "The woman knows birds better than we ever will. She'd pluck out my eyes and skin me like a rabbit."

"Then fight with her. Contradict her. Argue with her. She'll probably take it as a challenge and enjoy your wit."

"That would just come across as ill-mannered and possibly abusive. The very thought of it is disturbing." Conall pointed a threatening finger at him before putting the king in check with his bishop. "My goal is not to have her pack up and leave for Folais Castle."

Bryce studied him for a moment before moving his king away from the attack.

Conall knew what must be running through his brother's mind. The younger man never imagined he'd see the day. The thin, wounded man that he brought back home last winter was now a man with dreams.

Bryce rested an elbow on his knee and smiled.

"No more idiotic suggestions," Conall ordered.

"Gifts. Women love gifts," he suggested.

"I've done that. I gave her a book. She was impressed. But Innes was raised needing nothing. Her affection cannot be bought. Of that, I'm certain."

"How about your strength and finesse as a warrior? You do have a reputation. As to that, Ailein says that her sister watches you train."

Conall held up the stump of his right hand. "I can only go so far with that."

"True, and I suppose while we're at it, your face and scars make you something of a beast, so you won't be charming her with your looks."

"Check."

"I'm trying to help you, but I'm running out of ideas." He moved his king.

"You've said nothing useful."

"Have some new clothes made."

"I want to woo *her*, Bryce. Innes. The woman wears black. Do you really think clothes are a priority?"

"Then . . . shave," he threw out in desperation.

"Checkmate," Conall said, disgust on his face. "For the life of me, brother, I don't know what Ailein sees in you."

Chapter 15

"My mistress would never have taken her own life."

Sitting on wooden benches in the cottage, Innes and Ailein exchanged a side-glance and then watched Teva paw through the basket of food the visitors brought as a gift. Outside the open door, in a small garden that spread out behind the cottage, three goats grazed contentedly.

"You say you want to know about her? Then we can start there."

The woman seemed to be old, but her true age was difficult to judge. Her gray hair was thinning and her back bowed from the years, but there was an energy in her that belonged to a much younger woman.

Two Sinclair warriors had escorted them to the village. Innes was happy about that, considering what had happened when she went out with Wynda.

The stone and thatch cottage was one of the largest in the village. From the outside, it appeared that it was well cared for. Before they left, Jinny told her that the women in the castle believed Bryce was very generous in settling Teva here comfortably after he decided that she was no longer needed at the castle.

Teva had been waiting at the open door when they arrived. She knew they were coming. And there was one thing the old woman wanted to talk about: Shona's death. That suited Innes, for the sake of her sister.

"That's why we couldn't find her grave in the family crypt?" Ailein asked.

"Aye, damn them all," the woman snapped. "Buried out in the cold with her unborn bairnie. Sometimes I think I hear her."

Innes sat and listened, reminding herself that this was her sister's query.

"But why would they say it was suicide?" Ailein asked. "Who would decide such a thing, if it weren't true?"

"Fingal, curse his bones. False, blackhearted priest. It was Fingal," Teva barked. "Said he knew her as he'd confessed her often enough. He buried her in unconsecrated ground. Put her out in a shallow grave with nothing to mark where she lies. Just like a dog."

"That's a serious accusation to make against a priest," Ailein said.

"The devil take him. He's no priest, but a son of Satan," the woman fumed. "And what's worse, that man came *with* us to Girnigoe. Aye, Shona's welfare was entrusted to Fingal. He was to be her protector. He was to make certain she received what was agreed upon."

"So you served her for many years."

"Aye. Many fine years. Never was there a lass like her. I raised Shona from the time I took her from the arms of her wet-nurse. I did everything for her. I saw her grow through the years. I watched her lose both parents, God rest their sainted souls. And we came to Girnigoe together." Teva no longer saw them. As if lost in her memories, she stared at the peat fire burning on the hearth as she spoke. "She was a breath of fresh air in that ancient pile of stone. She infused life into everyone she met. She taught these barbarians what a real lady—"

"How did the priest justify himself?" Innes interrupted. "The family could not have been happy about such a decision."

The woman's eyes cleared. She looked at Innes. Her face hardened. Then her gaze fixed on the gloves Innes wore.

"Are you cold, m'lady?"

"Nay, I am quite comfortable." Innes slowly removed her gloves and tucked them into her belt. "You haven't answered the question. The laird would never have accepted such a judgment unless he believed the priest was correct."

Teva stood and picked up the basket, taking it to a table near the window. With her back to them, she emptied out the contents one by one, taking her time.

Ailein had warned Innes of the possibility of unpleas-
antness before coming here. After all, she was the laird's
new wife. She'd replaced the woman Teva obviously
adored. No matter what the topic of their conversation
might be, she knew this visit would be somewhat
strained. Right now, however, the older woman appeared
to be dismissing them.

Innes opened her mouth, but Ailein took her hand.
They looked into each other's eyes. Her sister reminded
her that she still wished to find out more. She didn't want
Teva to ask them to leave.

"Teva," Innes said, trying another tack, "they say
Shona was a striking woman."

The praise captured the old woman's attention. "Striking? There wasn't a bonnier lass in all Scotland. And
when she grew up, there wasn't a more beautiful woman."

"So she was fair then?"

The old woman took a deep breath and nodded. "Hair
so light that it rivaled the rays of the morning sun. Eyes
so blue they put the summer sky to shame." She reached
into the neckline of her dress and drew out a locket.
"Hardly anyone knows, but this treasure was painted the
year before we came to Castle Girnigoe. Shona's mother
gave it to me on her deathbed—as a gift, for my promise
to always look after her daughter."

She opened the locket in front of the two sisters but

held it out of their reach. They were allowed to look but not touch.

The years had been rough on the piece. The image was faded beyond recognition.

"This is watercolor thickened with gum arabic," Innes commented. She was more interested in the process than the person depicted.

"It wasn't any Arab that painted it. Two monks passed through on their way to the shrine of St. Brigid in the west. One of them was a painter. Why, even he said he never saw a more beautiful child." Teva pulled the locket away and tucked it into the neckline of her dress.

"I can see she was," Innes said. "In fact, I don't believe I've ever seen a likeness more striking than this."

Ailein arched a brow at her.

Innes continued. "Shona arrived at Girnigoe with the intention of being the next laird's wife."

"Not just the laird's wife. She was to be the countess of Caithness. She planned to make Castle Girnigoe the center of culture in the north." Teva sat down again.

"She must have been... well, distraught when the news of Conall's death reached her."

"It was hard, to be sure. Her grief was fierce—like the rest of the clan—but she survived it." There was a small shrug. "Conall was so in love with her. But he had his chance. She was ready to marry, but he put off the wedding so many times, running off to do battle instead of fulfilling his promise to marry her. After Solway Moss, Shona didn't want to wait a year or two and let Bryce play the same game as his brother. She reminded him of his obligation and demanded the terms of the marriage agreement be met."

Innes took her sister's hand again. She was relieved to see Ailein's heart ached for her husband. He'd married because of duty.

"So they married," Innes asked quietly, "but how long was it before the news came that Conall still lived?"

"Shona and Bryce married in March. The news of Conall arrived in November."

"That must have upset her again. Surely, she had to feel something for the man for whom she'd been intended, and now she was married to his brother."

"Aye, m'lady, she *was* upset. But not for the reason you're thinking. She thought . . ." Teva stopped, catching herself.

Innes realized she could finish the sentence. That marriage had nothing to do with love . . . for either of the brothers. Teva was about to say that Shona thought she was going to be countess. Now she was not. And *that* was what upset her on hearing about Conall.

Innes thought of how much Conall already meant to her. For her own sake and her sister's, it relieved her that love and affection didn't seem to play any part in the decisions made. At the same time, every life was precious and two had been lost—and for what?

"You said she wouldn't end her own life. What do you think happened?" Ailein asked gently.

"Murder. And I don't think it; I know it."

It was clear now why the old woman was no longer welcome at Girnigoe. Innes exchanged another look with her sister. "That is a strong accusation."

"Aye. I know it. I'm not a fool." The woman set her jaw stubbornly. "My mistress was an angel, but she had her enemies, as I've said already."

"Who would do such a thing?" Innes asked. "And why? What could anyone hope to gain?"

Teva looked away a moment, then her gaze moved from one sister to the other.

"If I tell you the truth and you go back to the laird, he'll have me thrown out of here." There was a quaver in the old voice. She realized that she might have already said too much. "I'll die cold and alone on the moor. I'll have no clan or kin to take me in."

"We came here to see you because we wanted to hear you," Ailein assured her. "Whatever you say will stay with us. I'll not repeat this to the laird. You have my word on that."

The woman's gaze fell on Innes, who nodded.

A heavy silence hung in the air for a few moments before Teva finally spoke. "It was one of three. But to speak truly, it could be any of them . . . or all of them together."

"Continue," Innes ordered. "You need to explain."

"Lachlan," Teva said. "The man is old and lame. He has no skills, no abilities that warrant him being the steward of such a place as Girnigoe. And he steals."

Innes saw her sister open her mouth and then close it. Ailein wanted to defend the steward, but she realized it was best to let Teva continue.

"My mistress planned to have him replaced," Teva added. "He knew it."

"You're saying that he may have killed her, even though it was Bryce and not she who would make that decision."

The woman's jaw hardened. Obviously, she did not like having her word questioned. "Bryce respected Shona. He listened to her."

"As he should," Innes said, deferring to her. "Who else?"

"Wynda, of course."

Innes bristled. Stern as she appeared, Bryce's aunt had shown her and Ailein nothing but kindness since they arrived. Wynda was competent and ran the household with an iron fist, but most of all, she loved the Sinclair brothers as if they were her own sons.

"Why Wynda?" Innes asked.

"From the very day we set foot in the castle, Wynda never once tried to hide her dislike of my mistress. Their relationship only worsened over the years."

"Not liking someone is a long way from murder."

"Aye, but the woman saw that her bitterness was about to come back on her. You see, Wynda knew she'd be sent back to that convent her father had exiled her to when she was younger."

"What exile?" Ailein asked. "What do you mean?"

"So you don't know about her past?"

The conversation was going astray, and Innes suddenly questioned their decision to come here. Already she understood why the Sinclairs didn't want Teva living among them. The woman's words were like a snake's poison.

"When Wynda was just a lass, she ran off with a man that her father didn't approve of. She was carrying his child when the laird caught up to them."

"How would you know such a thing?" Innes asked.

"I'm a Sinclair, too, remember. On Shona's side of the clan, everyone knew about the disgrace Wynda brought on her folk," Teva said smugly. "Her father killed the man and sent her off to a nunnery. Had her bairn there—a son, they say—but they took him from her. She never saw him again. She would have rotted there if her brother hadn't sent for her. He needed her when Conall and

Bryce's mother died young."

"What was Shona doing with this knowledge?" Ailein asked, her voice rising. "Bribing her? Tormenting her? Threatening her?"

"My mistress treated Wynda no worse than she deserved to be treated."

"All of this is nonsense," Innes cut in. "Those two lived for years in that castle. If you knew about Wynda's mistake—if that's what it was—everyone else must have known as well. And people have their differences. That is no reason for murder."

"If you get any of those tight-lipped Sinclairs in that castle to talk to you, they'll tell you that Shona and Wynda had a terrible argument the day my mistress died. Right in the Great Hall, it was. I was there, and it was ugly."

"What did they argue about?"

"My mistress thought—and rightfully so—that it was foolish to pay a colossal ransom to get back Conall. The reports came that he was barely alive," Teva said proudly, as if she'd been consulted about the decision. "Wynda started screaming like a madwoman. Called my mistress horrible names. And she threatened to kill my sweet lass if she ever said such things again."

Ailein took Innes's hand. Innes wanted to get out of here. They'd accomplished nothing by coming here, except to become angry.

"Whom else do you suspect?" she asked, squeezing Ailein's hand and letting go. "Who is the third person?"

"The priest."

"What animosity would he have for Shona that would drive him to murder her? You said he was brought here to look after her."

"He never approved of anything she said or did."

Innes shook her head. "This is too much."

"He sided with Wynda in every disagreement. His allegiance wasn't with his own people but with these Girnigoe Sinclairs. And he went to my mistress's room that day. He could have done it."

Ailein stood up, motioning to Innes that it was time, and walked toward the door.

"Thank you for talking to us," Innes said, going to Teva. She wrapped her hands around the woman's thin fingers.

"We're truly sorry for your loss. It had to be very difficult. It appears that you've lost a loving mistress."

Innes flinched. She closed her eyes for an instant to tolerate the pain.

"Justice will come," Teva said, rising. "Her killer will be exposed. As sure as God above watches us, justice will come."

Ailein led Innes out of the cottage, and the two walked

together to where the Sinclair warriors waited with the horses.

"It made me sick to listen to her," Ailein said.

Innes nodded. "But she believes everything she says."

"You saw something else, didn't you?" she asked. "When you took her hand."

Innes looked back at the cottage. "Teva has had a stick laid over her back, and more than once. Shona used to beat her."

Chapter 16

Jinny paused inside the doorway to the East Tower and put a hand on Innes's arm.

"To be honest, I was a wee bit nervous when he walked right up to me, with his wild look and . . . Lord, the size of him!" She giggled like a lass of fifteen.

"He is imposing, I'll grant you that. But why—"

"But such a *man*, he is! Quite handsome when you look at him close. Those eyes, they just draw you in. And those scars. He's seen life like few do. Why, I couldn't breathe. I stood there, mute as a stone, just staring at him. He had to ask me twice before I found my voice. What was I to say but, 'Aye, m'lord. This way, m'lord.' I tripped on my own feet twice leading him up here."

Innes went up the stairs with the older woman at her heels. Jinny had been waiting for them in the Outer Ward and grabbed Innes as soon as she returned from the village with Ailein.

"But why did the earl want to get into my room?" she asked.

"I cannot say. Sworn to secrecy, I am. Besides, I'd not

spoil it."

Innes's mind raced, trying to imagine why Conall would want to come up here.

"Did I tell you how polite he was? Talked to me like I was a lady of quality." Jinny put a hand to her heart when they arrived at Innes's door. "By the Virgin, I'd never tire of waking up to the sight of that man's eyes and shoulders and—"

"You sound like a woman in love, Jinny."

"How could anyone not be?" the older woman answered coyly. "Aren't you?"

She was. But she wasn't going to admit it to Jinny. Innes pushed open the door, realized what he'd done, and immediately sighed with pleasure. A small table was set up by the window, with two chairs beside it.

"A chess set. He is so . . ." She stopped, not wanting to say too much in front of Jinny, who was watching her as if it were her own gift to Innes.

She crossed the room. This was an even finer set than the one he kept in his own chambers. She removed her gloves and picked up one of the pieces.

"Did you see the chairs?" Jinny prodded. "Finer than any you'd find in the North Tower, I'll be bound."

Innes held the chess piece in her palm. It was carved from walrus ivory. Half of the pieces were stained red; all the major pieces depicted human figures. The knights rode horses and held spears and shields. The rooks were ferocious-looking berserkers furiously chewing on their shields in their eagerness to do battle. The pawns were smaller, with rounded tops and runelike designs carved on them. She ran her fingers over the board of inlaid wood, a treasure on its own.

No one had ever given her gifts like Conall Sinclair. He couldn't read her mind, but he knew how to make her heart glow.

She put the piece back on the board and went to her writing table.

"Jinny, I need you to go to the West Tower and ask for a man named Duff."

"I know Duff."

"You do?" She glanced up. Jinny looked away, but it appeared she was blushing.

Finishing her note, Innes folded it. "Please have him deliver this to the earl. It is for his eyes only."

Innes handed the letter to Jinny and watched the serving woman hold it to her chest as if it were the jewels of the royal family. She started for the door and then stopped.

"So these are no rumors," Jinny said with a broad smile. "He's really taken with you."

"Out with you."

"Is it safe to say there may be another wedding?"

"Go, Jinny."

Innes closed the door behind the woman and leaned her back against it. Her eyes immediately teared.

She was in love with Conall Sinclair, but she couldn't say what was in her heart. Not yet. Only when she made him aware of her gift could he really know her . . . and accept her for who she truly was. But would he?

She stared at the precious chess set. She had no doubt about the gift's intent. Her sister's advice came back to her. *Tell him sooner and not later . . . before you fall in love with him.*

But her heart had already crossed into *later*.

———

Conall opened the letter and smiled. A chess move. That's all. She led with the queen's knight. A challenging position to put herself into for the start of the game. She wasn't making it easy for herself. He turned to Duff.

"Did she say anything more?"

"Nay, m'lord. Jin . . . uh, the Munro woman said that her mistress sent this, and I was to bring it to you right away."

He couldn't believe it. He was actually nervous. When had he ever asked a woman to marry him? Never.

He wanted Innes. He wanted her in his bed. He

wanted to open his eyes each day and see her face next to his. To plan, to live, to look forward to this day, and the next day, and the next, with Innes at his side. But what did he have to give her in return?

He had to go before he lost his courage. He headed to the door with Thunder trotting after him.

"You stay here, beast."

The wolf sat back on his haunches, wearing a dejected look.

He got to the door, but the wolf's whimper stopped him. "By the devil. Very well, come on. My chances might be better with you alongside me."

Thunder pranced over and ran down the stairs ahead of him.

Taking the tunnel under the castle to the East Tower, he wondered if Innes would see him alone or if someone else needed to be present. His plan for this visit was honorable. The rumors circulating about them would very shortly disappear, though. He intended to make their news public as soon as she agreed to marry him.

Of course, there needed to be a visit to Folais Castle. He needed to work out the details with her father and secure his assent. The Munros had provided support for the Sinclairs in all the battles he and his father fought. He knew that if Innes accepted him, Hector would as well.

Thunder was already scratching at her door when he reached the landing.

"Sit."

The wolf obeyed.

"Let me be doing the talking," Conall ordered.

Thunder jumped at the door again, scratching away.

"You are a bloody beast."

The door opened and before Conall could catch him, the wolf had his paws on Innes's shoulders and was kissing her face. The sound of her laughter was a caress.

"Down, Thunder," Conall commanded.

For once, the animal listened. A quick glance around the room told him it was only the two of them. He fought the urge to do what Thunder had done. She stood within his reach, wiping her face dry with a kerchief, a smile lingering on her lips. Her face was flushed. Her eyes shone. Had she been crying? He couldn't tell.

A moment of doubt edged in. *Nay,* he thought. *Don't be a fool.*

Thunder jumped on the bed across the room.

Conall glared at him. He needed no reminder of where he wanted to be with Innes. If he were to kiss Innes, or touch her right now, that wolf would need to move over. He'd been thinking of making love to her, dreaming of it. He couldn't wait until she was his.

"Down, wanton," he ordered.

The wolf only made himself more comfortable on the bedclothes.

"I'm sorry that I brought him with me." He took a step toward the bed and Thunder, sensing imminent threat, jumped back down. "He forgets he's a wild animal when he's with you."

"That's because he's not a wild animal." She petted Thunder's head as he came and sat like a perfect pet beside her. "In fact, I prefer his company to many humans."

"If you're saying that I have to compete with him, too, for time with you, then I'll be wearing this beast as a cloak next winter."

She laughed and shook her head, a blush rising into her cheek. "No competition. I'll be available to you any time you wish."

Innes walked away just as her words settled in his mind. *Did she just give her consent?*

"This chess set is magnificent," she said. "Who made it?"

She sat down on one side of the board, motioning to him to take the opposite seat. She'd already made her move, the same one she'd sent him in her letter. Thunder sided with her, lying down at her feet.

As he sat, Conall noticed the items she'd stacked up on the table beside the board. Her portfolio of drawings. A pouch that she always wore at her belt. Her gloves.

"The set was carved by one of the Norse craftsmen who built Castle Girnigoe nearly eighty years ago. It's been in our family ever since."

She winced and sat back. "What is it doing here? Shouldn't it be kept safe somewhere?"

"Bryce hates chess. He only plays it because I force him to. This set has been sitting in storage."

"Still, you should never have brought it here."

"It's a gift, from me to you."

She shook her head. "This is too valuable."

"It is a gift, Innes, from the earl of Caithness to the woman he's proposing marriage to."

Conall braced himself. He didn't know what he expected, but it wasn't tears. Confusion tore at him as she stabbed away at beads rolling down her cheeks. She refused to look into his face.

The two of them sat in silence for what felt like eternity. He finally found some words. "I take it my offer is not . . . acceptable."

She took an uneven breath and looked up. "Nothing has *ever* made me happier than the offer you've just made."

That only compounded the confusion battering away at him. Her assertion of happiness did not match the sadness she clearly felt.

He couldn't bear it if she refused him, not after daring

to hope. He wanted her to be his wife. He *needed* her in his life. He reached across the board and took her hand. "What is it? Talk to me. Don't make me sit here feeling helpless."

"You know nothing about me."

In so many ways, she was an innocent. Beneath the armor, she was vulnerable. For whatever reason, she'd suffered since her mother's death. He wished he could take away that pain. "I know enough."

Innes shook her head again. Freeing her hand, she sat back and motioned to the board. "We'll play this game. With each piece you take, you can ask a question."

"About what?"

"About my past. About the unknown in my life. You can ask anything you want to know about the woman you want to marry."

"I ask a question and you answer?"

"Aye. And I promise to tell you the absolute truth."

"What about me? The pieces that you take. Are you also going to ask about my past?"

"Nay." She smiled gently. "I won't. This is my gift to you. The gift of truth."

He stared at the board for a moment before looking up into her face. She appeared to have her emotions under control. He wanted to reach over and kiss those crystal pearls off her cheek. He wanted to tell her that there could be nothing in her past as dark as what lay buried in his. She had nothing to hide, but his demons haunted him.

"Does it matter who wins?" he asked.

"The game we are about to play is not about winning. It's simply about learning, as life is."

"Will you agree to marry me after this game?"

"Will you agree to finish the game?"

He studied her beautiful, tearful face. There were words that he'd still not spoken. He wanted her not because of suitable arrangements for their clans, or her dowry, or causing elation in his brother and her sister. He wanted Innes because he loved her. "Aye. I give you my word."

"Then I will marry you." She brushed the last of the tears from her face. "But only if you find it in your heart to repeat your proposal."

Chapter 17

"The villagers are coming for me now. I see their torches on the brae above my glen. The priest has found me out and will have his vengeance. I know the fiery death that awaits me. The good lass I have chosen awaits this chronicle. I must stop here and make good her escape. I pray she finds a place of safety among Clan Munro. She is a young woman of quality. God protect her . . ."

From the *Chronicle of Lugh*

This was the best way. He needed to know all of it.

She wouldn't trick him. She couldn't lie to him. He needed to know the burden Innes brought with her, and how much of it would fall on the shoulders of her husband, if she ever were to marry. He needed to understand that he wasn't only joining his hand with hers in marriage; he was opening his soul to her for as long as she lived.

It was time. With chess, there were rules. He'd promised to finish the game. Now she could set the pace.

The first piece he captured was a pawn.

"That shock of bonnie white hair." His blue eyes caressed it. "Did you always have it?"

"This?" It had fallen across her face. She pushed it behind an ear. "It went white the day of my mother's burial."

"But you were just seven, you said."

"You'll not find a great deal of logic to my life."

"What do you think caused it?"

"That's another question. You'll have to earn the answer."

His smile made her heart swell. She stared at the board, not allowing herself to hope. She captured a pawn and his bishop in two turns. He was forced to take out her king's knight.

Innes had started the game recklessly, daring him to capture her pieces. Conall, on the other hand, was playing cautiously, allowing her to make mistakes. There were no mistakes on her part. Every loss was intentional.

"The black dress. Do you ever wear another color?"

"Never. Except what I wear to bed. I meant to say, my shifts are all white."

His gaze flickered to the bed and back, then moved down the front of her dress. Her cheeks warmed as she remembered what went through his mind back at Wick and again by the loch. She prayed there would come a day when she could fulfill every one of his desires.

"Do you have to sacrifice another of your pieces before I ask when you started wearing it, and why?"

"That's two extra questions, but I'm feeling generous, so I'll answer."

He laughed. "I like this way of playing chess. And I appreciate your generosity."

She patted Thunder's head. He lay at her feet, his head resting against her knee. Innes wondered if the wolf sensed the inner chaos she was trying to keep hidden. "I was seventeen. I wore black when my father's wife introduced me to one of her cousins. I knew the man had come to Folais Castle to ask for my hand in marriage."

"And he was discouraged by the color of your dress?"

"That and my cool treatment of him. Also, I gave him some odd responses to his questions."

"What do you mean?"

"He asked what I was mourning. I told him I was mourning the loss of innocence in the world. He asked how long my mourning would last. I asked how long he thought the world would last."

Conall laughed. The loud heartfelt sound made Innes smile.

"You were too much for him," he said.

"I suppose he came looking for a bride, rather than a philosopher in black. In any event, he didn't stay very long."

"It all worked so well that you decided to adopt the habit."

"Aye. I felt a change in myself from that point on," she said, making her move. "I began to speak my mind. Stand up for myself. Protect my sister. My father knew I was different, but he's a good man. He has always stood by me, allowed me to be who I needed to be. With each passing year, my armor became stronger, my tongue a wee bit sharper."

"You don't frighten me, you know."

"And yet many men find me terrifying."

"I'm glad of that." He reached across the board, cupping her face with his hand. "Dear Innes, I respect and admire the woman that you've become. If you were less strong, or less direct, I believe I wouldn't feel this way."

His thumb caressed her bottom lip, and Innes's breath caught in her chest. She wanted to lose herself in his touch, in his affection and passion. But they were far from finished with this game.

As he captured the next piece, his gaze wandered to the items on the table. "The gloves. Are they part of your shield, too? Did you start wearing them the same time you began wearing black?"

Her heart beat so hard in her chest that Innes thought he might hear it. "The glove is my greatest shield. The one I use to protect those I meet."

"I don't understand."

She stared at the chessboard, at the gloves, at the

leather pouch with the relic on the table. She couldn't look him in the eye. It was time to tell him the rest of it. It was time to show him.

"I need you to make a vow to me," she said.

"Of course. That is exactly what we're playing for."

She took a deep breath. "With the exception of my father and sister—and Wynda, as of last week—no one else knows what I'm about to reveal to you about myself."

Her hands were shaking. She tucked them between her knees. Now that the moment was here, doubt ripped at her will.

"Speak to me, Innes," Conall said. "I promise you that I will never repeat anything you tell me now."

She recalled some of the accounts she'd read in the chronicle her mother left. "You understand that if you do, it will mean my death."

He paused and then took her hand. "Whatever it is, I shall safeguard your secret."

She looked into Conall's eyes, reading the thoughts rushing through his mind, understanding that he would protect her regardless.

"Do not fear. I am no witch. There is no sorcery. What I am about to show you has come down to me across generations. I had no choice about accepting it, until it was too late."

Innes freed her hand. She couldn't stand seeing his

thoughts, hearing the questions before he said them. And he was worried about her. She was giving him pain.

She picked up the pouch. "Open your hand."

There was no hesitation. He opened his palm. She dropped the relic into his hand.

"What is this?" he asked.

"This was given to me by my mother on her deathbed."

He studied the carved stone in his palm.

"What do you see?" she asked.

"A stone tablet. The edges are rough, as if it was broken off of a larger tablet." He lifted it to the light of the candle and stared at the unusual markings that had smoothed with age. "It looks to be very old."

"Do you feel it?"

"Feel what?" he asked.

"Is it warm to your touch?"

"Nay."

"Do you feel the power that runs through it?"

He met her gaze. "I feel nothing. It's just a piece of stone."

"Hold it out in your palm."

Innes placed her own hand over his, with the stone between their palms. Her fingers warmed. The heat radiated wherever their skin met. The stone channeled the power from Innes and extended it to Conall. She'd tried this only once with Ailein. Her sister had been terrified of the power.

Innes saw Conall's mind flood with questions and concentrated on reaching him.

I'm telling you the truth, she thought. *Believe me when I tell you that I have no choice in this gift.* Her words repeated in his mind. She then thought back to the two of them at the loch, and she knew he was seeing it too . . . except he was seeing the moment through her eyes, through her memory. He understood how she felt.

The relic dropped onto the chessboard as he pulled away his hand. He looked into her eyes. "You spoke to me, and yet you said not a word."

She nodded.

"I heard it. I felt it. By 'sblood, I saw it. I saw us!"

"You were in my thoughts. You were seeing my past, my memory."

"How?" A look of suspicion had edged into his face.

"It's the tablet."

He picked up the piece again. "Anyone holding this can read someone's mind? See their past?"

"Right now, it only empowers me and no one else," she explained. "Except when I extend that power through the stone. As we just did. But that's only momentary."

He stared at it in silence. She knew how much this was to sort through.

"Is this what you were talking about when you said

your life changed when your mother died?" he asked.

She met his gaze. "Aye. You asked about the patch of white hair. It was the stone. It was the realization that there could be no more secrets in the world. Souls were exposed to me. Lies were revealed. My childhood was shattered, finished. I wasn't joking with my first suitor when I said I mourned the loss of innocence."

The game was forgotten. His interest gave her hope that perhaps he'd understand.

"How did your mother come to have it?" he asked.

"She received it from a line of women who had it before her. At Folais Castle, we have a chronicle that is kept under lock and key. It's a narrative written by those who possessed this stone from the time it arrived on our northern shores, fifty years ago. It also explains the greater power behind other stones that are out there," she explained. "My mother's is the last entry in the chronicle. Someday, when I know the person I will pass the relic on to, I will add my account to it as well."

He stood up, looked around the room. He was lost, and her heart was breaking. He took a step toward the door but came back and sat down again.

"What are your memories of this before your mother died?" he asked.

"I was so young." She thought back. "She always wore gloves when she was in public. And I remember she wore this pouch around her neck or at her belt. She never parted with it. I had no idea what it was until the days before she died. She held me at her side and kept talking to me. But none of it made sense. I didn't believe. Not until she was gone. It is only with death that the power shifts to another. Not before."

Innes couldn't tell him that the first thoughts she read had been of her father's disappointment in not having sons, and of his plans to remarry. Hector Munro was a good man; he was an excellent father. And to this very day, he'd kept his promise to protect Innes and the stone.

"No one knew what your mother could do?" Conall asked.

"No one, except her husband."

"And who knows about you?"

"As I said before, only my father, Ailein, and on our outing this week, I told Wynda."

"Why Wynda?"

There was no denying him. Innes told him everything that transpired that day and how she used her gift to scare away those young men.

"So now there are others who know it, too. Young reivers wandering through the countryside looking for helpless women to rob."

"They didn't know who I was." She had to put his mind at ease. Her intention was for Conall to learn about the stone, not to rattle him about her safety. "They were not bad people. Only young lads who'd lost their way. Ask Wynda about it."

It took a few moments before he focused on the items around the chessboard again. "Do you need to touch the stone while you're reading someone's mind? As we did now?"

She shook her head. "After my mother's death, the stone attached its power to me. It became a part of me. I carry it with me because I was told that's what I should do. It's for the purpose of safekeeping. But I don't need to touch it."

He looked at her hand. "The market square. The toddler. You knew his name."

"Kade. I knew his name from his memory of his mother calling for him. I knew where to take him for the same reason."

"And at the warehouse when I took your hand."

She blushed. "I knew you wanted to kiss me."

"And at the loch."

Her gaze fell to her lap. "I . . . I knew you wanted to make love to me."

Conall lifted her chin and looked into her eyes. There was tenderness, a passion banking in the depths of his blue eyes. Innes realized that he still didn't understand the extent of her gift. She had to tell him the rest of it.

"There is something more that I need to show you."

She picked up her drawings and opened them for him to see. The two drawings she wanted were at the top. The battlefield with the dead, and with his severed hand. The second depicted a dungeon. Her fingers shook as she extended those to him.

"Twice we touched when I had no time to prepare, no time for a glove," she said. "Both times you didn't know me, and you were fighting the memories of your past."

He stared at the drawings.

"The first one I drew after the day of the wedding, when you caught me falling down the stairwell. The second time was when you were returning to Castle Girnigoe and Thunder knocked me down. You pulled me to my feet."

He continued to stare at them.

"I wasn't prying into your past. I'm no thief, stealing one's secrets. The images that came to me were the ones that were in the forefront of your mind when my hand touched you."

She spoke softly and quickly, trying to hide her raw emotions. She knew he resented any hint of pity.

"When I touch a hand, I am swept into a person's mind. I have no choice in what I see. Sometimes, it is the smell of death. And I feel that, I smell that, I taste that. Sometimes, there is violence. I feel the pain. Many are consumed by their nightmares. And I *feel* those nightmares, *live* those nightmares.

"The past that lives in our thoughts is heightened, sharpened, exaggerated. And it becomes mine. I share it, feel it, try to endure it along with them. When I am swept into the pasts of so many of us, I know that Hell is empty and all the devils are here."

She stared at her hands. He hadn't moved at all.

His silence was killing her. Her throat burned with mourning the grief of what she knew was to come. Her vision swam with unshed tears. "It's not by choice that I do this. But here I am. No secrets. The real Innes Munro."

"Enough," he said, rising to his feet. He strode to the door and opened it. He paused and then looked over his shoulder at her.

"Thank you for your honesty and your trust," he said, his voice thick. "Your secret is safe with me for as long as I live. Thunder, come."

The wolf licked her hand and ran after his master.

As the door closed behind them, a knot in her chest threatened to choke the breath out of her, and the tears began to fall.

Innes knew this would be the way. This was the end for them.

Chapter 18

It all made sense to him now.

The first time, she'd gasped in pain. The second time, she'd nearly passed out in his arms. This was exactly what life with him would be for Innes. A life of misery and torture every time she touched him.

He couldn't do that to her.

Conall stood on the rocks, looking out at the sea. The waves crashed at his feet. The darkness was spreading across the sky, choking the life out of the lingering dusk.

Alone . . . again. How his own misery was compounded now. He'd caught a glimpse of a possible life—a real life with her—and now he must walk away from it.

Sitting in her room, he'd needed a moment for what she was saying to sink into his thick head. But when it got through to him what she shared, he'd felt a moment of intense relief. She wanted him, too. She trusted him as the one man to whom she could unburden her soul.

She understood. It explained the connection when he touched her, the invisible bond that joined them.

The moment of relief didn't last. Reality quickly raised

its ugly head. Living with him meant she'd feel his pain. Always. Every day. She'd feel the scorching heat of his shame as he did. She'd suffer the pain of the lash, as he suffered.

How could he care for her, love her, and still sentence her to such a living hell?

He closed his eyes and raised his face to the wind as his throat burned with emotion. He wanted to run, to disappear so he wouldn't have to look on her face and re-member how much he still wanted her.

But he couldn't do that. She deserved better. She de-served his respect. She'd told him the truth, and he owed her at least that in return. It was essential for her to know that it was because of him, and not her *gift*, that they could never be together. She'd seen just two brief mo-ments. Hundreds more haunted his memories.

First, he had to rein in his emotions so he could speak to her rationally. He had to make her understand that those battles—and the pain of the dungeons after-ward—still lived in him. The shame of surviving when so many of his clan fell around him would haunt him always. And what of the torture he endured to keep his captors from knowing who he was and bleeding his clan dry with ransom? That nightmare came true, anyway, when an-other prisoner exposed him.

He walked along the rocks. Perhaps tomorrow he

would speak to her. Explain. Make her understand why they could not be together.

Next week would be better. He could use more time to try to smother his feelings for her. And then he just needed to wait out the time until she returned to Folais Castle. He had no doubt she would go this time.

But what of the days and weeks and years after that?

The howls drew his attention to where Thunder stood by the sea door. The wolf jumped and scratched. For a fleeting second Conall imagined Innes coming out to find refuge here, just as he had. Perhaps their talk would happen now. But the thought of being alone with her again this soon didn't sit well. Even with all he'd faced in his life, walking out of her room had been the most difficult thing he'd ever done. That was a memory he would live with always—the tears shimmering in her eyes as she tried bravely to hold them back.

The wolf was not giving up.

Resigned, Conall walked up the incline, but his heart pounded in his chest as he opened the door. He fully expected to see her, but there was no one inside. Thunder disappeared into the darkness.

He ran after the animal. There was nothing to stop Thunder from ending up in the kitchens or in the stables.

He caught sight of the wolf racing down the tunnel, heading toward the stables. When Conall got there, he emerged to find the entire area in a complete chaos. Horses were being pulled out of stalls. His own was missing. Men were moving about, and he could smell smoke. He grabbed a length of rawhide and quickly fashioned a leash for Thunder.

"What's going on?" he asked one of the stable hands.

"Taking all the horses out into the yard, m'lord."

"Fire?"

"The laird," the man responded, struggling to pull a stallion from his stall. "He's out there giving orders."

Keeping Thunder at his side, Conall went out to the stable yard. A fire burned in the center, but he looked back at the tower, still expecting to see flames engulfing the upper floors. But there was nothing amiss.

The bedlam in the yard was worse than inside. He saw his brother holding Conall's stallion by the fire and ordering people about.

"Bryce!" he called out.

His brother paid no attention and walked away, still issuing directions. Men led horses into the fields, where Conall saw another fire burned.

"Bryce," he called again, lengthening his steps until he caught up to him. "What the devil is going on?"

"Nothing to concern yourself with. I'll talk to you in a while."

"What are you doing with my stallion?" he demanded.

"The weather looks to be dry for a time, so I decided it's a fine night for gelding," Bryce replied. "We'll start with the yearlings and do the entire herd tonight."

"You don't think you're gelding my stallion without asking me. And your horse, too? Are you planning to geld our finest stud horses?" He didn't wait for an answer as the realization came to him. He looked around him. "Every older mount that can travel any distance seems to be here."

"We've talked about this before. It's time it was done."

Their conversation last month had to do with improving the quality of their herd over the years.

"I see. And here it is, the middle of the night," Conall barked. A stable hand went by, leading two horses. "And these mares, Bryce. How do you plan to geld them, I'd like to know?"

Not waiting for an answer, Conall stalked away.

"And no one," he shouted over his shoulder, "better lay a hand on my stallion."

Bryce caught up to him in the stable. "Look, Conall. I'll do whatever needs to be done to keep you here at Girnigoe. And if this means gelding every stallion or having the men drive every one of our horses halfway to Inverness or locking you up in your lair, I'll do it."

It was foolish to ask how Bryce knew what transpired with Innes. These were flap-tongued Sinclairs, after all.

And where, he asked himself, did they ever get their reputation for taciturnity?

"What makes you think I'm going anywhere?" Conall demanded.

"It's become your nature to disappear," Bryce said. "But I am warning you, brother. If you leave this castle, I am coming after you. I'll bring you back, and I'll use force if I need to."

Conall scowled. "And what will you do if Innes decides to leave? Will you use force to keep her here, too?"

"She is Ailein's responsibility. And knowing my wife, I'd say she's prepared to lock her sister up if need be."

Moments after Conall and Thunder left, Ailein had burst into Innes's room.

"This was just your first conversation about the stone," Ailein said gently, sitting beside Innes on the bed, caressing her back. "You've given him a great deal to untangle. What did you expect?"

Innes turned her face away. She couldn't stop the sobs. She loved him but he'd walked away. She knew he wouldn't be able to accept the curse that was part of her life.

"I'm leaving," Innes murmured. "Tomorrow."

She hurt more than she could have ever imagined. A tight fist wrapped around her heart, squeezing the very life out of her body. For as long as she lived, she wouldn't forget that wounded look on his face as he walked out.

"Nay. You're not. You're staying here with me."

Innes shook her head and lifted her face off the pillow. "Can't you understand? My heart is broken."

"Look at you. I've never in my life seen you like this." Ailein caressed Innes's hair. "I will not allow you to go away. You will stay here and see this through."

Another sob escaped Innes's lips. "You can't stop me. Let me be."

"Don't make me lift this mattress and roll you onto the floor."

"You're being cruel."

"Aye, cruel as the winter wind."

"Don't throw my own words back to me. You might come up with your own."

"Yours will do." Ailein frowned. "Tell me this, if you go back, will your life be your own?"

Innes sat up in the bed, clutching a pillow in front of her. "He rejected me. He doesn't want me. What I have . . . these things . . ." She held out her hands as if they were diseased. "They are an intrusion into his past. Don't you see? I *understand* why he doesn't want me."

"Did you tell him anything about the pain you feel?"

Innes stared at her sister through a cloud of tears.

"Did you tell him that you see not only a picture of the past, but that you also feel the pain of whatever horror is fresh in that person's mind?"

"I don't remember." She looked away. She had.

Ailein shoved a dry kerchief into her hands. "Think, Innes. Try to remember what you told him."

"I might have. I was getting so desperate. I needed to make him understand that what I did was not by choice. That I had no control over it. I might have admitted more than I should have." Innes wiped her face.

"Did you show him your sketches?"

"Only what pertained to him," she said quietly. "Two of them."

"I want you to listen to me and think clearly for a moment. I've learned a great deal about Conall Sinclair lately. And you know him far better than I do."

Innes remained silent. Fresh tears started gathering on her lids.

"But I know this," Ailein continued. "The man is smitten with you. He spoke to Bryce about ways of wooing you. My husband said his brother sounded like a love-struck swain."

Innes wanted to hope, but she couldn't. Could her sister be right? Was there any sliver of possibility that they could have a future? "So what are you saying?"

"I'm saying that he doesn't see you as an intrusion. Just the opposite." Ailein paused. "You've had a glimpse of his past, of the demons that haunt him, and you've felt the pain as well. And now he knows *that,* too. Think, Innes. Perhaps he walked out of this room because he's worried about *you.*"

Chapter 19

"If I've told you once, I've told you a hundred times. I'm not going down there." Innes stood by the door, waiting for her sister to give up. "I refuse to go anywhere that I'll be studied by your Sinclairs like some wounded gull."

Ailein pushed her way inside the room and closed the door behind her. "Actually, they probably think of you as a wounded blackbird, but no matter. You've locked yourself away here for days, and that's long enough."

That was to give Conall enough time to think.

And she wasn't totally locked away here. She still walked. She just went out earlier and later than usual, leaving before the household stirred at dawn and late at the night when fewer folk lingered in the courtyards.

Innes knew that Conall hadn't left Castle Girnigoe. She saw his candle burning in the West Tower late into the night. Like some thwarted thief of hearts, she stood in her darkened window, pining for him.

"When will he have an opportunity of speaking with you if you keep yourself confined like this?"

Innes returned to the worktable and her sketchbook.

She closed it before her sister had a chance of seeing her latest drawings. Ailein would be shocked by the images she'd been sketching.

"He can find me if he wants."

And he hadn't. She should have followed her first instinct and gone directly back to Folais Castle.

"Have you given much thought to what I suggested last night?"

Ailein had mentioned that Innes should "accidentally" run into him in the castle, just to remind him that she was still here.

"It's out of the question. I am not chasing after him. I'll not force him to speak to me."

"Why not?"

"Because it's over, Ailein. I am . . . I've heard what he has to say."

Innes knew the truth was that seeing him would tip her over the edge. She wouldn't allow her emotions to pour out in front of him. She'd decided before not to lie to him; she wouldn't try to influence him with tears now.

The decision to see her or not must be his.

"Well, you're coming with me today." Ailein picked up Innes's gloves and held them out to her.

"Didn't you hear anything I just said?"

"Don't worry. We're not leaving the East Tower, so

there is absolutely no chance of us running to your precious Beast." Ailein tossed Innes a glove. "It's time you got past this misery you're wallowing in and paid some attention to me, if even for a short time."

"Where are we going?"

"Upstairs."

"To Shona's chambers?"

Ailein nodded. "I spoke to Bryce. I told him I wanted to see the rooms."

"What did he say?"

"It was perfectly fine with him." She stood contemplatively for a moment. "The more time that goes by, the more I understand him . . . and why he became so angry on our wedding night."

"Why did he?"

"Think of what he went through." Ailein walked to the window and looked out at the bluffs. "Shona was always intended for his brother. Then the devastating news comes that Conall is dead. He assumes the position of laird and marries her to fulfill a family agreement. Months pass. And then the news reaches him: his brother is alive. He wants to get him back. Nothing else matters. He didn't want the title in the first place. He has no wish to be laird. Wealth means nothing to him. He just wants Conall back."

Innes knew of the bond between the two men. She'd

never forget Conall's words to her the day on the rocks.

Ailein turned to her. "But Shona fought him. She preferred to let Conall rot in a dungeon rather than ransom him."

Anger washed through Innes. To think of what Conall had gone through, and the woman who had once been promised to him wished him dead. "She was a troubled person. The more I know about her, the more upset I become."

"My husband says he never told any of that to Conall. But none of it mattered. By the time they were back, Shona was dead and Fingal had decided how she died and where she should be buried."

"But why was Bryce angry about the brooch?"

"Because he knew his brother must have gone upstairs to fetch it. He was upset because he thought it meant that Conall still cared for a woman who didn't deserve his affection. He was angry because it was a reminder of Shona." Ailein walked to the center of the room. "And of course, I didn't help things by losing my temper."

Innes was relieved those two had resolved their troubles. It warmed her heart to know Ailein could speak openly to her husband about his first marriage.

"I disliked Teva," Innes said. "And I'm certain I would have detested Shona if I'd met her, but what you just said makes it more obvious that she was not a woman to end her own life. She would have fought her husband and

Conall when they returned before giving up anything she saw as hers."

"I know."

"Did you tell Bryce about Teva's accusations?"

"Nay, I couldn't," Ailein said. "I gave her my word. And Bryce has been kind to her. I wouldn't wish to taint for him whatever good feeling he gets from his charity. It would hurt him if he heard her accusations. Those are three people that he respects."

Innes understood her sister's decision. "Why are we really going to Shona's room?"

The younger woman shrugged. "I don't know. To put it behind us? I would like to finally decide that whatever happened, it's finished. With the room open and people coming and going, perhaps I could lay Shona's ghost to rest."

How many minds had Innes touched only to find them plagued by that sense of unfinished business? Innes looked at her sister with new sense of appreciation. This new Ailein was brave and direct. She knew how to fight. She deserved to be happy.

"How are we going to get into those apartments?" Innes asked. "I distinctly remember hearing that they're locked."

"I spoke to Wynda," said Ailein. "She asked Lachlan to open the room for us and she suggested having Fingal come along, too."

"Why the two of them?"

"They're worried about you. The estrangement between you and the earl is an ongoing topic of conversation among the Sinclairs. No one knows the reason, but everyone is eager to offer a suggestion about how to bring you two back together."

"Am I going upstairs so these people can give me advice?"

"Nay," her sister said innocently. "They just want to see you."

Innes pulled on her gloves and followed Ailein up the stairs. The door to Shona's room was open.

The chambers were furnished very much the same as Ailein's rooms in the North Tower. But it was apparent that no one had lived in or visited the place for quite some time. A thick coating of dust covered the surfaces. All the windows were open and a warm cross breeze wafted through the room.

Wynda stood by a window overlooking the bluffs—the same window from which Shona fell. Like those in the room below, this one opened wide enough for a person to pass through.

Innes tore her gaze away. She didn't want to imagine Shona's death.

The priest stood near Wynda, speaking to her, but he

stopped when he noticed their arrival. Lachlan was studying a wall and a section of the ceiling where it appeared there had been some leakage. All three came over and greeted them, and were most solicitous of Innes.

"I'll have the mason come up and see to that leak," Lachlan told Wynda. "We'll want to get him up on the roof before the next storm. If you want to leave everything open, I'll come back and lock it up myself."

Wynda nodded and Ailein walked the steward toward the door.

"From the water marks on the floor, the damage to the roof must have been there a while," she said.

"Aye. You could be right about that. There's no telling it wasn't there even when Mistress Shona lived up here."

"Wouldn't she tell you," Innes asked, "if there was a problem?"

"Nay, not that one. Not until it became a much greater job than it had to be. Of course, then it'd be my hide for not noticing it sooner. But that was her way." Lachlan shook his head. "By the way, m'lady, the earl is coming with me to Wick again in two days. I know we'd both enjoy your company if you'd consider coming along."

"Thank you, Lachlan," Innes said softly. "But I promised to spend the day with my sister. Perhaps next time."

Innes didn't miss the cross look her sister sent her. The

two of them had made no such plans.

The steward doffed his cap and disappeared out the door.

Wynda and Fingal were standing quietly by while Innes walked around the room, studying the personal items left on the table and on a dresser. Being here, realizing this was the room of another woman who had disappointed Conall, brought on another wave of sorrow.

"Are we planning to use this room in the future?" Ailein asked Wynda.

"Since Lachlan will be bringing workers up here, this might just be as a good time as any to clean it up and make it ready for guests."

Innes's attention was drawn to them. "Why did Shona decide to live here and not move to the newer ward and the new rooms in the North Tower?"

"She was always set on having her own way," Wynda said flatly. "This was where she lived when she arrived as a child, and this was where she decided to stay after her wedding. It mattered naught to her that her husband's chambers were not even in this ward of the castle."

"One would think it would have been inconvenient for her here," Ailein commented, "considering the distance to the Great Hall and the kitchens and everyplace else that her rounds would have taken her."

"Inconveniencing folks was never her concern. Shona

thought of only one person, and that was herself."

Wynda's gaze went from Innes to Ailein and then to the priest. After their arrival, Fingal had taken a seat in a corner, listening and watching.

"She was a spoiled child who grew to be a spoiled woman," Wynda continued, unable to keep the edge out of her voice. "I don't like to speak of the dead this way, but it's the truth. And both those lads, thankfully, grew up knowing her nature."

Teva's attitude toward the Sinclairs of Girnigoe was nothing compared to the hostility in Wynda's tone. There was no question that she did not approve of Shona.

"Is that why the earl waited and did not marry her?" Innes asked.

The priest spoke up for the first time, drawing all eyes as he stood. "Conall Sinclair would have gone to the gates of Hell to fight Lucifer himself if he thought it would buy him more time. He had no interest in marrying the lass. But he would have done it eventually, I'm sure, for he is an honest man. Is that not so?"

Wynda nodded her agreement but said nothing.

"And I never blamed him or urged him to do any different," Fingal continued. "I came here with her. I knew her. She was a mean and selfish lass from the time she could talk. I place no blame with her upbringing at Girni-goe. She arrived that way and, because of her loss of parents, folks gave way to her. As a result, she respected no authority. She learned no obedience. No respect. As you say, Wynda, she valued nothing more than her own welfare."

"But why would a person like that kill herself?" Innes's question silenced them all for a few heartbeats.

"It wasn't because of any love for Conall," Wynda explained. "She didn't want him back. She was angry with Bryce for going after his brother. Her position was selfish, cold, and harsh, but she didn't care who knew how she felt. That was the last straw for me. The morning of the day that she died, she and I had an argument in the Great Hall. We never settled it, not that it matters now."

Clearly upset, she sat in a chair by a window and stared out.

Innes looked at Fingal. "And yet, with all of this unresolved, there was no doubt in your mind that she took her own life?"

The wiry little priest shook his head.

"None," the man said with all the gravitas he could muster. "Shona committed a mortal sin, and she did it to punish her husband. With full knowledge, she deliberately ended her life, and in that same act, she murdered the Sinclair heir in her womb. Her actions warranted the loss of our charity and the salvation of Heaven. And she did this to herself. She brought upon herself her exclusion from Christ's kingdom. She condemned herself to the fiery pit of Hell."

He moved across the room and then stopped at the doorway. "You ask if I have any doubt that she would harm herself and an unborn child. I know she did it, and I know it was done in revenge. She *told* me she would do it."

———————

Where does it come from, this pride, this arrogance that makes a lass believe she is a queen? Shona had that. Everyone around her lived only to serve her, or so she believed. We were only fit for her to wipe her boots on. I tried everything to teach her that this was wrong. Nothing worked. Nothing reached her.

When I found her whipping a serving lass, I put a halt to that. She stopped, for a time. Then she became . . . cleverer and more secretive. And for my trouble, she hated me. Not with any outward display, but I knew.

And when I saw how she treated my lads, our own war began. No one would treat Conall and Bryce badly and get away with it.

And on it went . . . until she was nearly of age. But before she and Conall could marry, he was cut down and taken at Solway Moss. My boy was gone.

But it made no difference to Shona. She would marry the new heir, and she would be queen of her domain all the same.

Chapter 20

"I know him," Wynda had told her. "I raised him. I could tell you stories for days about his moods. Conall will brood in silence forever. If you care for him, then go after him. Make him see you."

Innes heard the words echoing over and over in her mind. Last night, as they were leaving Shona's chambers, Wynda had put her hand on Innes's arm and told her what she needed to do. Unfortunately, Ailein heard her as well, and spent the next hour lecturing Innes until she relented.

So here she was, a pawn in these women's hands ... albeit, willingly. She was to become the pursuer. The enticer.

She was out of her mind. But she knew deep down that she had to try or forever look back on this chapter in her life as the time when cowardice prevailed.

A gale blew in through the west-facing windows. The weather today resembled late fall instead of early summer.

"Jinny, if I'm dead from a chill, none of this will matter.

Maybe we should close those shutters."

"I know you're a far hardier lass than that, Innes Munro. You'll not touch those shutters. And you'll not blow out the candles."

Innes frowned in frustration as the serving woman ran the brush repeatedly through her hair.

"And you'll definitely not put on any cloak over this bonnie white shift I had sewn especially for you," Jinny continued.

"He's probably sleeping, you know," Innes grumbled. "We're going through all this deviousness for nothing."

"You don't worry about any of that now, hear me?" Jinny scolded. "You listen to your sister's advice, and all will work out. She's a married woman now. She knows what to do, and her husband is on your side, too, don't forget."

Innes wondered how Conall would feel if he knew that practically his entire clan was scheming against him on her behalf.

Jinny's voice dropped to a whisper, as if spies lurked in the shadows. "Nothing would make me happier than to have you two settled here together. My two precious girls."

Innes looked down at the sleeveless shift she was wearing. Made of fine linen, it was also extremely thin. "I might as well be wearing nothing at all."

"That's the idea, my darling lass. But give it time."

Sighing with resignation, she allowed the older woman to finish brushing her hair, but as soon as Jinny left, Innes went around the room blowing out the candles. When she extinguished the last two, she stood by the open window and looked out at the West Tower. A man's figure was silhouetted in the window, watching her.

In spite of herself, her insides thrilled at the thought of it, but she closed the shutter.

"I just hope that was Conall watching," she murmured, running for the bed.

———

If he went right now through the tunnels and knocked at her door, or if he ran straight across the bridge and scaled the wall to her window, he wondered if Innes would let him in.

This was the first time Conall had seen her after far too long. And by 'sblood, he was seeing her now, moving about her chambers, wearing practically nothing. The fire ignited in his loins, and he knew he couldn't look away if the Second Coming occurred directly behind him.

"I said close that shutter, Conall, not stand there gaping like some shepherd who thinks he may have heard a pack of wolves in the darkness. No offense, Thunder."

"Not a word out of you, measle," Conall barked at his brother, keeping his gaze fixed on the window in the East Tower. "These are my chambers. You sit quietly and stare at the board for a spell and maybe Thunder will give you a hint as to your next move."

Innes stood at the window and blew out the last of the candles in her chambers. *Damn.* He still waited for few heartbeats more, hoping that perhaps she'd change her mind and light another candle.

"I don't see what the attraction is out there. And as much as I absolutely love this game, I don't have all night. Do you want to continue or no?"

Conall stalked back to their game. "The next time we train together, I'm going to kick your scrawny arse all over the Inner Ward."

"Terrifying," Bryce responded, yawning.

"Check."

"Bloody hell." His king started to run.

"I don't know why I waste my time playing with you," Connell complained.

He really wanted to play with Innes. He imagined what it would be like to sit across from her, trying to strategize, when she was dressed only in that shift. It would be the most enjoyable loss ever, he decided.

"You should send one of the lads off to Saint Andrews to hire a tutor," he grouched at Bryce. "Take some bloody lessons. There's a great deal to be learned from chess. Check."

"She's leaving, you know."

His brother might not have a great deal of finesse, but he knew how to deliver a fatal stab. Conall did not lift his eyes from the board.

"When?" he asked.

"Tomorrow, if it were up to her."

Conall should have been relieved. He told himself to *be* relieved. But he wasn't. He was aggravated.

"Ailein is trying to keep her here for as long as she can, but she's fighting a losing battle," Bryce continued. "What happened between you two? What went wrong?"

"Nothing that concerns you. Checkmate."

Bryce sat back and stared at him. "She *will* be leaving in a sennight, I can tell you that. And this time, it's definite. She's not relying on Sinclair escorts. She sent off a letter to Folais Castle, asking her father to send some of his men. Think, brother. Do what you have to do. Your time is running out."

Chapter 21

To develop a winning strategy in chess, you need to know your rival, what they want, and when they will make their move to get it. To accomplish that, Innes thought, information was invaluable and timing was key.

And with Ailein marshaling her league of informants, Innes had everything she needed.

Innes got word the moment that Conall and Lachlan left for Wick, and she knew when they were expected to return. His man Duff was in charge of Thunder whenever the earl was away from the castle on day trips. Bryce assured her that the manservant would be compliant.

Shortly before Conall and the steward were expected back, Innes knocked at Conall's door in the West Tower. Duff let her in and handed her one end of a makeshift leash with an excited young wolf attached to the other end. As always, Thunder's enthusiasm at seeing her was a challenge to control.

"Don't let him near the horses, m'lady. Those stable hands will have my hide hung and drying on a wall if you do. But more important, and I'm begging you, the kitchens. Please keep the beast well clear of the kitchens."

"Don't fear, Duff. We are going down to the rocky beach on the sea side of the castle. I'll keep him there until . . . until someone comes for him."

She hoped that someone would be Conall Sinclair.

Initially, Innes intended to kidnap Thunder and keep him in the East Tower with her. The more she got into this scheming, the more devious her mind became. But a simple plan was often the most effective, so she reined in her guile.

Descending to the tunnels, Innes struggled to hold Thunder until they passed through the heavy door onto the stony beach. She then removed the rope and let the wolf go free.

The animal went wild, running in circles, jumping on her, running into the waves and back.

"At least *you* aren't afraid of being with me. Are you, pup?"

———————

"Where's Thunder?" Conall demanded, stomping into Duff's work area. "If he's gotten away from you again, I swear, I'll—"

"The mistress has him." Duff raised his head from the leather collar he was making for the wolf. "Didn't think you'd mind her taking him down along the strand."

Conall glowered at him. He didn't mind. And he did. Bloody hell. She missed the wolf enough to come get him. Did she miss him?

"Did she come here for him herself?"

"Aye." The man put aside the leatherwork. "I'll go get him now if that's what you want. Just say so."

He knew he should let him go. Damn. "Nay. Not yet. Keep on with your work."

Conall stalked upstairs to his bedchamber and opened the window overlooking the bluffs. He couldn't see much of the rocky beach below from here.

Today at Wick, everything reminded him of Innes. The wool warehouse. The village urchins. The market cross and the smattering of vendors.

Thunder ran into his view across a stretch of the beach. A few steps behind him, Conall saw Innes run after the wolf. She was barefoot, with her hair flying loose behind her. He wanted to thread his fingers through those silky strands, take a handful in his fist, and draw her face to his. He wanted to taste her lips, devour them.

The two ran off and disappeared where he could no longer see them.

"She's determined to torment me," he muttered, heading back down the stairs. Duff lifted his head but said nothing as Conall passed through the room.

As he moved quickly through the tunnels, he continued to argue with himself about whether he should go out and confront her. He had every right to take his wolf back from her.

He'd planned to speak to her when the time was right. He'd even practiced a few of the lies that he would deliver. He needed to convince her that their marriage would not be a good idea. She deserved that. She needed a way to move on from their conversation in her room.

But he couldn't do it. He didn't trust himself to be alone with her. It was cowardly, but he just wanted to get through these next few days until she left.

When he reached the turn that led to the beach, he instead climbed to the ramparts that looked out over the sea.

Beneath him, she was throwing a piece of driftwood over the incoming whitecaps. Thunder dove out to retrieve it. A dozen seals watched with interest from deeper water.

Innes stood in the water with the waves breaking around her. The tide was coming in, and he wondered if she knew how dangerous the currents could be there.

As she picked up the branch Thunder dropped in the water, she seemed to sense his presence, for she turned and looked directly up at him. Before Conall could back away from the edge of the wall, she raised her hand and waved.

His throat knotted. The urge to hold her in his arms threatened to overwhelm every shred of common sense in him.

A wave crashed at her feet at the exact moment Thunder jumped on her to take the stick out of her hand. She fell in the water, and the next wave was on top of her. He waited a heartbeat but her head didn't surface.

He rushed back down through the passageway. He had to get to her. The currents would pull her out to sea. The waves would dash her against the rocks. This shoreline was treacherous. A few fishermen died every so often, one last year just pulling in his boat.

Conall broke out onto the strand. He could see her. She was struggling to get to her feet, only to be knocked down by the next wave.

Thunder saw him but he wouldn't leave her side. The wolf tugged at her clothes, pulling at her but only managing to keep her from getting her feet under her.

"Out. Away, Thunder," he shouted as he rushed into the water.

Thunder backed away, and Conall wrapped an arm around her waist, lifting her into his arms as another wave crashed around them.

She clutched at his neck, holding him tightly, coughing up seawater as he staggered toward the shore.

"That was the most insane thing you just did," he lectured. "You could have drowned there. You could have been pulled right out to sea."

Worry had his heart pounding in his chest. The thought that he could have lost her made him want to shout at her. What the devil was she doing stepping into these waters with no one watching? If he hadn't come, who would have saved her? He felt sick.

She tucked her face into the crook of his neck.

He wanted to take her straight up to the West Tower where he could lecture her some more. That was after he stripped her naked and dried every inch of her and tucked her into his bed. The image of Innes at her window rushed through his mind. All night he'd dreamt of tearing that white shift off her body and kissing the skin beneath it.

By 'sblood, the woman was driving him mad.

He stood her on her feet once they reached the stony beach, but she continued to hold on to his neck for few moments longer as she tried to catch her breath.

He held her, justifying it in his head that it would only be for a few more seconds.

Meanwhile, an array of erotic fantasies paraded through his mind. His dream of Innes naked. The day at the loch and how close he'd come to throwing caution to the wind and making love to her. He ached for her. He was growing hard, and he knew he needed to stop this. He needed to step away from her before she noticed his body's reaction.

"You should go in. Change right away. The water was cold. You don't want to catch your death."

She nodded and released him. She was shivering, but he saw the blush in her cheeks.

Those magical gray eyes lifted for a moment and looked into his. "Thank you. Thank you for saving me . . . again."

Conall watched her as she hurried toward the sea door. Before she reached it, she paused and picked up her stockings and shoes. And her gloves.

Her gloves. Bloody hell.

Chapter 22

"My hand begins to shake from the poison. I know they have killed me. Someone in the castle. This relic, this fragment of the Wheel, is no gift but a curse, to be sure. We thought I would be safe . . . still not safe. My beloved child, my dear, sweet Catherine sits weeping at my bedside. She is promised to the son of the clan chief, but I fear for her safety . . . his honor . . . but I must . . . my vow . . . no choice . . ."

From the *Chronicle of Lugh*

The sharp ring of metal on metal filled the air, punctuated by grunts and shouts and laughter from both fighters and onlookers. Watching the men train from the safety of Ailein's window was so different from being right here, so close.

"Are you certain I'll be safe walking through there?" Innes asked her sister.

Ailein backed up onto the steps to the Great Hall. "Bryce vowed that he'd watch for you. This will be a test of Conall's affection."

Innes thought her sister was insane, and she was insane to go along with it. But desperate times called for desperate measures. Her days at Girnigoe were coming to an end. She had to make him act. All she needed to do was walk through the yard, concentrating on the sketch in her hand as she headed toward the East Tower.

Innes's eyes were drawn to the flashing arcs of the swords as the pairs of Sinclair warriors fought. She saw no sign of Conall in the crowd of shirtless, sweaty bodies. She hoped he was here. She prayed he'd notice her and come to her rescue.

Madness was quickly becoming the best description for her behavior. She dressed scantily in her bedchamber at night, parading before the window. She nearly got herself drowned in the sea. And today she would walk through a fierce company of warriors, hoping she wouldn't be punched in the face or lose a limb to a slicing sword blade.

What wasn't she willing to do in the name of love?

Focusing on the paper in her hand, she took the first step.

———————

Bloody hell. What now?

Conall fended off the slashing blows of the two warriors fighting him and looked again at the small figure in black wandering into the tumultuous chaos of the training yard.

What did she think she was doing?

The fighters came at him again. Beating back their ferocious onslaught, he realized Innes was paying no attention to what went on around her. Swords clanged and flashed in the sun, but as the men realized with alarm that she was there, they moved aside, contorting their bodies and parting like the Red Sea as she moved through them.

Conall's own sparring partners, unaware of the action behind them, continued to attack him. As he fought them off, he suddenly realized that Innes was heading for trouble.

Bryce and one of the men were fighting with short swords, and neither of them was aware of her presence. Bryce lunged with the point of the weapon toward his fighter's chest, and the man spun away from the attack, driving at him with a frenzy of strokes.

Conall couldn't watch any more.

She was about to step right into the sword's path.

His intention was to push her out of the line of danger. But as he passed, Bryce stepped back, catching his hip and sending him stumbling toward her. Going down, he caught Innes by the waist. Before they hit the ground, he rolled and she ended up sprawled on top of him. Her silky hair blanketed his face. Her breasts pressed against his naked chest. His arm remained around her waist, holding her where she landed.

Her eyes rounded with shock. Boots quickly gathered around them.

"Here we are again," he said. "How many times must I save you?"

"I'm sorry. I didn't realize this would . . ."

She tried to push herself up, but the devil in him made him hold her tighter. She smelled so good, her lips were so close, and her breasts were crushed against his chest.

"What are you thinking? Let me go."

"If you weren't wearing those gloves, you'd know what I'm thinking." His gaze was fixed on her mouth.

Before she could respond, a dozen of his cursed warriors helped her to her feet.

Conall sat up. She glared at him, snatched up her fallen paper, and then turned away. The spirals of dark hair reached the tops of her buttocks. She'd stopped braiding and putting her hair up just to drive him mad. He was certain of it. He looked up and frowned at the line of Sinclair warriors, standing stock-still, their training forgotten. Every one of them grinned from ear to ear, watching Innes walk away.

He wanted to pound every dog-faced one of them. He jumped to his feet and Bryce was there.

"You and I are done for today," said Bryce.

"I'm not. There are a few brains out here that I need to rattle."

"Brains? You certainly won't find any in this bunch." Bryce put an arm out, stopping him. "Besides, I have more important business with you. Clan business. One of the merchants is waiting for us, some complaint about our wool. I have no idea what he wants. Why don't you clean up and come to my receiving room, so we can straighten this out?"

Conall would have liked to put his brother off, but he understood the validity of Bryce's concern. No one wanted any setbacks after the gains they'd begun to make.

Back in the West Tower, he climbed the stairs to his chambers and cleaned up. All the while, his thoughts kept going back to Innes. She was doing this intentionally; he knew it. She made sure he saw her, touched her, smelled her, felt her soft curves against his body. She wanted him to suffer and know what he'd given up.

He pulled on a clean shirt. If only she knew that he was doing this for her own good.

Blasted woman. He should tie her to a horse and send her back to Folais Castle now, before he lost his mind.

The storm brewing in him must have shown in the blackness of his frown, for everyone scurried out of his way as he strode to the North Tower.

In the Great Hall, Wynda took a step toward him but then veered off, choosing to talk to Fingal. Lachlan limped away and disappeared through the door to the kitchens before Conall reached him. At the door to Bryce's room, he didn't bother to knock.

Bryce was dragging a chair across the floor. There was no one else there.

"Where is he?" asked Conall.

"Where is who?"

"The bloody merchant."

"Oh, he left. It was nothing. Just a misunderstanding."

The grin on his brother's face didn't sit well with Conall. He slammed the door shut behind him. "You knew this before you asked me to come here."

"Aye. That I did."

"What the devil for? So I wouldn't crack a few empty skulls?"

"In part," Bryce replied, leaning against his desk. "You have one fist left, and I'd prefer not to have it bloody and useless all the time."

Conall cursed and began to turn to the door. As he did, his gaze lit on the chessboard and he stopped.

"That's the other reason," said Bryce.

The chess set he'd given to Innes—his gift to her—sat there with two chairs arranged on either side.

Conall's eyes narrowed, his muscles tensed. "What's this doing here?"

"Innes sent it to me. She said she wasn't about to take it back to Folais Castle. Said such a valuable set should remain with the Sinclairs. Quite a remarkable woman, that one. She also offered to give me few lessons before she left. Ailein tells me her sister is quite proficient at the game. Among the Munros, no one can defeat her, apparently. Weren't you just saying I should hire a tutor?"

Blood was pumping so hard in Conall's head that he could barely hear his brother's words.

She returned his gift.

"Have that taken back to her chambers," he said through clenched teeth.

"She won't take it back. She told me—"

"She *will* take it back," Conall barked, storming out. "I'll make sure of it."

Chapter 23

The chess set had done the trick.

Innes had no doubt who was pounding on her chamber door.

Fighting the nervousness and excitement shaking her to the core, she took her time, glancing in the mirror at her reflection. Keeping her hair loose made her look younger, despite the blaze of white hair. But her face was flushed, her breathing uneven. She needed to be calm.

The black dress she'd worn this morning was dusty from the tumble in the training yard. There was no time for her to change into another one.

The knock became even louder, almost violent.

She wiped away the worst of the dust. He probably wouldn't notice.

"Innes, I know you're in there. Open the door."

She glanced at the high neckline of her dress and wished she'd taken her sister's advice and worn something more revealing. But she couldn't bring herself to do it, not while she paraded herself among those half-naked men.

"You open this door, or I *will* take it down."

She pulled on her gloves, slowly, methodically, taking her time, and finally unlatched and opened the door.

Conall Sinclair, wild-eyed and disheveled, looked like some creature of the darkness ready to tear her to pieces. She bit her lip, remembering how slow he'd been in letting her go in the training yard.

"Why, m'lord, what a surprise!"

He charged past her. "We need to talk."

She looked down the hall outside.

"What are you looking for?"

"I was hoping you had Thunder with you." Innes shrugged, trying to look disappointed.

She closed the door and turned to him. She didn't think she'd ever seen him looking angrier.

He stalked to the open window overlooking the bluffs, obviously trying to cool his temper. She waited patiently. When he finally turned around, his gaze immediately went to the white shift draped across the foot of the bed. The same one that she'd worn at night to tease him.

"What can I do for you?" she asked casually, drawing his eyes back to her.

"That bloody . . ." He stopped and took a breath. "The chess set. My gift to you. You returned it. To my brother."

"Aye. It seemed to be the right thing to do. And I offered to give him some lessons, too. He was quite happy about it, I think."

"That is my gift to you. It is yours to keep."

"That set is too precious. It belongs to the Sinclairs."

"Blast the Sinclairs!" he exploded. "It's *yours*."

"As I understand it, that chess set was a gift from the earl of Caithness to the woman he was proposing marriage to," she said, fighting back emotions that suddenly threatened to burst loose. She couldn't cry. She wouldn't. Not after everything she did to bring him back to this room. "Since that offer no longer stands, I have no desire to keep it."

He stared into her eyes, and she recognized the struggle. What she saw there was no longer anger but torment.

"About my offer—" he began.

"You don't . . . you don't have to explain anything." Her voice broke slightly. "I understand. This curse that is part of me is too much to ask you to bear. You said everything that needed to be said when you walked out that door."

The emotions packed in the blue depths of his eyes told her how hard it was for him to stand back, how hard he was fighting the urge to come and take her into his arms. Yesterday along the shore, as he'd carried her out of the water, she'd seen much more into his soul than he could have ever imagined. He loved her. Right now, she didn't have to touch him, but she understood his thoughts. *If I go to her,* he was thinking, *I fail her. Not just now, but for the rest of her life.*

"My proposal . . . the reason why I did not repeat it is not about you," he said. "It's about me, about my past. About the privacy I need. You might call it selfish, but it's my right to keep hidden what's mine. I cannot allow anyone to intrude."

Innes watched him in silence. He was lying.

"You're going to move on, and I'm certain that happiness awaits you," he continued. "You are beautiful, Innes. Intelligent. You are exciting and passionate." His gaze caressed her slowly from head to toe, lingering on her face, her lips, her hair. "There is a man out there who will be lucky to have you as his wife. He'll be worthy of your love. And your gift. He'll be a much better man than I could ever be." He tore his gaze away from her face and looked at the door. "Part of me wishes I could be that man. But I'm not."

At the bottom of the stairwell, Conall pushed open the heavy door to the tunnels. The door hadn't been latched since the first day she accepted his invitation and came to the West Tower to play chess.

He didn't want to see anyone. He said what he had to say, and now he wanted to disappear and grieve for what he'd done, what he'd needed to do.

Leaving Innes's room, seeing her standing there disheartened but brave, listening to his words but respecting his decision, was torture. And he was a man well versed in torture.

He'd go away. This was the answer. Bryce couldn't hold him here. No one could. He couldn't see her again. He couldn't be near her and not give in to what he wanted more than anything in the world.

He passed through to the West Tower. Arriving at his chambers, Thunder greeted him.

"Duff, go down and get my horse ready."

"Ready? For what? Where are you going?"

"Go and do as you're told. And, by God, I'll beat you within an inch of your life if you take the news to my brother or say a word to *anyone*."

The servant scurried out the door.

Today. He'd go right away. Conall started toward the stairwell leading up to his bedchamber when Thunder rushed toward the door. He turned around and was shocked to find Innes leaning against the doorjamb, catching her breath.

"You walk quite fast," she said, panting.

A ray of hope squeezed into his heart. She'd come after him. But why?

"What are you doing here?" he demanded.

"I just saw Duff on the stairs and he told me you're

leaving." She motioned over her shoulder. "I'm glad that I took the tunnel, too. If I came through the courtyards and over the bridge, you'd have been gone by the time I got here."

Confusion tore at him. He'd spoken his piece. Told her they could never be. He expected her to leave and hate him for his cold words.

"Why did you follow me?" he asked.

"Life is like a game of chess. To win, you have to play."

"I am not playing."

Her eyes flashed, challenging him. "You gave me your word of honor that you'd finish the game we started."

"That game is over."

"Then we're starting a new one." She stepped into the room and the wolf jumped on her in excitement. "Sit, Thunder. Stay."

The wolf obeyed like a trained lapdog.

"I said I'm not playing," Conall said as sternly as he could manage. But his heart was working independently of his brain; it pounded harder with each step she took.

"In that case . . ." She studied him from across the room and started removing her gloves ever so slowly.

"What are you doing?"

"You are going to tell me again why you withdrew your offer of marriage."

"I just told you . . . only minutes ago."

She dropped her gloves on a nearby chair and approached him. "This time you'll say it holding my hand."

"Innes," he warned, taking a step back. His gaze traveled down the front of her dress. He didn't remember the top handful of buttons being open when he was in her bedchamber. "I think you should leave. Now."

"Oh, I'll leave. And I promise never to come back . . . to you, that is. I have every intention of seeing my sister in the future." She continued to move toward him.

Conall took another step back, wanting to laugh, but he couldn't. She didn't need any more encouragement.

"But before I go," she said, "I want you to know that I believe in honesty. In truth. I'd like to know that what came out of your mouth matches what's in your heart and your mind. I have to make certain that you believe your own words."

"What if I don't care for that . . . that intrusion?"

"Well, then. I'll have to force you."

He stared in disbelief as she charged at him. For an instant, he didn't know if he should laugh or run. She was a little thing, practically half his size and weight, and yet she was clearly set on handling him.

And he wanted to be handled. She wanted the truth? He wanted her tackling him to the ground and pinning him down and straddling him right here.

He maneuvered around a chair, and she eyed him. The

wolf tried to get in the game. This time Conall was the one who ordered him to sit.

"Give up," she said. "I won't hurt you."

He laughed, backing toward the stairs. Her smile was the most precious reward.

"This has gone too far, Innes," he said, trying to be serious. "Think of your reputation. These are my private chambers."

"This has gone too far, Innes," she mimicked. "Let me lecture you on what's best for you. On whom you can love. Whom you should marry. Let me decide for you, Innes, if I'm worthy of you or not. Let me decide for you if you can handle my past."

She backed him up the stairs.

"You're mocking me," he said.

She followed him up. "Only one of us is speaking the truth."

He backed through the door at the top. "You're wrong. I meant what I said."

She closed the door and latched it behind her. "Then I guess it's time to confirm or deny it, wouldn't you say?"

He was finished. She had him. He couldn't have held back if his life depended on it. He went to her.

The joining of their lips might have set the entire castle ablaze. Like a starved man, he kissed her, devoured her, and she was as zealous in her response.

He dug his fingers into her hair, holding her tightly as his lips tried to get the taste of her. Her hand touched his, then her arms wrapped around his neck, her body arching, pressing tighter against him, pushing him to sheer madness.

Moments later, she tore her mouth away from his and placed a hand against his lips. His heart pounded, his body throbbed with need, and he looked down into her flushed face. The intimacy of her fingers on his lips was almost more than he could stand.

"You lied," she whispered. "You want me. You said those things to protect me."

Her lips were full and tender, her cheeks the color of wild roses. She was by far the most beautiful woman he'd ever held in his arms.

Damn, he loved her. But this was no time for talking. He wanted to touch her. He wanted to taste every delicious bit of her skin.

She read his mind and started unfastening her dress. His lips moved from her mouth and traveled across her cheek to her ear, down her neck as quickly as she opened the dress, inch by inch. His hand traveled everywhere, roaming her back, feeling the curve of her bottom, pulling her hard against his manhood.

The bed was only a few steps behind them. He was afraid that he'd lose control once he laid her down on it.

"Take me there," she whispered. "Make love to me."

He'd died and gone to Heaven. He swept Innes off her feet and carried her to the bed.

"We have to go slow," he murmured, "even if it means I lose my mind. This is your first time. We need to go gently."

Her fingers combed caressingly through his long hair. She traced the soft ridges of his ear, the line of his bearded jaw. He laid her down and looked at her hair spread across the pillow.

"You take my breath away," he said.

His hand smoothed the material of her dress. He pulled open the buttons slowly, moving with deliberate relish downward.

She gasped as the front of the dress parted and his hand brushed over her breast.

She opened her arms. "Come to me."

He pulled the shirt over his head and kicked off his boots. He unfastened his kilt and let it pool at his feet. He climbed next to her.

"You might be frightened by what you see in my head, by everything that I want to do to you. But I promise to go slowly."

"Kiss me, Conall," she whispered against his lips. "I'm not afraid."

The Highlander's blood, already roaring in his head,

surged at the huskiness in her voice. Desire took on a life of its own and pushed him to the edge of his control. He rolled toward her, crushing her against him.

She arched her back as he moved from her mouth and trailed his lips downward over her chin and her throat. Her fingertips stroked his bare back.

He caressed her ivory skin, from her throat to the tops of her breasts. He could feel the warmth of her body, the firm flesh, the trembling shudders that his touch brought on. A moan of pleasure deep in her throat filled him with certainty.

He drew down the neckline of her shift until her breasts sprang free. His lips locked on the erect nipple. He heard her gasp and felt her bloom beneath him. Her hands tugged at his hair, pressing his face even tighter to her breast. Then, as he continued to suckle, moving from one nipple to the other, her knee rose instinctively and took possession of his thigh.

The rush of heat scorching through her body lit Innes's senses with explosive energy. Her mind whirled with confusion at these newfound sensations, while her body screamed for more. She writhed as his tongue laved her breasts, and she lost the ability to breathe when his hand pulled her skirt up over her legs. She gasped with shock and pleasure as his fingers stroked the skin of her legs. When his hand found the juncture of her thighs, Innes reveled in the waves of white heat that cascaded through her and threatened to obliterate all reason.

As he lifted his head from her breasts and looked deeply into her eyes, she slid her hand downward over his buttocks and his hip. She could feel his arousal, thick and hot, pressing against her. She knew what he wanted, so she wrapped her hand around him.

Fighting for control, Conall gazed down at the beauty in his arms, knowing that he would certainly die if he did not take her now. More than anything else, he wanted to bury himself deep within her, bring her to heights of unimaginable pleasure, and pour his seed into her. His eyes took in her swollen lips, her heaving breasts, reddened in spots from his rough, bearded face.

"I was trying to protect you from my past," he said raggedly, using his final shred of willpower. "This is your last chance, Innes. Tell me if you want to stop now, for I won't be waiting much longer. I take you now, and you will be my wife."

His body was rigid, every muscle tensed and hard as steel. His lips hung only a breath away from hers. But his gaze never left her, sweeping over her features, continuing its soft caress of her face.

"I've already made my move." Innes lifted her mouth to his. "It's time you made yours."

Chapter 24

He possessed her. He enthralled her body in a timeless, frenzied world of sensation and passion. The climax exploding within her matched what she saw in his mind. The two of them joined and cried out and were caught in the stunning power of a summer storm. Somewhere in a more conscious world, Innes heard a woman's voice—her own voice, she realized—crying out exultantly. She couldn't breathe.

And then she was simply sailing through a crystalline sky, colors she had never before seen flashing around her as she soared.

Conall held her as she descended, kissing her softly, cradling her in his arms.

The sensations in her body receded in waves. Innes's bones had dissolved into liquid. Her flesh tingled. The room was slow to come into focus. The sounds were a distant beat. And then they grew closer.

"That monster is howling," said Conall.

She listened, at first not comprehending his words. There were thumping sounds against the door, followed by Thunder's howls.

"I will let Bryce have him stuffed after all," Conall growled into her neck, not letting her go.

The next howl was even louder and more heartrending.

"He misses his pack," she said. "He wants you."

"It's you that he's in love with." He rolled off her reluctantly. "But the damn wolf is a Sinclair, too. All that racket is just to report to the castle what we're doing."

She pulled the blankets over her face. It was midday, and she had chased Conall Sinclair into his bedchambers and forced him to make love to her.

He pulled the blankets down, and she looked at his magnificent body standing naked beside the bed.

And she wasn't a bit sorry.

Thunder howled again.

"Please let him in," she said.

"I will, but first . . ." He turned her slightly and began peeling what remained of her clothes from her body.

"What are you doing?" She laughed.

"I want you here in my bed as the Lord made you. We're only getting started."

Her clothes dropped onto the floor. She tried to hide her body, but he pulled the blanket off again, letting his gaze lovingly caress her face, her breasts, her belly, her thighs.

Her desire and excitement started building again.

"Don't move," he said.

She stared at his magnificent back and buttocks and legs as he walked toward the door.

Innes could hardly believe what she'd done. Ailein was right in encouraging her, in convincing her, to stay and fight for the man she loved. Her heart soared to think they had a chance. That she wasn't cursed for life because of her gift.

Innes knew he was still concerned. She needed to train herself to be aware of it. Her fingers were the conduits of power. She had to hold back from touching him—unless both of them were prepared. Innes needed to make sure he knew that she was mindful of it. He needed to trust her in managing her gift.

Conall opened the door, and Innes quickly pulled the blankets over her, for Thunder paid no attention to his master and leaped onto the bed looking for her.

She laughed as the wolf growled and dug at the bedclothes, trying to get to her.

"I told you," said Conall. "You're the one this beast loves."

Conall crawled in with her just as the wolf found Innes's face and the tongue-lashing began.

"Fine. Fine. I love you, too." She petted the giant animal.

"Get off the bed, Thunder," Conall ordered.

The wolf moved to the other side of Innes and pressed himself against the covers, taking refuge at her side.

She couldn't stop the laughter from bubbling up in her. The two of them hemmed her in. "I now have my own pack."

"When we're outside, when you need protection, we'll be there." Conall's arm wrapped around her waist, and he pulled her against him as he shoved the wolf off the bed. "But listen to me, Thunder. She is *my* human."

The wolf tried to jump up once more, but decided his master wasn't having it. Growling, he moved to his straw bed and settled down, watching them.

"In spite of his size, he acts like a pup," said Innes. "Do you have any idea how old he is?"

"About six months."

"So he is a pup. Where did you find him?"

He propped himself on an elbow, his leg draped across hers. He looked from Innes to the wolf.

"I found him when Bryce and I were riding back from England," he said. "Here I was—broken, miserable, not understanding why I was still alive. I saw no purpose left in my life, and then I find this one—the last of his litter—by a stream in a glen we were passing."

The wolf's eyes never wavered from them, as if he understood every word.

"Hunters had killed his mother and the other pups," said Conall. "I don't know how he survived."

She smiled up at him. "And you brought him home."

"And I brought him home, aye."

Innes rolled toward him and tucked her hands under the pillow. "Will you tell me about the battle?"

He looked into her eyes, worry darkening his brow.

"You started telling me that day at the loch," she said softly. "If I know what happened, if I understand the source of your pain, I'll be better prepared. And I'm not speaking of the physical pain of losing your hand. The first time I touched you, I felt something much more powerful. A feeling so deep that tore at my heart."

He caressed her face, coiling her hair around his finger.

"Please, Conall. I know that being with me, marrying me, is forcing you to bare your soul," she told him. "But I don't want to be stealing bits and pieces of your past. I want you to tell me what I should know."

"I've not spoken about how that battle and the loss affected me. Not once since I've been back."

Innes brushed her lips against his. She wouldn't force him to speak, but at the same time it broke her heart to know there were demons that haunted his memories.

"I know a little about Solway Moss," she offered.

"Of course. Your clan lost good men. But what do you know?"

"I know we always dredge up a good reason to fight the English—land, alliances, succession, and now religion. I know King James snubbed Henry and refused to meet with him at York, and that resulted in English troops raiding the Borders. But I also know that Henry Tudor will conquer and rule all of Scotland, if he gets the chance. We fought the battle at Solway Moss to try to stop him."

He caressed her face. "You amaze me."

"Tell me your involvement in it," she pleaded. "And here are my hands. Tucked away. You will not harm me by thinking of it, speaking of it. Instead, you'll help us both."

He looked into her eyes for a moment more and then rolled on his back, staring at the ceiling. "It was November, two years ago. Initially, we were to be an army of twenty thousand. The Sinclairs have a long history of fighting for the crown. We've always stood by the king, and been favored for our loyalty. Not long before we set out, King James chose me to command three thousand fighters."

She propped herself on an elbow, so she could look into his face. She was mindful of not touching him.

"We moved south into England. They were waiting for us between two rivers with their cavalry and their cannons. Other Scots troops were supposed to join us, but none came. Without the king there, his commanders wouldn't support each other. When the battle started, the English outnumbered us three to one. In the first encounter, they gunned us down and then threw their cavalry at us. We found ourselves penned in between the river and the Moss. That's where the fiercest fighting took place."

He paused and looked into her face, as if assuring himself that she was not suffering. Innes said nothing, fighting the urge to comfort him. She knew what would come next.

"The riverbanks and the field all about were painted with Scots blood. We were no match for the English Border Horse. They rode over us time and again. Hundreds of my men were cut down and left to die in the marshes and the river." He paused again. "You drew that scene."

She did. Innes remembered the sorrow she felt as only an outside observer. She couldn't imagine the extent of Conall's loss at his position.

"And then you were taken prisoner," she said.

"I should have died on that field with my men."

"You fought bravely and honorably," she said softly, unable to stop the tears that sprang into her eyes. "You didn't surrender. You were taken from that field by force. Fate had other plans for you."

He kissed her lips. He kissed each of her eyes and brushed away her tears.

"Tell me what happened after," she said.

"The English captured so many after that battle. They were to be bargaining tokens to break down the Scottish crown. Others were part of vast ransoms," he told her. "While I lay in prison, I heard that King James died not long after, humiliated by our loss and ill with fever. Even the birth of our infant queen could not rally him. He was too distraught. He died lamenting the death of his Sinclairs, they say."

"And that only added to your unwarranted guilt."

"Not unwarranted. I was their commander. It was under my direction that so many lost their lives."

She propped herself up. "If there is anyone who should harbor guilt, it is those villains who did not arrive, those supposedly loyal Scots who left you unsupported while you fought a larger army alone. This shame—this guilt you feel—it's only right that they should bear it, not you."

A smile tugged at a corner of his lip. "You're angry on my behalf."

"Aye, and who wouldn't be," she said, shaking her head. "And while you languished in captivity, you wouldn't reveal your identity. That's why it was a year before anyone knew you were alive."

"I knew what gold we as a clan had in our vaults. And I knew that those English bastards would take every bit of it. It was just bad luck that I was discovered."

"Your life was worth it. Bryce knew it. Your clan wanted you back. You were needed here," she told him, not wanting to imagine how empty everyone's life would have been if Conall had never returned. How purposeless her own life would be now. "But that is in the past. Now is the start of a new chapter for you and Bryce and the Sinclairs."

"My little warrior." He traced her bottom lip. "Now you also understand why I care so much about Bryce's happiness."

"It's because of what you saw as your brother's sacrifices."

"There were sacrifices, to be sure. He married Shona because I failed to do it sooner. He impoverished the Sinclairs to save me. And there was a time when I thought he was sacrificing himself again by marrying Ailein, just because of the size of her dowry."

And he'd not been the only one thinking that. Innes remembered her sister's doubts even on her wedding day.

She kissed him. "When it comes to those two, I'm actually glad that their marital difficulties started on their wedding night . . . before I left for Folais Castle with my kin."

"Not as glad as I am," he said. "You've been my undoing and my salvation."

His fingers caressed the column of her neck and gently

squeezed her breast before moving down over her stomach. She gasped with excitement when he touched her wet folds with his fingertips, parting her, teasing her. A moment later, she was moaning with pleasure.

She opened her legs to receive him, but he smiled and moved his lips down her body. He tasted her breasts and still continued downward, lifting her hips and kissing the inside of her leg. His gaze met hers, challenging her silently to watch.

Innes's heart sang in her chest, her skin tingled, her body shook with erotic anticipation.

He moved his mouth to the juncture of her thighs. She cried out with a startled gasp at the shock of the intimacy, and her entire body lifted upward toward the ceiling. But he pushed her back and continued his sweet torment.

The sky opened overhead. She could muster no control. Her body shuddered in wild spasms of release and waves of pleasure that continued to roll through her. Moments later, her hands clutched desperately at his hair, pulling him back up to her.

She could no longer hold back. She needed to feel him, touch him the same way. She pushed him and he rolled on his back, bringing her with him. She straddled his hips and flattened her palms against his chest.

His gaze was drawn to her hands, then to her breasts.

She smiled. "You have to realize that there are rewards

in me reading your thoughts."

"Are there now?" He tried to touch her breast, but she pushed his arms above his head.

She started with his mouth, leaning over him and kissing him with the same thoroughness that he'd kissed her. Her breasts brushed against his chest, her hips teased him where she touched his stomach.

His eyes lost focus, strain showed in his face, but he was bound to her wishes.

Innes let her mouth travel down the hard planes of his chest, her fingers tracing down to his powerful thighs. They flexed under her touch.

Innes's breath caught in her chest at the sight and the feel of his full manhood rising so intimately between her breasts.

Her fingers moved down slowly and encircled the smooth flesh. Placing her mouth again on his stomach, she followed the path he showed her in his mind, descending slowly until her lips caressed the pulsing shaft.

She heard him draw in a deep breath and hold it. Building her courage, she let the tip of her tongue trace the length of him. Fiercely, he thrust his hand into her hair.

"Innes, I cannot take much of this." His voice was hoarse. Glancing up, she could see the sweat glistening on his brow.

She wanted him to be undone the way she'd been undone. She opened her mouth and took him in.

Innes heard him call her name as he pulled her roughly up and turned her facedown on the bed.

She spread her palms flat against the bedclothes, lifting herself to receive him as he searched for the moist opening. She gasped softly with the urgency of his penetration.

Conall leaned forward over her back, his mouth kissing her neck, the sensitive spot beneath her ear. His hand caressed her breasts, teasing her erect nipples, before moving lower to stroke her very center with expert fingers.

Now it was she who would lose control again, and she panted for breath, rocking back into him, hardly realizing that she lifted off her knees as he drove into her with fast and powerful thrusts.

A growling sound vibrated in his chest as he took hold of her writhing hips, plunging into her over and over.

As the heavens burst open before her eyes with a million dazzling shocks of reds and golds, Innes did not know if she cried out. Vaguely, she felt him grip her shoulder, toppling her forward as he convulsed with a loud cry. Instinctively, she clutched his arms as he wrapped them around her, pressing her into the bed.

How long they stayed that way, Innes had no way of

knowing. She gradually became conscious of their fast and uneven breathing, relishing the sensation of their heated bodies molded together both inside and out.

Eventually, he stirred, gently withdrawing from her and placing tender kisses on her spine, on her neck. He rolled to the side and turned her, drawing her against his chest and kissing her lips.

His mouth slipped to her ear. "I apologize for the audience."

She looked down at the foot of the bed. Thunder had his paws on the blankets, waiting for the invitation to jump up.

Chapter 25

"This is more like my Ailein," Innes teased as her sister wiped away the tears racing down her cheeks.

"What do you expect? My sister is getting married. I'm the one responsible for it. I arranged it." She beamed through her tears. "Bryce says Conall insists on leaving for Folais Castle the day after tomorrow to speak with Father."

"Aye, he's trying to give Fingal three weeks for posting the banns. They'll do the same thing at home." Innes smiled, still dazed from everything that was happening. She was going to marry Conall Sinclair. Their betrothal would take place in private tomorrow night, before he left. Even though he hadn't met with her father to settle any arrangements regarding dowry, the two of them were capable of making their own decisions.

"You do know that Bryce is going with him," Ailein told her with a smile. "Like me, he is taking all the credit for your romance. He wants to make certain everything goes smoothly with Father and that the wedding date is set and that the ceremony will be here at Castle Girnigoe."

"I don't believe Father will object to any of that," Innes said. "Besides, I'm going with them, so there shouldn't be any prob—"

"You can't go!" Ailein cried out in dismay.

"What's wrong?" Innes immediately jumped to her feet, went to her sister, and took her in her arms. As soon as she touched her, she knew.

Ailein burst out laughing.

"Is it true?" Innes asked.

Ailein smiled, wiping her cheeks at the same time. "Jinny thinks so. And I saw the Sinclair midwife this morning. They both say I'm expecting."

Innes hugged her sister again, this time not letting her go. Years of memories rushed into Innes's thoughts. Memories of the toddler she used to hold in her lap after their mother passed on. The child that followed Innes every moment of the day and crawled into bed with her every night. The one who wouldn't allow anyone else to soothe or comfort her. And now Ailein was going to be a mother herself.

"Have you told Bryce?" Innes asked, pulling away.

"I did this morning. He's quite excited. But he also wants to make sure I'm not left here alone. He asked . . . I'm asking that you stay."

Innes rattled off in her mind all the reasons why she was going back to Folais, and they all had to do with

Conall. She wanted to make certain he was well received and well treated. Most importantly, she wanted to be with him while he traveled.

"Please, Innes?" Ailein begged.

"Of course." She took her sister in her arms again. "Of course I'll stay."

———

Innes stared at her reflection in the mirror, not recognizing the woman looking back. The underskirt of heavy ivory-colored silk, with its low square neckline and elegantly embroidered sleeves, swept to the floor. Ivory lined her gown of deep blue silk, edged with intricately stitched beads of silver and laced in front beneath her breast. The blue gloves matched the gown perfectly.

Her loosely braided locks fell to her waist over one shoulder. The silver edging on the gown accented the blaze of white in her hair.

"Thank you, Jinny. You've wrought a miracle, and I'm struck speechless."

"Nay. It's you, mistress. It's your beauty shining through," the old woman said happily. "You look bonnier than any princess, I'd wager. Just wait until the earl sees you. He asked you to marry him, seeing you only in those black dresses. Wait until he sees you without them."

Oh, Conall *had* seen her without them, Innes thought, walking away from the mirror so Jinny wouldn't see her blush. After that first day when she followed him to his chambers, they had tried to be discreet. When Conall came to her late at night, he used the passageway under the castle. She burned, thinking of the things that he did to her body. How he made her soar every time they made love, leaving her breathless and spent . . . and still wanting more.

"Please remember to tell no one of tonight's betrothal," she said, turning to Jinny. "The earl wants just the two of us there—with Bryce and Ailein and Wynda as witnesses—when we exchange our promises before the priest."

Conall and his brother would leave for Folais Castle tomorrow. He knew their wedding plans were out of his control; Ailein and Bryce had already taken charge of it. But for tonight, he wanted their affair to be private. And Innes would do anything for him. She'd run off with him, if that's what he wanted.

The knock on the door told her that he was here for her. Jinny hurried to the door and opened it.

For a long moment, there was absolute silence. From where she stood, Innes could only see Jinny. She appeared to be frozen in the middle of a curtsy.

"Jinny, is your mistress ready?" The very sound of

Conall's voice resonated in her heart. She went to the door and, like her servant, all she could do was stare.

If not for his eyes, his voice, and the portrait of him she'd admired the first night they'd arrived at Castle Girnigoe, she would not have immediately recognized him.

"You've shaved," she said.

His gaze swept over her before returning to her face. "You're wearing blue."

He looked handsome, incredibly so. She let her gaze move over his strong chin and the chiseled jawline, the straight nose and piercing blue eyes. His scar was more noticeable with the beard gone. But she loved him, regardless of how he looked.

She smiled. "And you cut your hair." It was still long, but he now tucked it behind his ears. It barely reached his shoulders.

He looked from Ailein to Jinny and back and then stretched out his hand. "Ready?"

Innes nodded, still flustered by his new looks. She put her hand in his, and he led her down the steps. He said nothing as they descended. At the bottom landing, he didn't step out into the courtyard, but instead opened the heavy door to the tunnels.

She giggled when, a moment later, the darkness of the cavern enveloped them and he began kissing her senseless.

"What have you done with my beloved?"

"I could ask you the same thing." She laughed, caressing his cheek and kissing him back. She leaned into his touch as he traced the neckline of the dress and cupped her breast. "I was getting so accustomed to having your beard marks on my skin."

"I can't wait to take this thing off your body. I plan to run my smooth face all over you."

"I'll get rid of Jinny as soon as we get back. I know you and Bryce want to get an early start."

"After the betrothal, we're as good as married. I'm spending the night in your room." He kissed her lips again. "And I don't care who knows."

Before leaving the passageway, he pulled off her gloves and handed them to her.

"We're about to exchange our promises of marriage," he told her, looking into eyes. "I want you to know what's in my mind and in my heart."

When she thought she could not love him more, he surprised her even more.

"I love you, Innes," he whispered.

"And I love you, Conall, more than life and eternity and everything that may lay in between."

His lips claimed hers in a kiss that thrilled her to the depths of her soul. He held her in his arms for few moments longer before taking her by the hand. They moved down the tunnels and climbed the steps into the North Tower.

She was excited, and she knew he was, as well. They'd decided to make their promises to each other after the supper in the Great Hall was long over and the inhabitants of the castle had retired. They had made appearances for the past two nights, but Conall had been reserved, as always. He remained on the fringe of the crowd. He didn't want to be at the center of attention. Innes respected his wishes. She understood it would take time before he realized that his clan did not harbor any ill will against him. But she couldn't tell him. Words were not enough. Conall had to see it and recognize their love on his own.

The Great Hall was empty and in near darkness as they walked through it. Only a low fire burned in the hearth. All was quiet. The two hurried to the door of the laird's reception room, which stood open. Inside, Ailein, Bryce, and Wynda waited with Fingal.

Candles were lit in every corner. Sprigs of rosemary and rosebuds had been woven into a wreath, and Ailein placed it on Innes's head as she kissed her cheeks. Bryce held a strip of Sinclair tartan to be used for their handfasting.

The two faced each other, and Fingal began.

Innes looked up into Conall's eyes as his left hand took her right. Her heart joined with his. She saw in his thoughts more than the words repeated after the priest. She saw the eternity of love—the passion, the promise to cherish and protect her to his last breath. Tears rolled down her cheeks as she gave her consent. Bryce wrapped the tartan around their hands, joining them in the promise of matrimony.

Conall kissed her and for those few moments, no one else existed. It was just the two of them and their love and their promise of a future.

Bryce and Ailein burst in, congratulating them. A smiling Wynda kissed Innes, but then tears rolled down the old woman's cheeks when Conall enfolded her in his arms. Innes knew of Wynda's love, of the loss of her own child, and of how much this man meant to her.

A moment later, they turned to go. But as Bryce swung the door open, a sudden roar erupted and cheers enveloped them. Out in the corridor, all the way to the Great Hall, a crowd of people waved and cheered. For as far as Innes could see, jubilant Highlanders were waiting.

The Sinclairs had arrived to congratulate their earl.

———

Clan Sinclair finally had the opportunity to celebrate

their returned warrior.

As she lay in bed beside him, the event came again before Innes's eyes. It would forever be branded in her memory. Conall moving through his people. Men, women, and children cheering him on, congratulating their earl on the betrothal, and giving him the long overdue hero's welcome.

Walking beside them through the Great Hall, the priest had told Innes that because of the period of unsettled sadness after the death of Shona and the unborn child, there had been no fanfare after Conall's return to the clan. This was the people's first real chance to show their gratitude.

Conall needed this. He needed to realize how much he mattered to these people. He needed to learn that he was the greatest source of pride to them. And he was touched. Innes's hand had been in his. She was witness to the groundswell of emotions within him and around him.

He'd felt as he should feel. Their hero.

Nestled against him now, Innes traced his ear with one finger. She touched the line of his jaw and the beard that was already sprouting. She smiled when he opened his eyes.

"I can't believe I fell sleep," he said.

"This has been an important night for you," she said,

putting her head next to his on the pillow. "Not to mention that you made love to your intended twice already."

"Tradition has it that if a couple has sex after handfasting, they're then married," he said. "So I made love twice to my *wife*."

"Bryce and Ailein will still insist on a wedding. We cannot avoid it. My father will as well. He's a hard and tough man. But I guarantee he'll still cry during the ceremony. I don't think he ever thought he'd be rid of me."

Conall laughed, holding her tight. "I'm going to miss you so much. Are you sure you don't want to forsake that promise to your sister and come with me instead?"

"I think I'm doing this as much for Bryce as for Ailein." She kissed his chest, pressed her lips against his chin. "Just think, the same week you get back, we will be married."

"I've been thinking about where you might want to live after the wedding," he said, caressing her back. "The hunting lodge is mine, but it's not the most protected of places. There's a tower house just south of Wick that we can renovate and make more comfortable. It might be a convenient place, whenever we come north, if that's what we decide on."

She pulled back, looking into his face. He looped her hair around a finger.

"Twice now, since I have been back, the earl of Arran

has sent an emissary with an offer," he said.

"The Regent? The protector of the infant queen Mary?"

He nodded. "He sent the second offer after the burning of Edinburgh last month. He wants me at court."

"Please tell me, not to fight."

"Nay, he wants someone on the council to stand behind him." He traced her lip, looked into her eyes. "I haven't agreed to anything, and I won't, unless you'd be happy living at court, too."

Wynda had told her this would happen. Conall was too valuable to be left alone.

"But we don't have to make any of those decisions now." He gathered her against his chest. "I want to make you happy. And we can always travel."

"I'll be happy wherever you are," she said, meaning it. "I would like to see more of the world, but the urge is not what it was before I met you. And as far as where we live, if you decide to accept the Regent's offer, I can speak for Ailein in saying she'd be overjoyed if we were to spend our time here whenever we are north, especially now that she's with child."

"The same is true with Bryce," he said. "Growing up, our intentions and our interests were always focused on the clan. Neither of us ever cared much about being laird. But regardless of what position I accept, now that my fighting days are over I believe I can be of use to him and to our clan folk."

Innes could not find enough words to express her relief at Conall's acknowledgment that his fighting days were over. And as far as being at court, she'd spent much of her life shying away from a public life. But at her husband's side, she'd go to the end of the world. She'd do anything to help him heal the wounds of Solway Moss and his year in captivity.

"Can I bring you back anything from Folais Castle?" Conall asked.

Innes thought about his journey ahead. "When you arrive, please bring the chronicle back with you. That account should be with me now. I'll write a letter to my father and explain. He'll understand."

He looked into her face. "You told me there are other stones like yours out there."

"Mine is one of four pieces of the wheel. Each fragment holds a different power. Like me, each bearer carries the gift until death. Then the stone transfers it to whoever possesses the piece."

"Different powers? How so?"

Innes never had a chance to explain any of this to him the day she'd told him about the relic. "One stone heals wounds. It can even bring a person back from the shadows of death, from the very gates of the next world. The second empowers the bearer to speak to the dead. The person possessing it can raise a soul and speak to them no matter how long the dead have been at rest. The third stone bearer can see into the future. You know what I can do. But I am also the keeper of the past. I keep the chronicle. I doubt that any of the others who hold the pieces of the wheel know the disaster that awaits if the four fragments are reconnected again."

He caressed her hair. "And you fear that."

"You know man's nature. The greed, the selfishness, the insatiable need for power. Can you imagine if one of these pieces were to fall into the wrong hands?"

"Do you have any knowledge of who holds the other pieces?"

"None at all. But when you bring back the chronicle, I want you to read it. The first entries refer to the men who held each stone fifty years ago," she said. "They took them far away to keep them safe."

"With the exception of them coming together, or a chance of discovery, is there anything else to fear?"

"I fear the stone that can raise the dead. There is no end to the power of the man or woman who possesses it." She shivered. "Can you imagine, an army of the dead?"

For days, Sir Ralph Evers's troops had been combing Easter Ross, the foothills of Ben Wyvis, and the lands north of Moray Firth. Farms had been pillaged, cottagers interrogated, but they had come up with nothing. No word of the Munro woman. Until now.

Word had reached Evers near Cromarty Firth that three young Highlanders were running their mouths about a 'witch' who could read a man's mind and see into his past.

Finding the men took only a day.

A short distance upriver, thick smoke and sparks billowed high into the black sky from the burning farm cottage. The family living there claimed to know nothing about any Munro witch or about the men who'd been hiding in their sheepcote and escaped on foot when the soldiers arrived. They paid dearly for their ignorance.

"Two of 'em run off into the night, Sir Ralph," the soldier said nervously, trying to avoid the steely gaze of his commander. "This one drowned trying to get across the river. He's dead, m'lord."

Sitting astride his black steed, Evers looked down at the dead Highlander stretched out on the bank of the river and then at his four soldiers squirming behind the body.

Evers waved them away. "Go back to the farm and wait for me."

The men needed no more persuasion and immediately disappeared into the darkness.

Sir Ralph Evers dismounted and approached the body. Holes in the back of the jerkin indicated that more than the river was responsible for the boy's death. Evers touched the pouch at his belt and kicked the body until the corpse rolled on its back.

He looked at the freshly killed face. The Highlander's vacant eyes dully reflected the full moon climbing into the black Scottish sky.

In a tower fort in the Borders, Evers had conjured the spirit of the old man Cairns. On the church altar in the Lowlands, he'd raised the dead abbot and learned the secrets of their treasure vaults. He'd even conjured up the ghost of the long dead Red Comyn. They were powerless before him.

Evers had forced from them what he wanted to know. He would do the same here.

"Rise," he ordered.

Before him, something stirred in the body of the dead Highlander. A wisp of smoke emanated from the corpse, and then the shape of the young man formed, rising and hovering over its former self. The spirit stared at Evers.

"Tell me about the witch."

There was no hesitation in his response. "She took hold of Jock's hand, and she knew everything of his past. She read his mind. She knew where we lived. She knew his secrets."

"Aye. That's the one. She's a Munro. This is Munro land. Tell me where she's hiding."

"*I know nothing of her being a Munro, only that we saw her.*"

"*Where?*"

"*On Sinclair land. She was with an old crone who said she spoke for the laird.*"

"*What laird? Those lands are extensive.*"

"*Girnigoe,*" the spirit told him. "*She's at the castle at Girnigoe.*"

Chapter 26

FOLAIS CASTLE

The laird's receiving room was a snug, comfortable affair with French tapestries on the wall, a map of the German Sea, and displays of ancient swords and weaponry. Conall sat in a Spanish chair of elaborately carved oak strategically placed in front of a cozy wood fire. Hector Munro sat in a matching chair.

"I'm grateful for the hospitality you've shown me and my brother. I need to apologize again for not receiving you at Ailein's wedding to Bryce," said Conall.

"Let's say no more about that. I'm happy that my lass is well settled," Hector said with a satisfied look. "And I'm even happier to hear all this about you and my Innes."

"Aye, she's brought about changes already, I can tell you."

Hector looked into the fire for a moment before beginning again. "I suggested that your brother go off to see our new cannons in the gun house because I wanted to speak with you alone."

Conall expected this. Innes was a precious gem and he'd make any assurance the baron needed to ease his mind about his daughter's happiness.

"You said already that we shan't worry about her dowry," said Hector. "It isn't that . . . though she'll come with her fortune, as Ailein has."

Conall began to speak, but the Munro laird waved him off.

"Our time is short, and I need to ask you something." Hector's gaze fixed on his face. "Has she told you of the . . . of the added responsibilities that fall to you as her husband?"

"She has," he replied. "I know of her special gift, and the stone, and she told me that we are to carry back the chronicle that she received from her mother."

The baron was clearly relieved as he leaned back in the chair. "Innes said as much in the letter you brought, but I needed to hear it from your own mouth."

"I've vowed to protect her," Conall said. "You can be assured that I mean to do it."

"I know you will. You're a fine man and a fine warrior. As I said, I'm happy that Innes has found you and you her. She could do no better if she searched out the entire world. Our families are now knitted together for eternity."

"She is the finest of women," he said. "I'm a fortunate man."

"Aye. I feel that way about her myself. I shall miss her here at my side, believe me. And until now, I thought I'd have her counsel till I'm old and gray."

"She says your son Robert will be at your side soon. By all accounts, he's a fine lad."

Hector looked happily into the fire for a moment and then called for a servant, who opened the door and looked in.

"Bring in our other guests," the Munro ordered. Seeing the question on Conall's face, he explained. "Some people have come looking for Innes. I know them, and I trust them. Their mission here is of some urgency . . . and it concerns you now."

Before he could explain further, the door opened, and the two men stood.

"Let me introduce you to Alexander Macpherson and his wife, Kenna MacKay."

While the Sinclairs served the crown with their swords and their lives on land, the Macphersons were a force to reckon with at sea. Conall knew by reputation the commander of the Macpherson ships and future laird, but this was the first time they'd met. For generations, those ships had ruled the Western Sea, terrorizing the English coast and growing rich from the Spanish gold being plundered in the New World.

Alexander Macpherson was tall and muscular, but he moved with the smooth power of a large cat. He had the clear eye and steady hand of a warrior. And his protectiveness of his young wife showed; he stayed within arm's length of her at all times.

Hector Munro wasn't much for ceremony. He pushed them past the pleasantries and explained Conall's knowledge of the relic before arriving at what mattered most: the danger to Innes.

"I was hunted," Kenna told them. "My husband and I were chased through the Western Highlands by English soldiers and Scots Lowlanders. They serve a man named Sir Ralph Evers."

"Evers," Conall broke in. "I know the man. He's a butcher and a marauder. He's terrorized the Borders in the name of the Tudor king."

"He's broken free of his master now and he's come north," Kenna continued. "He's been cutting a bloody swath through Scotland to get his hands on the remaining stones."

"He has two of them that we know of," Alexander explained. "One belonged to an old man named Cairns. He was one of the original four who were shipwrecked with the relic."

"And the second?" Conall asked.

"He has Kenna's stone."

Conall recalled Innes's words. The power of the relics and how they transferred was fresh in his mind.

"But the power remains with you," he said. "And it will always stay with you."

"Unless he kills me," Kenna responded, moving to Alexander's side. "And my husband can attest to the attempts."

The Macphersons knew Innes had the relic. This meant so could Evers. Conall's mind immediately turned to Innes's safety. Before he left, she'd promised to not venture out of Girnigoe without an escort. But that wasn't enough. Villagers, travelers, merchants, strangers arrived at the castle daily. Any of them could be an agent of Evers. He had to get back to her.

"Which of the stones does he have so far?" Conall asked.

"I had the healing stone," Kenna told him. "Cairns died under torture. His power of speaking to the dead lies with Evers now."

"We believe that Innes will be his next target," Alexander asserted. "Although the baron here insists that his daughter's secret has been well kept, the rumor is out there and it has spread. The same thing happened with Kenna."

"We know Evers now has Innes's name," she added. "We have no doubt that he is coming for her."

Chapter 27

Innes and Ailein followed the steward through the chapel into the dimly lit oratory. Fingal was standing by the door, murmuring in Latin and taking the stopper from a bottle of holy oil. The sight of the priest confirmed the information Lachlan conveyed to them on the way there. Fingal was preparing to give the sacrament of extreme unction.

"The poor creature . . . stabbed and beaten and . . . and worse . . . then left for dead," Wynda told them, her voice faltering.

"When did they find her?" Innes asked, grief taking hold of her heart. "And where?"

"Around noon, on the way to the village at Keiss. Not an hour's walk north of here." Wynda looked at the young woman, who was breathing with difficulty. "The animal that did this just left her to die."

Ailein touched the aunt's arm and leaned over the injured. A blanket covered her battered body.

"Do you know her?" Ailein asked.

"Aye, she's one of our own," Wynda said. "Her name is Dona. She works in the kitchens. Brought her daughter

333

here last year to help, as well. Every fortnight or so, the two of them walk back to their village to check on her folks. The mother's crippled and they're both aging. Dona and her daughter left yesterday. That's the last anyone saw of them . . . until today."

Innes approached the table where they'd laid the woman.

The eyes were closed, but the eyelids fluttered as she moaned weakly. Her breathing was growing more labored with every passing moment. Innes guessed her suffering would not last much longer.

"Have you found the daughter?" she asked.

"Our men are searching along the coast," Lachlan put in. "They've been to the village. There's no sign of her yet."

"Does this happen often?" Innes asked.

"Never," Wynda answered firmly. She did not look away from the dying woman. "But what of the daughter? I can't stop thinking what might have happened to her. Just ten years of age. A happy lass, she is. Eager to please. She loves . . . loved . . . working alongside her mum."

"And the husband?" Ailein asked.

"Dead," Lachlan replied. "A fisherman. Drowned two summers ago."

Wynda picked up Dona's hand, caressing the fingers.

"We have womenfolk out traveling the countryside all

the time," Lachlan added. "They'll all be afraid to venture out their door if we don't find out who did this."

Innes slowly removed her gloves. She saw her sister reach out to stop her, but Innes shook her head. She knew what she was doing. Dona was the victim of a vicious beating. She'd been stabbed and violated. Touching the woman's hand, all that pain would become hers. She'd relive the horror of it all if that's what was in Dona's mind right now.

Innes moved around to the other side of the table, drew up a stool, and sat down. "What's the daughter's name?"

"Cari," Wynda told her.

"Cari," Innes repeated softly, leaning close to the woman's face. "Where is Cari, my sweet? Where is your daughter?"

"I don't believe she can hear you," Wynda said, wiping away a tear. "That poor lass. What did they do to the wee thing? Throw her into the sea?"

Innes put her lips close to Dona's ear. "Where is Cari? Can you tell us where she is?"

Ailein hurried around to stand behind her. Her sister had seen this before. Innes could cry out, show the pain on her face. Ailein was trying to set herself up as a shield between Innes and everyone else in the room.

"Has anyone spoken to the parents?" Ailein asked.

"Aye," Lachlan spoke up. "The old man is out with the men searching for his granddaughter."

Innes reached for Dona's hand and put her ear to the woman's lips. "Where is Cari?"

She gasped in pain as the man kicked her in the stomach. She looked up at the faces. She saw how they'd arrived at the shore. Another man's fist connected with her jaw. She fell to the ground and raised herself on weak arms, seeing her daughter. *Run, Cari, run.*

Moments later, someone forced Innes's grip away from Dona's. Innes sat back on the stool shaking, her chin dropped to her chest. Ailein leaned over her, sheltering her from the other three in the oratory. She'd put an end to it.

Tears fell from Innes's cheeks. She tried with difficulty to draw the curtain of discretion around her.

"I'm sorry," Wynda said gently.

Innes looked up. The older woman understood. She'd guessed what Innes had just gone through.

Wynda looked around, aware of their audience and continued. "Here, with your wedding nearly upon you, you should be seeing only the best of us. But I want you to know this is not who the Sinclairs are. This had to be the act of an outsider."

"It wasn't one man," Innes whispered. "There were two of them. And they *were* outsiders. Lowlanders. They had a boat."

Wynda stood up, looking down at the unconscious woman.

"She spoke to you?" the priest asked.

Innes glanced at him. "She whispered to me."

"And Cari? Did she say anything of the lass?" Wynda asked.

"The *old fortress*. She was running to hide there."

"Is there an old fortress near the place?" Ailein asked.

"Aye," Lachlan put in. "Not far to the north of it. We just call it that. It's a crumbling ruin of who knows what."

Dona died only minutes after Fingal finished administering the last rites, anointing her forehead and seven other places on her body.

After it was over and the two sisters had returned to the East Tower, Innes lay quaking in Ailein's arms late into the night. Touching the suffering woman had thrown her into a chaotic and tortured world. She could not push the horrors out of her mind. Over and over, she relived the young woman's terror and pain as the men attacked her. But thankfully, a sense of relief occasionally crept in at the thought of seeing Cari run away to safety.

Dona had told her where her daughter had gone as if she *knew* Innes was listening.

Violence, especially against women, was the hardest for Innes to bear. When she experienced those memories, she was only a helpless observer. She couldn't fight. She could only witness the horror... and feel it. She was fortunate that she'd not touched many minds with that kind of past. But of those that she had experienced, Dona's was the worst.

Finally, very late, one of Bryce's warriors knocked on her door to tell them that Cari had been found, terrified but unharmed. They had taken her to the cottage of the grandparents in the village.

Ailein left her then, and Innes tried to sleep. But every time she dozed off, the faces of those who attacked Dona appeared in her mind, and she sat up in a cold sweat.

She couldn't wait until Conall returned. She recalled his warnings, their argument on the strand about the hazards of this very same thing. How many mornings and evenings had she walked along the bluffs, not paying any attention to the dangers lurking around her?

At dawn, she finally dressed and went to the West Tower. Thunder greeted her happily. Like her, the wolf missed Conall badly. She would have slept there to keep him company, but she didn't want to complicate things for her sister. Besides, Conall would be back soon enough.

She took the wolf down onto the stony beach, but the

morning mists were thick, so they stayed close to the castle walls.

It was still very early when she left Thunder with Duff. Walking out of the stable yard, she was about to cross the drawbridge when Lachlan, driving his cart, reined in next to her.

"Morning, m'lady," he said, touching his cap. "Heard the good news?"

"What is it?"

"We found the two men. Sailors from a merchant ship put in for repair."

Dona was dead, but this way more lives would be saved. "That is good news, Lachlan. I'm very relieved."

"It's a good thing all around, I'd say."

"Does my sister know?"

"Aye. Told her myself. In fact, I've just come back from taking her to the village. Wanted to see the lass and give her condolences to the old folk. She sent me to fetch you and bring you there."

Reaching out to her, the steward took hold of her gloved hand and helped her into the cart. With a flick of the reins, they were off a good clip through the morning mists, with Lachlan chatting about the planting of the crops and the sheep shearing and castle business. He even talked about the upcoming wedding.

"This is an early morning for my sister," Innes broke in

sometime later. "Did Wynda go with her?"

"Aye. And Fingal came along on his old mare as well. They all need to decide what to do about the lassie, I suppose."

So many of Wynda's routines required her to be about the kitchens in the mornings, Innes thought. It was curious that she wouldn't wait until the afternoon to make this visit. And Ailein had been throwing up every morning since Bryce and Conall left. These early weeks of pregnancy were difficult ones for her.

Innes turned to the steward. "Did you take all of them to the village yourself?"

"Aye, that I did. With the priest riding alongside."

"How did my sister fare on the cart?"

"Fare?" Lachlan looked at her in surprise. "Why, no problem at all. Except for the business of the lassie, we talked about the wedding nearly the whole way."

Innes's gaze lingered on the steward before looking away. She had never come this far north of Castle Girnigoe. To the right of the narrow cart path, the cliffs dropped off sharply to the sea. The rolling waves broke and crashed on the rocks below. The mists swirled around the cart, and Innes regretted not taking the time to grab her cloak before they left.

"When did you go down to Wick?" she asked.

"Wick? I've been there thrice these past eight . . . ten

days, I'd say. A busy time of year, it is. And of course, the merchant ships are dropping anchor now fairly regular. I was there just yesterday morning. Why do you ask, m'lady?"

"The men who were captured. Have you seen them?"

"Nay. I haven't."

"How do you know they're the right people? Did they confess?"

"Why, I think . . ." The steward looked over his shoulder and flicked the reins, encouraging the horse to quicken the pace. "I think we'll just get along to the village."

A knot of anxiety formed in Innes's stomach. She looked ahead; she looked back. They'd seen no one since starting out. Still, she wanted to be sure she was worrying for no reason.

"Did my sister mention that she wanted you to take us to Wick this afternoon?"

The steward thought for a moment. "Aye. That she did. Wanted to go sometime after midday."

Anxiety turned to cold dread. He was lying. They'd made no such plans.

Innes stared down at her gloved hands gripping the seat. She let go and pulled off the gloves.

"Don't," he said harshly. "I know who you are. I know what you can do. I saw it with my own eyes last night in that oratory." Lachlan glared. "You'll not be touching me with those hands."

"It's not what you think," she said, trying to stay calm. What did he think, that she was a witch? And where was he taking her?

"I know exactly what to think. I heard it in Wick."

"What did you hear? Who has been talking about me?"

"The word is out. I didn't believe it at first, but I believe it now."

"What word?"

"Everyone knows it. There are men looking up and down the coast. Lowlanders and even Englishmen, looking for a woman from Clan Munro. They say she's a witch. She has a magic relic given her by Satan himself. She can turn a person into stone if he looks into her eyes."

"Lachlan, you know me. Have I turned anyone to stone? Do you really believe any of that foolishness?" she asked.

The steward said nothing. And then the sickening truth dawned on her. "You're taking me to them."

He flicked the reins again.

"But why? Please don't tell me it's for gold."

When he didn't deny it, Innes knew she'd guessed right.

"But you seem so happy," she said. "You have a good

position. You want for nothing."

The man's hard gaze snapped at her. "I saw what you did last night, mistress. You touched Dona's hand and read her mind."

"That's true. It's a gift I possess. But I don't use it. Haven't you seen me always wearing a glove?"

"It's too late, m'lady. You'd know and I'd be dead."

"Know what?"

"You'd know I've done the Sinclairs wrong for years. Taking a little here. Putting away a little there. But you're to be the earl's wife, and there will be no hiding anything from you." He shook his head, like he'd fought a battle with his conscience and lost already. "I can't risk it."

"Lachlan, I have more wealth than anything those people can pay you. If you stop now, I can keep your secret."

"Nay. I can't. It's too late." He reined in his horse and the cart rolled to a stop. "They're waiting for us. Waiting for you."

Before she could reply, a group of men climbed into view from the cliff edge. More men came toward the cart from behind a small rise.

It took only an instant for her to take it all in.

The mail shirts they wore were like the ones she'd seen in Dona's mind. Two of these men had attacked and killed the young woman. She was certain of it.

A cloaked rider spurred his steed up a steep path leading down to the sea. More men waited by two longboats on the rocky beach below.

Cold sweat ran down her back.

The end had come.

Chapter 28

"My days are nearly finished. I thank the Virgin for giving me a man I could trust. I could not give him a son, but Hector has protected my secret, as well as my life and the lives of my two daughters. I only pray that my precious daughter Innes grows to have the strength and wit to preserve this gift that I pass on to her. I grow weaker. I have more to tell her. I must finish my writing here . . ."

From the *Chronicle of Lugh*

The commander nudged his black steed forward to the cart. This man was no Highlander, of that Innes was certain. As he came closer, from beneath his leather cloak he drew a long sword from its sheath.

Lachlan stood up in the cart and bowed slightly. "As I promised, m'lord, I've brought the woman you seek."

The rider's eyes locked on her face for a moment, then flicked to the pouch at her waist. Lachlan had delivered what these people were after.

They didn't just want her. They wanted the relic.

"You promised a reward of English gold, and I trust that a gentleman such as—"

The commander's sword whispered through the air, and Lachlan stood frozen in time as the blade swept toward him.

The steward's blood spattered her as his head tumbled onto the ground.

Innes wasn't going to die like a dog. Not sitting still. Springing out of the cart, she lifted her skirts and sprinted back in the direction they came.

"Go after her," the commander shouted. "Bring her to me."

She knew what these people were capable of. She saw what they did to Dona. And now Lachlan. With her, it would be worse. Far worse. She might not outrun them, but she'd die before surrendering.

Conall and the group traveling from Folais Castle were still a mile from Girnigoe when a dozen Sinclair warriors galloped up to meet them. Conall's worst fears came true as soon as one of them spoke.

"Lady Innes is missing."

They were still on Munro land when they heard the stories of Englishmen and Lowlanders being seen in the hills. But after all that the Macphersons told them, Conall knew who these men were and what they were looking for. Sir Ralph Evers would not waste his time on Munro land once he learned where Innes would be.

Cold fear washed through him. He had to find her. Get to her. He'd led so many men into so many battles. He'd never allowed fear to paralyze him when action was needed. And he wouldn't now, even though his fear for Innes's life made it hard for him to think.

"Where was she last seen?"

"In the stable yard," the Sinclair warrior reported. "Lachlan is missing, too, m'lord. But we don't know if the two left together or if someone's taken her. A woman from the castle was killed yesterday . . . by Lowlanders."

"Enough," he ordered. "Ride with me."

Spurring his horse, he galloped ahead as the Sinclairs raced to keep up, shouting answers to Conall's questions. As far as anyone knew, Lachlan hadn't planned to be away from the castle. Others coming back from Wick confirmed that they hadn't seen the steward there or on the road.

Conall slowed his steed only when he rode into the stable yard. Bryce and the Macphersons reined in right behind him. Innes's father and her family would be arriving in a few days.

Ailein ran out across the bridge into the stable yard as they dismounted.

347

"Innes isn't here. She's not in the castle," she told Conall and Bryce, panic evident in her voice. "We've looked everywhere. Someone took her. I'm sure of it."

"Duff!" Conall shouted up at the windows of the West Tower. "Bring Thunder."

Perhaps, he prayed, his wolf could find her scent and show them the way. He knew he was grasping at straws, but what other chance did they have? Evers hadn't taken Innes for ransom. From what Kenna MacKay told him, the Englishman would kill her as soon as he had his hands on the relic.

Duff barreled out of the West Tower with Thunder pulling at a short leather lead. As soon as the wolf saw Conall, he yanked free and raced to him.

"Innes," Conall told the excited wolf, trying to undo the leash. But the animal was too excited to remain still. "Find Innes."

Thunder darted off through the gates, and Conall leaped onto his horse in pursuit.

Innes stood with her back to the cliffs. The mists swirled around her. A dozen filthy soldiers hemmed her in.

The commander barked his order and they rushed forward. She turned to leap from the edge, but she hesitated.

She couldn't. And then they had her... and the stone she'd received from her dying mother's hand.

Pain cut into the deepest core of her being. She'd failed. Her sworn duty was to protect this tablet, and she'd failed. When the rider produced two more pieces of the Wheel of Lugh and fit her fragment together with them, something died within her. She knew there could be no escaping her fate now. But unlike the others in the chronicle, unlike those women who died to protect it, she... Innes Munro... simply gave it up into the hands of monsters who raped and killed the innocent and the defenseless. Guilt ripped at her heart.

And what of Conall? What of the love they had just found? Would he ever even know what became of her?

A movement drew her gaze to the top of the rise behind these killers.

Thunder.

The Englishman nodded to his men. "Kill her. I want to see her dead."

The Lowlander holding Innes by the hair jerked her head up and raised his knife to cut her throat.

Before the blade could leave its lethal mark, a flash of gray fury was upon the man, knocking him from her and ripping open his face.

Over and over, Thunder attacked the head and neck as the warrior screamed. Stunned by the sudden ferocity of the beast's assault, the other men staggered back a step. That was all Innes needed.

Picking up the fallen knife, she slashed at the closest warrior's face. The man spun away, howling in pain. But before she could bolt through the opening, the others snapped out of their stupor. One of them grabbed her wrist, and wrenched the knife from her.

Thunder's shrieking yelps yanked her head around. A soldier was pulling his sword from side of the writhing wolf even as another raised his weapon to finish the animal.

"NO!" she screamed, ripping her wrist free and diving forward.

She landed on the wolf as the sword point descended, thrusting into her. Hot as molten metal, it cut straight through flesh and bone. Her breath caught in her chest, and the searing pain inside of her radiated outward from the blade, scorching her until something snapped in her head and there was no more pain.

Suddenly, pounding hooves were directly in front of her. The clanging sound of sword blades mixed with the grunts and cries of wounded men. The horse moved away a foot, a yard, and then she saw her fierce defender.

Conall, driving the men back with ferocious rage, his sword swinging as their foes fell away before him.

And beyond the fray, she saw others coming over the rise.

The mounted commander saw them, too. She watched him spur his horse back toward the cart before disappearing down the path to the beach.

———————

Conall slashed at anything that moved around him. With blind fury driving him, he carved through the animals that dared to touch her.

The dead and dying littered the cliff top by the time Bryce and the others reached him. It was a miracle that Conall recognized his brother before attacking him as well.

Throwing down his sword, Conall leapt off his horse and ran to Innes. Her body lay against the panting, bloodied wolf. Her head rested against his heart.

"Conall," she said softly. "The leader. He has the stones."

"Never mind that, my love. Let me look at you."

Blood was flowing freely from the gaping hole beneath her breast, and his soul withered within him. He'd seen such wounds before. He knew that she . . . he knew . . .

She turned weakly to clutch at the wolf's fur. "Thunder. He saved me." She looked back at him. "You saved me."

Bryce was shouting as he ran up to them. "Alexander has gone after Evers. He has two boats on the beach, but . . ." He stopped and then murmured. "Oh, God."

Conall didn't look up at his brother. His eyes were fixed on his beloved. Her face was growing more ashen with each passing moment, her breathing growing shallower.

A figure suddenly appeared and put a hand on his shoulder.

"Let me help," Kenna said gently, kneeling down beside him.

Innes looked up at the face of the brown-haired woman silhouetted against the sky. She didn't know her, but she was offering her help.

Innes had known severe pain in the past, touching others. But this was different. With this stab wound, the metal drove through her, taking her breath away, making her vision grow suddenly sharp. This time there was no possibility of taking her hand away and finding relief. This was death.

She continued to caress Thunder. His blood and hers were soaking the sandy ground beneath them. She wanted to talk. She wanted to pretend that she was fine, for Conall's sake, but she couldn't. Her lifeblood had once filled a jar, but this wound cracked the vessel, and her time on earth was draining away. Others moved around her, but she couldn't see them. She didn't have enough strength to turn around. She was losing her ability to focus. The end was here. Death was upon her.

"I'm Kenna MacKay," the woman whispered, crouching down next to her.

Innes heard Conall's voice. "Tell me what to do."

"Hold her. Comfort her."

He sat himself behind her, pulling her gently against his chest. She saw Thunder try to lift his head. The wolf looked briefly at his master before laying his head back down.

"Do I know you?" Innes asked the woman.

"Nay, but we're sisters, of sorts." Kenna took her hand, and their skin immediately warmed. The sensation ran between their fingers, and she saw into Kenna's mind.

"You," she said. "The healing stone. But you've lost it, too."

"We'll talk about that later. First, let me see to you."

"Thunder. The wolf." She caressed the animal lying by her. "You cannot let him die."

"I'll help him if I can. But for now, close your eyes."

Conall's lips brushed against her hair, her temple. He whispered words of love and encouragement in her ear. Innes pressed her face against his heart, listening to the strong beat.

"I love you," she whispered. "The few days we've had together have been the happiest of my life."

"And we have the rest of our lives, my love."

Kenna's fingers skimmed over Innes's wound. With feathery touches, she moved her hand around the bloody gash and over it. Innes closed her eyes, giving herself over to the heat that emanated from the other woman's hand, and losing herself in Conall's whispers of affection.

She'd lost the stone. The man possessing it now had three of the four pieces. She wanted to mourn the tragedy of failing her mother in losing the relic. And she kept thinking of Lachlan. The steward's words repeated themselves in her mind. He'd stolen for years. And he had been willing to kill—or have someone kill for him—to avoid discovery. This was the truth about the knowledge of secrets. Everyone had them; many would destroy her to keep them hidden.

She wanted to focus on the dangers still around them, but her mind continued to pull toward the other woman and her touch. Kenna, she said her name was. Her power ran through Innes, making her mind release all the tension, all the fears. Her body followed.

The heat spread through her limbs, centering on the wound. The pulsing blood slowly decreased. Innes opened her eyes. Kenna appeared to be almost in a trance. Her fingers continued to move over the wound.

Innes reached up, her fingers brushing against Kenna's. There was no change in the woman's awareness, no interruption of the ritual. But as she touched Kenna's hand, Innes realized Kenna was hovering, suspended within something Innes had never before experienced. It was an intangible, spiritual otherworld. Kenna existed at this moment within the infinite soul of healing. Innes heard the echoes of voices speaking in different tongues. She saw ancient faces appear, then flicker and fade and become someone else. And she knew this all had to do with the relic. The stone had been stolen from Kenna, but she still embodied the power.

The pain's departure came quickly. It faded suddenly, like the memory of a dream. Innes realized she'd stopped bleeding. She looked at her clothes; the tear in the fabric and the bloody stain made the wound appear worse than it actually was. Shapes became people, and faces came into focus.

A huge, blond-haired man was crouched protectively behind the young woman. Some moments passed before Kenna opened her eyes. Their gazes locked.

"Your gift is a blessing. Thank you," Innes whispered. Her fingers were still resting on Thunder. "Can you heal him, too?"

Kenna smiled, moving over to the animal. "A first time for me, mending a wolf."

Chapter 29

Innes was confined to her bedroom, not because of any pain or need for rest, but to give the appearance of recovery. Kenna and her power needed protection as well.

The Sinclair warriors following Conall and Bryce had seen all the blood she'd lost on the cliffs. Kenna shared Innes's fear of other people knowing about her power. The difference was that Innes had known about it early on; Kenna had only discovered her gift this year.

Kenna and Alexander Macpherson would stay for the wedding, and Innes was glad. There was so much the two women needed to talk about.

"The stone sat for many years among some other gifts left to me by my mother after her death," Kenna explained on one of her visits to Innes's room. "I only found it when I was about to marry. Even then, I didn't know what it meant or what I could do with it until months had passed. I had no one to teach me. My father told me later that my mother didn't think it would be fair to place that much responsibility on a child."

Innes laughed and touched the band of white in her

hair. "This is what happens when you're told at age seven. A quick end to childhood."

Kenna smiled. "Both of our mothers thought what they were doing was right."

"Aye. There's not much point in second-guessing them," Innes said. "Conall told me you finished reading the chronicle and returned it to him."

Kenna nodded with a frown. "A fascinating account, but terrifying to know that Evers now has three fragments of the Wheel. I still have so many questions."

"That makes the two of us."

"Alexander is still furious the Englishman escaped."

"It doesn't make our situation, or our families' situation, any easier. And thank you for confiding in Ailein about your gift. She's known the other stones were out there for a long time."

Kenna's response was cut off by a knock on the door, followed by Jinny's appearance.

The older serving woman looked worriedly at Innes. "Your sister says that if you promise to take it easy, you can leave the room and walk in the Inner Ward with his lordship."

Innes tried to hide her delight at finally going out. "Does Conall know this?"

"Aye. That he does. He and your husband are waiting downstairs now, m'lady." Jinny nodded to Kenna. "And they have that wolf with them. Before the day you went missing, I didn't see much use in keeping such a dangerous beast. But you should have seen it. The way he tore up that coast road after you, he looked like he'd run through the gates of Hell and take on Satan's legions to rescue you."

"He practically did." Innes would never forget Thunder's attack on her captors... nor Conall's, either. Her heroes.

Conall had Thunder on a short leather lead and was standing with Alexander Macpherson when the two women stepped out. Innes's eyes drank in the sight of Conall in his white shirt, kilt, and boots. She couldn't stop the tremors of excitement that raced through her every time she saw him. Because of the arrival of her family, along with the influx of other guests, they'd had no time alone together, not even after everyone retired for the night. The floor above her was now used for guests—and that's where her father and Margaret and the boys were staying. After the wedding nothing, she swore, would stop them from sharing the same bed.

The wolf jumped up on seeing her, lunging to get to her.

"I'll be getting one of these for you," Alexander told his wife, "as soon as we get back to Benmore Castle."

"But I already have a courageous beast of my own,"

Kenna said, looping an arm through her husband's. "Mine is a lion."

The two of them made a striking pair. Innes had heard bits and pieces from Kenna about their rocky courtship. The young woman ran away right after her wedding. Then, six months later, her own husband kidnapped her. And that coincided with the appearance of Evers and his butchering minions, who chased them through the Highlands. Looking at them now, Innes found it nearly impossible to believe they'd ever been at odds.

Conall pulled Innes into his arms and kissed her—not caring in the slightest that they had an audience.

Still enjoying the embrace, she noticed the additional armed Sinclair warriors. They were everywhere, on top of the walls, in the courtyard, by the passageway to the Outer Ward.

"Are you expecting an attack?" she asked Conall.

"Nay, but we want to be prepared."

"This is also the way at Benmore Castle now," Alexander Macpherson told her. "Since Evers took the stone from Kenna just over a month ago, we've had four attempts on her life. And that doesn't include those who decided to take *our* gold instead of his and not go through with their plans."

"They really are trying to kill you." Innes voiced what she already knew, but it suddenly became very real, seeing the warriors. "Evers has the stones. It's the only way he can get the power."

Kenna nodded. "And he'll do the same thing to you now."

"And now we've learned our lesson that he doesn't need an army. He simply offers gold." Conall was still holding Innes in his arms while Thunder sat attentively at their feet. "Lachlan was a trusted kinsman. See how easily he was persuaded."

"Aye, all it takes is an archer with good aim," Alexander told them. "Someone working in the kitchen who knows which trencher of food is yours. With a price on your heads, Evers need never approach you himself."

"It is not death that worries me, but I have no desire to live in fear for those I love," Innes said. "We cannot allow him to govern our lives."

"Alexander and Kenna are going to stay the sennight following the wedding. I believe we have more decisions to make before they leave," Conall told her. "But right now Bryce and Ailein are waiting for us in his receiving room. If you'll excuse us."

As they walked away from the couple, Innes turned to him. "Did you tell Bryce about the stone, as I asked? Is this why he wants to talk to us?"

Innes already knew how damaging rumors could be. It was essential that her brother-in-law, as laird, know the trouble she'd brought to his door and to his clan. Knowing the truth would also help him understand Lachlan's betrayal.

"Aye. I told him," Conall said. "He didn't say straight out that he already knew, but I have a feeling he and your sister will not be ones for hiding things from each other."

She was relieved. And she absolutely understood her sister's decision to tell Bryce. While Innes still had possession of the relic, Ailein was the one who would have inherited it. It was important for Bryce to know.

"Do you know then why he wants to see us?"

"It's Wynda who asked to see us," he told her. "You, me, Bryce, and Ailein. She said it's urgent that she talk to all of us today."

———

When the four of them and the wolf joined her in the receiving room, Wynda closed the door, shutting out the din coming from the Great Hall. She'd been searching for words, but memories kept intruding on her thoughts, distracting her from her purpose.

Even now, seeing their faces brought a surge of emotion in her. Thinking back to that day when she returned, she recalled the exact moment when Conall and Bryce changed her life. Sadness that had become a part of the fabric of her exis-

tence had suddenly been replaced by unexpected joy. Wynda looked at her boys, now strapping and powerful men. She looked as well at the two Munro sisters, so clearly in love with them.

For the past sennight, Castle Girnigoe had been brimming with anticipation of the upcoming wedding and the festivities surrounding it, but another feeling lay like a shadow around them. Shame lay just beneath every smile. Shame that the dead steward had brought to their door.

The castle folk did not know all of it—they only knew he had betrayed his trust as steward—but Wynda knew the depth of his betrayal. In the oratory that night, Lachlan and Fingal both saw what Wynda already knew: the stunning power that Innes wielded.

For all her years working with Lachlan and Fingal, Wynda didn't know their secrets. And she had no idea to what extent the steward would go to avoid exposure. No one could, but it hurt her nonetheless.

Secrets. Wynda had secrets. And they were festering inside of her.

How strange then, Wynda thought, that she saw Innes not as a threat to her, but as her salvation. She would tell the truth, and live with the judgment brought on by exposure . . . or die with it. But she would do it of her own free will; she would not live in fear of Innes's power. She welcomed it and blessed the lass for it. She met the young woman's gray eyes.

What did she see in them? Kindness. Concern.

She turned to Conall and Bryce. This was their story, too, as much as her own. Hearing it from her lips would bring . . . what? Pain? Anger? Perhaps. But also a sense of salvation, she hoped, from a past that had to be haunting the edges of their lives.

"*I was there, that day, in Shona's room when she died,*" *she began.*

All eyes locked on her.

"*Wynda,*" *Conall said, trying to stop her.* "*We don't need to speak of this. The past is behind us.*"

"*Nay, it isn't. Not yet.*" *She shook her head.* "*Let me have my say. I need to get this out into the sunlight.*"

She waited until both men nodded.

Wynda addressed Bryce directly. "*When you left Girnigoe to go bring your brother home, Shona became wild. I know you saw that even before you left. Her world was coming apart. Conall was alive. When she thought he was dead, she married you. Destined to be Countess Caithness and wife of the clan chief. But now, you were going to free him and bring him home. She was afraid you would relinquish your position to Conall, as you said you would do. She knew she was about to lose it all.*"

"*That's true. We argued about it before I left.*"

"*But she didn't stop,*" *Wynda told them.* "*You were barely out the castle gates and she started again. She badgered who-*"

ever would listen. She complained to clan elders and stable lads. To scullery lasses and cotters' wives. She thought she could divide the clan. She pretended that she spoke for you, insisting that you wanted a show of power when the two of you returned, supporting you over Conall."

"That was a lie," Bryce said with clenched teeth.

"Aye, and she knew it. But that didn't stop her. So, I confronted her with her lies that day in the Great Hall. And we fought."

Wynda paused and led Innes to a bench, where they sat down side by side. She took the surprised young woman's gloved hands in her own and looked into her eyes. "Will you remove these? I want you to hold my hand as I speak. I want no doubt about the truth of what I am about to say."

"Wynda, we will believe you, whatever you tell us," Conall asserted. "You've been like a mother to us."

She shook her head and asked Innes again. "Please, my dear. Help me unburden my heart."

The young woman looked up at Conall first and waited for his nod, then pulled off her gloves.

Innes's hand was warm. Wynda took strength from that.

"That afternoon," she continued, "I went to her chambers in the East Tower. We were far from finished with our argument, to my thinking. She blamed me. She blamed the world. And we fought. The words were ugly, the accusations fierce. Then she even brought up my past. She accused me of bring-

ing shame to the Sinclairs. She spoke openly, mockingly, of secrets that I kept hidden for years. Secrets about the child I
bore out of wedlock, about the child that was taken from me
and given away. I fought back with my own hurtful words,
telling her that everyone knew she cared nothing for either of
you. She wanted only power and position for herself. I told
her she didn't deserve to be carrying the bairn in her womb."

Wynda paused as a tear dripped from her cheek onto her
lap.

"She grabbed for my apron. She intended to fling me
about, as she did her servants. Perhaps she intended to cast
me out through that open window. But I tore her hands away,
and she fell back. Heavy with that child, she stumbled at the
window. And then she was gone."

No one moved and silence gripped the room for a long moment until she spoke again.

"It was an accident, but I said no word of it to anyone. I
ran from the room. I was afraid. I thought everyone would
simply assume I killed her. Truth would mean nothing. It was
my word against that of a dead woman. So I fled and said
nothing. Fingal, having gone up later to Shona's room, discovered what had happened. The uproar in the castle that
followed hid my involvement."

She paused and looked at Innes. The young woman
squeezed her hand, giving her encouragement she needed.

"With Bryce gone, the priest stepped in. Fingal knew

Shona, and he had no love for her. He decided it was no accident. He'd heard her threaten to hurt the child she carried, to punish Bryce," she said. "I stayed quiet when Fingal said Shona's death was a suicide. I said nothing when they buried her in the fields in the dark of night. I knew the truth, but remained silent. I feared for myself."

Wynda lifted her eyes to Conall and Bryce.

"Innes can tell you that I've spoken the truth. But I'm also telling the truth when I say I'm ashamed of my silence. I was afraid. I didn't have enough faith in my own people to believe me. So I allowed Shona . . . I allowed that child . . . to be buried . . ."

Emotions overwhelmed her. She let go of Innes's hand and stood up. Fighting back a flood of tears, she looked up at Bryce.

"You are the laird. I wronged your wife and your bairn . . . and you. I've brought scandal to our people. I wronged the Sinclairs," she said in a broken voice. "Your judgment, whatever it might be . . . your punishment . . . I will accept. I . . ."

Ailein came forward and took her into her arms. Wynda could no longer hold back the tears. She cried for loved ones she again might lose.

Innes joined her sister, and Wynda felt her touch.

"First of all," Bryce spoke up, drawing their attention. He stood next to his brother. "We'll have the body of Shona and the child moved to the crypt."

Conall nodded in agreement.

"What will you say to Fingal?" Wynda asked.

"I believe after what he saw at the oratory, he will not question me," Innes said gently. "We can tell him I know the truth, and that it was an accident. That should be enough for him."

Clutching the hands of the two women at her side, Wynda looked up at Bryce and Conall. "And what of my punishment?"

Bryce looked at Conall and then back at her. "You will remain here to guide and protect the next generation of Sinclairs. Where would we be without you?"

Chapter 30

A hush fell over the congregation as the sound of a lone bagpipe commenced. Straining for a first glimpse of his bride, Conall squinted toward the brilliant light spilling through the open doorway. He did not have long to wait.

Innes and her father entered the chapel, and Conall froze at the sight, unaware of anything but her and the drumming of his own heart.

Innes's hair hung loose beneath a jeweled coronet. Her gray eyes flashed with her love as they focused on him, and her gown of ivory, ornately embroidered with threads of gold, glittered as she crossed the threshold. The heat of a thousand suns rushed into Conall's face as he gazed upon the beauty advancing toward him.

Moments later, Hector Munro delivered Innes's steady hand into Conall's and, beaming proudly, retreated to his place with his family.

Fingal started the prayers, then encouraged the two to exchange their vows of love and fidelity, before God and their community.

What the Lord hath joined, let no man put asunder.

After he thoroughly kissed his bride, the Sinclairs and Munros and other guests approached the altar, congratulating them. After the night of their betrothal and the welcome by his clan, Conall was far more at ease with the attention. And it warmed his heart to watch the Sinclair warriors, one by one, pledge to protect Innes as they welcomed her into the clan.

When Kenna and Alexander Macpherson approached to congratulate them, Innes told them the news. "Conall and I decided yesterday. We'll be joining you to search for Muirne MacDonnell."

The Macphersons had learned weeks earlier the name of the woman who supposedly possessed the last relic. It was only rumor, but it gave them a place to start looking. Even if it were correct that Muirne was the one, her exact whereabouts were unknown, except that she'd been last seen at the Shrine of the Cloak in Monyabroch. Their intention was to begin the hunt there.

Kenna hugged Innes. "I'm very glad. Our chances of defeating that qualling blackguard will be so much better if we fight him together."

Sometime later, when Conall and Innes finally made their way out of the chapel into a courtyard filled with friends and family, they were greeted with the melodious sounds of pipers and pealing bells. Laughing children from the villages, dressed in new clothes and wreaths of greenery, danced around them as Bryce and Ailein joined the procession through the crowds to the Great Hall, where a sumptuous feast awaited everyone.

As soon as all were seated at the tables and the celebrating began, Conall leaned over and kissed her lips.

"There will be no escorting us out of the hall," he said. "No waiting for bed linens. No busybodies outside our door."

"I love the fear you instill in them."

"And you'll not leave this hall without me," he whispered in her ear. "And you will not have Jinny undress and prepare you for bed. That is a duty I insist on performing for my wife."

She smiled mischievously. "How soon do you think we can leave? Jinny looks quite anxious to be about her duties." She nodded toward the serving woman, who was sitting next to Duff and laughing.

Conall turned back to Innes. "Would *now* be a good time?"

Taking her hand, Conall pulled her to her feet, and the two ran from the hall to the cheers of the assembly.

"They weren't even surprised." She laughed, running to keep up with him.

"Considering our reputations, I believe they were thrilled that we allowed any of them in the chapel."

Reaching the West Tower, Conall swept her up into

his arms and carried her to their apartments.

"Where's Thunder?" she asked.

"Duff has him locked in his work area for the night."

They could hear the wolf scratching at the door.

"Ignore him," Conall said. "He has a bed, water, food. He'll be fine."

He carried her up the steps to their bedchamber and kicked the door closed behind them. Depositing her gently on the bed, he kissed her slowly, his mouth lingering on hers with a tangible promise of what was to come.

"Don't go anywhere," he said with a smile, crossing the room and coming back with two cups of wine.

The candlelit chamber was adorned in a style befitting a royal couple. Everywhere Innes looked, she saw signs of Wynda and Ailein's thoughtfulness and taste. Every table held stoneware vases of budding flowers and greenery. A multitude of dishes of every imaginable food, prepared with care, were presented with artistic flourish. Pitchers of wine sat amid a sparkling collection of crystal goblets.

"You allowed them into your lair."

"It's our lair now," he reminded her, putting the cups aside and removing her coronet. "Just the two of us, locked away here for days."

"I love the thought of being locked up with you anywhere."

He combed his fingers into her hair, pulling her head

back and gazing into her face, her eyes. And then, his lips were on hers. Suddenly she wanted to lose herself in him, drown in him. Her body arched against him, her breasts aching to be free of the tight wedding garments, aching as she pressed against his hard body, aching for his touch.

With their mouths still locked together, Conall yanked at the laces of her gown. She helped him, loosening the garment, tugging at the bodice, fighting the confinement, until the gown dropped from her body and she stood before him wearing just her silk shift.

She didn't hesitate but began to help him to remove his clothes. The gold Sinclair brooch was undone. With one motion, Conall ducked out of the leather strap and the scarf of Sinclair plaid that crisscrossed his white shirt. The shirt was gone in an instant, tossed carelessly aside.

Conall was wearing only his kilt when she remembered the special gift she had for him.

"Wait. Wait," she chirped, slipping around him and running to the chair where she'd hidden it. "I have something for you."

"Do you need to give it to me now?" he asked smiling, pulling back the covers.

She hurried back to the bed, climbing up and placing it on the linen sheets.

He stared at the miniature chess set and smiled. "It's beautiful."

"I had Duff carve the pieces. We can take it with us when we travel."

"You know how much I love chess . . . but playing it in bed?"

"It's not chess."

He stared at the set. "The same board. The same pieces. Do they move the same?"

"They do." Innes looked at him coyly, edging around the board closer to him. "But the rules are different."

"How?"

"Let's play. I'll show you." She moved a pawn on the board. "Each move is a kiss." She leaned toward him and kissed his lips before sitting back.

Conall's gaze drifted over her, causing her to shiver. He made a countermove and dropped his head to kiss the curve of her breast just above the silk shift. Her breath caught in her chest.

"I like this game," he murmured.

"I thought you would." She slid the next piece across the board, leaned over, and kissed his chest, letting her mouth linger.

He answered her move and pulled the shift off her shoulders and downward ever so slowly. When her breast was free, he kissed her nipple. She moaned with pleasure.

"I more than like this game. I love your creativity." He removed his kilt and sat completely naked now on the bed. "What happens if I capture a piece?"

She looked at his body, her face ablaze, liquid heat running through her. "You'll have to wait until you capture one. Then I'll tell you."

On his next move, he pulled the shift down to her waist. He touched his lips to the faint scar beneath her breast, all that remained from the sword wound that nearly took her life. The sparks that ignited at his kiss flew through her.

"I love your scar," he said softly.

Two moves later, he captured a pawn.

"Very well," she whispered. "And now, an erotic caress."

His hand started at her knee, then moved along the inside of her leg under the shift until it reached the juncture. He touched her, teased her. Innes stopped breathing.

She could take no more of this. Pushing him onto his back, she climbed up, straddling him. As he entered her, she vaguely heard the chess set flying to the floor.

Later, when they both were spent from their lovemaking and she was sprawled across his chest, Conall chuckled.

"What?" she asked.

"I never had the chance to ask what happens when you put your opponent in check, never mind checkmate."

She laughed. "Let's play again and find out."

They peered over the end of the bed, looking for the chess set.

A large gray wolf lay on the floor, happily chewing the pieces. He looked up, a knight protruding from his mouth.

"Bloody *hell*, Thunder."

Author's Note

We're absolutely thrilled to have presented you Innes and Conall's story, the second installment in our Scottish Relic Trilogy. We hope you also enjoyed your brief visit with Kenna and Alexander from *Much Ado About Highlanders*.

In *Tempest in the Highlands,* the exciting conclusion of the trilogy, unseen forces play a hand in shaping the combined destinies of the women who possess the power of the stone tablets.

So, join us as Kenna, Alexander, Innes, Conall, and our new heroes—Miranda MacDonnell and Rob Hawkins—travel to the western islands of Scotland in a deadly race with Sir Ralph Evers to find the final spoke in the Wheel of Lugh.

As many of our readers know, we never seem to be able to let our characters go. Often, the people you meet in our stories show up in other tales. Be sure to check the family tree on our website for connections.

Finally, we need a favor. If you enjoyed this book, please leave a review of *Taming the Highlander* ... and recommend it to your friends. You, the reader, have the power to make or break this book. We greatly appreciate your support!

All the best!

You can contact us at:

www.MayMcGoldrick.com

About the Author(s)

Authors Nikoo and Jim McGoldrick (writing as May McGoldrick) weave emotionally satisfying tales of love and danger. Publishing under the names of May Mc-Goldrick and Jan Coffey, these authors have written over thirty-five novels. Nikoo, an engineer, also conducts frequent workshops on writing and publishing and serves as a Resident Author. Jim holds a PhD in medieval and Renaissance literature and teaches English in northwestern Connecticut.